In Short, Milo Overlock
William M. Schaefer

MARKHAM MEDIA LTD
795 Lakeshore Dr, Ste 307
Dorval, QC H9S 0A8

Markham Media Ltd
795 Lakeshore Dr, Ste 307
Dorval, QC H9S 0A8

Table Of Contents

1

Chapter One
Milo Overlock's Chance

I stood in the kitchen, perspiration pouring out of my temples and my heartbeat outpacing the frantic ticks of the clock. Mr. Overlock was in the parlor, all three hundred pounds and five feet of him curled into an armchair and waiting for his "duck dog," while the ground duck with which I was endeavoring to produce this item obstinately refused to make it from my fingers to the sausage-casing.

The bell rang again. I desperately held open the little balloon with my left hand and attempted to push the goop in with my right. It refused. Half of it slithered down one side of the casing and onto one of my newly-shined poindexters, while the other half collected in stock-pond fashion on my left hand. I sucked this off, and while my body briefly pondered turning itself inside out with the reaction, had a thought. I took a sausage-casing, put one end between my lips, and tilted my head back. Holding the outer end open as best as I could with one set of fingers, I took about two pounds of duck meat with the other and poured it over the casing, inhaling the while. I inspected it, and discovered the system to have worked—an inch of the bag was now filled. As the bell rang again, I quickly continued with the operation, coating my white moustache with a new grey-red hue, and inadvertently consuming ounce upon ounce of the revoltingly clammy, blood-fresh pond beast which an hour earlier had been quacking about outside on our duck pond. The casing now swelling with meat, I tied off the ends with the only knot I know (a granny) and placed the frank within a fresh roll upon a plate. Then I opened the icebox and hurriedly extracted a little bowl of something I had been working on for weeks—a special sauce from an old family recipe prepared from herbs I had carefully and secretly grown in my own room—and placed it, among some lesser condiments, beside the entrée. Hoping that it would make up for the fact that it had taken me longer than the ten minutes Mr. Overlock had allotted me to prepare his duck dog, I sauntered out of the kitchen and into the parlor, where I held the final presentation up to the Master's waiting nose.

The Master eyed the sandwich with subdued salacity, then directed his attention coldly to the sauce.

"Take that dog excrement away, Grave, or I will spoon-feed it to you until your nose bleeds it and your intestines are crawling on the floor," he said.

"Yes, sir," I frowned.

"I see that you have been helping yourself liberally to my meat."

I became aware that I had forgotten to wash my face off.

"It shall be the only meal that you receive today."

"Yes, sir," I said.

"You will also polish your shoes."

"Yes, sir."

"With your toothbrush."

"Yes, sir."

He began to eat his food. Apparently one of his better moods.

He chunked down the duck dog with a blank expression, big pieces falling from his mouth to the ground in a way that suggested the stall-end view of cows. Then suddenly his ten trained white mice came scurrying in from nowhere and gobbled up the detritus to the last entrail.

I am not certain which corner of hell first gave birth to these unearthly rodents, but they are no doubt its favorite children. My years of service with the Master had seemed tenfold under them, and despite the differences in our sizes, it had always felt like I was the one beneath the heel. One by one they used my trouser-cuff for a napkin, then swarmed up to Mr. Overlock's arms, where they formed two lines, five to a sleeve. The Master slowly processed his snack, then the mice licked his plate clean.

I held out my hand to receive the now-empty tray. Mr. Overlock threw it at my feet. I dutifully bent down to pick it up, and when I rose again saw the Master staring at me with a cold, contemplative, distant expression on his face. It was shared by his mice, and made me feel distinctly uncomfortable.

"Grave, there is a wart on my skin which I cannot cure," he said.

"Indeed, sir?"

"You are it."

A ball of mashed potato seemed to rise from my stomach to my throat. Invisible hands clutched my neck. I needed to use the water closet.

The front door bell rang.

I thanked almighty God, excused myself and went to answer it. On the other side, as if to brighten an increasingly grim day, stood a female. She was young, well-dressed, poised, and all eyes. I effected to be suave.

"May I be of any assistance to you, my dear young lady?"

"Who are you?"

"Why, I am Grave, Mr. Overlock's valet, butler, and cook."

"Then move your butt, butler. I'm here to see someone important, not casket-stuffing."

"Yes, miss."

Deflated but ever cognizant of my eternal duty, I led the abrupt popkin inward, and bade her stand in the entrance-hall until I could inform the Master of her visit. Exhorting me once more to "move my butt," she folded her arms and waited, while I, receiving the mandate with as much dignity as I am ever able to muster, transported the region so specified with poised alacrity. Once more I stood before the Master and his scowling mouse-kin, and announced the brusque visitation with a detached attitude I felt did me credit.

"Who is she, Grave?" asked Mr. Overlock.

"Er . . . a young lady of considerable description, sir."

"Her name? The purpose of her visit?"

"I was not able to determine either, I regret, sir."

"Why?"

"She was, er, determined in her motives, sir."

"Templeton," said Mr. Overlock, addressing one of his little white hellpods, "punish this irremediable simpleton."

The rodent, grinning evilly, came scurrying at me like a spider, and before I could do anything but gape, scampered up the underside of my trouser-leg all the way up to the top and bit me on the scrotum. Despite my many years of training in this regard, I was unable to keep from howling horrifically at the puncture, feeling something like an oat-bag under attack by a horse. My bellow being received in apparent disfavor by the Master, another mouse of his, Fiscus, came dashing toward me at this point, ran up my outerwear and stuffed itself in my mouth. Hence, one mouse tasted me while I tasted another mouse, and I'm not sure which sensation was worse. Mr. Overlock let them cling to their positions for about thirty seconds before snapping his fingers, but it had felt like thirty years to me, and I found it difficult to resume my fully erect stance after it was over.

"Throw the trollop out, Grave."

"I must request that you permit me to enter, Mr. Overlock."

It was the trollop—er, young lady, who, appearing to possess more in the testicular vein than I at the moment, had barged her way into the parlor.

"See here, miss—" I began.

"Silence, Grave," said the Master.

I shrugged helplessly and shrunk away into a corner.

"To what end do you risk my displeasure, female?" said Mr. Overlock coldly.

"I have no choice, sir," replied the wench. "It is an urgent matter of several persons' lives."

"Including yours, no doubt."

"Yes."

"And mine?"

"No, not particularly."

"Then what does it gain me to waste my time on your enforced company?"

"It may profit you monetarily."

"You intend to pay for my counsel?"

"No. It is a matter of one of your businesses."

The Master eyed me, and I filled his glass with grot. "I own many in Onwall, each of importance," he said, addressing his guest suspiciously. "And I find it highly unlikely that you could be aware of any matter concerning one of them that I am not."

"Believe me, Mr. Overlock, when it comes to money, I am aware of many things which are none of my business."

"Indeed?" said the Master. "Very well. You may speak until I've drained my glass."

"Thank you," said the girl. "My name is Heavenly Bodkin. I am married to a gambler, Mr. Sagramore 'Odds' Bodkin, who frequents the gaming establishment you own here in town. I am here to plead with you to forbid his patronage."

The Master sipped, his eyes unmoving. "Is he successful at his trade?"

"Sometimes," said Mrs. Bodkin. "More often he is not. When he loses, he becomes angry and uncontrollable. He is abusive to me, to his opponents, and himself. If his wagering is not curtailed in some way, and soon, someone will surely suffer."

"And how does curtailing him benefit my business?" demanded the Master. "At best, I can detect that it may produce no change whatsoever. If you could provide a reliable indication of which days he is likely to succeed, I could be convinced to ban him on those occasions. Otherwise, my interest is in Onwall, not private affairs between the maladjusted."

"And what if he kills another of your patrons, or a dealer?" said the girl. "Wouldn't that be detrimental to your affairs?"

"If he kills a patron, it will likely be an opponent who has bested him. Hence, I lose a competent gambler and retain an incompetent one, conditions any house would welcome. As for dealers, they are like Grave— replaceable cogs. Wipe my mouth, Grave."

I did, wondering why, if I was replaceable, he hadn't done me the favor of replacing me thirty years earlier.

"And I don't suppose my welfare interests you in the least," said the girl.

"No, it doesn't. You must pay the price for your lack of judgment, just as your master does for his."

"And others? Ones who are neither maladjusted nor lacking in judgment? What of them?" she demanded.

"Danger rarely goes unannounced," said Mr. Overlock. "A gambler is a creature of risk, who can weigh the advantages and disadvantages of his own perils himself. If he fails, he loses, as you did in your selection of a husband. The others must make their own judgments as well."

Mrs. Bodkin stood up haughtily. "Odds was a sure thing when I married him, Mr. Overlock. Not brilliant, perhaps, but polite, unselfish and well-situated. My real gamble was in coming here. You are so beloved throughout Onwall that I thought it was worth trying. Sadly, the few vague rumors I've heard about the real you were correct. You are demonic."

His mice growled at her, and she stepped back. The Master glared at her, but her defiance seemed to intrigue him a little as well.

"I warn you, wench, that I have trained my pets in the manner of piranhas when it comes to feeding. Do not risk my displeasure."

"What difference does it make if your nasty little friends do me in or Odds does? Your law forbids divorce, but my leaving him would not stop him anyway. I'm trapped. So go on. Tell them to attack. You were my last chance."

Occasions are few when the Master can be moved by a display of spirit. Integrity was mere defiance to his general perception, and those who practiced it usually ended up like one of his former cooks, who, having once stuffed a duck with a mincemeat paté Mr. Overlock wouldn't taste, refused to make alterations and ended up stuffed with it himself. Hence my surprise when Mrs. Bodkin's attitude gained her something other than mouse-bites or a gunshot to one of her lovely extremities.

"Very well," said Mr. Overlock icily. "We will examine the situation. It is possible that it may contain its distractions. If not, I may reserve the right to your company under different conditions in future."

Mrs. Bodkin appeared to remain composed. "You'll find it interesting, Mr. Overlock, I assure you. When will you go?"

"Tonight. You, like all women, are forbidden from entering the premises."

"I understand."

"You will be informed of my judgment by messenger."

"Yes. Thank you—"

"Dismissed."

I escorted the lady out of the parlor, unsettled in my mind about the sentence Mr. Overlock had used: "We will examine the situation." The word which bothered me in particular was "we."

I opened Mrs. Bodkin's door, beaming at her in congratulation for her success in winning over the Master.

She seemed unmoved. "Stop smiling at me, Snow White. You had better hope your master in there sees things my way, or it will be too bad for you."

It struck me as unbelievable that this lady could be bullied by anyone, husband included. However, ignoring the change of face she seemed to adopt when not in the Master's presence, I bowed gentlemanly before her and said "Good day, miss." To which she replied with an unladylike stomp on my foot and an even less ladylike "Eat shit."

Hobbling back inward, I cleaned up after Mr. Overlock and mice, and escorted the Master to his room. Pondering hopelessly the night's affair to come, and desperate to avoid it, I decided to take a risk and see if the beneficence Mr. Overlock had shown the girl might extend to me. It meant revealing something that I alone knew of.

"Excuse me, sir," I said, "but will you excuse me, sir?"

He looked at me like a volcano eyeing a little village. "What are you babbling about, Grave?"

"If I may be so bold, sir, I was hoping that you would relieve me of the responsibility of accompanying you tonight. It is my birthday, you see, and I was hoping to celebrate by retiring early."

He contemplated me briefly. "Which birthday is it?" he asked.

"My seventy-fifth, sir."

"And you wish to retire early?"

"Only insofar as my bedtime is concerned, sir," I said, knowing the impossibility of the other interpretation.

He gave my request all of the contemplation he apparently felt it was due—about two seconds. "No, Grave," was his answer. "I may require your services."

This gave me a chill.

"You may, however, bake a cake."

I was inexpressibly surprised by this, and it rather surpassed my earlier plan. "Thank you, sir," I flustered out sincerely.

"Do not, however, allow it to interfere with your other duties. I expect three visitors this afternoon, and you must attend to each of them. One is a new servant, a cook."

I couldn't have been more astonished. "A cook, sir?" I gasped. I had been performing the duty for over a year at that time, and it had greatly increased my pyramidic workload.

"Yes. His name is Wong, and is famous for his work with ducklings. He will stay a while and serve as your tutor."

I frowned. "He is Chinese, sir?"

"Late of the Isle of Wight. He speaks with a slight speech impediment, a lisp, so pay close attention while he is teaching you."

I gulped down my rising irritation. "And the other two visitors, sir?"

One is Nottingham White, a lawyer. An advertisement for Ludlum's appeared recently, describing the brand as 'Milo Overlock's favorite bourbon.' For this, I shall sue them into oblivion."

"But sir, Ludlum's *is* your favorite brand."

"Let them prove it."

"But if they fail as a result, sir, will you not be deprived of the product?"

"I will take over the company and help myself to their product."

I swallowed distastefully. "And the third visitor, sir?"

"A plumber of some sort. I do not remember his name. We have sewer access on our grounds, which he will give his yearly inspection, and he will also attend to our pipes. You will assist him."

"Yes, sir."

"Dismissed."

I left his room and, mentally putting aside the distasteful visitations so mentioned, made for the kitchen. Despite the news that I was about to be tutored by some displaced Chinaman, I was content, briefly, to dwell on my all-too-unexpected birthday-cake. I opened all the cupboards and drew up a fire in the oven. This was the nineteenth century, and we did not have luxuries like microwaves and instant cake-mixes such as we have today. It would be a toilsome task, and would take well into the afternoon, but I was more than happy to commit myself to it. Pulling out all kinds of flavorings and pounds of flour, I dove assiduously into the project until, three hours later, I was left with the biggest, pinkest balloon of a cake imaginable. Covering it with exotic icings and all sorts of fruit, I was just about to inscribe a sentiment to myself upon it when the front door bell rang. I set the cake aside and went off to answer it, skipping at the heels a bit.

Outside, to my surprise, stood a very Oriental-looking man. Cooks, in my experience, generally came by the kitchen door. Perhaps our customs were new to him, I thought. I also considered that he may have been Mr. White, if Mr. White had jaundice; however, I discounted the likelihood of his being the plumber, as he carried nothing which could have contained his tools.

"Mr. Wong?" I inquired.

"Wight."

I adjusted my thinking. "Mr. White?"

"Wong."

"Excuse me, but please tell me which is correct—White or Wong?"

"Wight is 'correct,' but I am Wong."

I tried to focus. "What I am trying to ask is, which name would it be correct to call you—Wong or White?"

"The wight one."

"You mean, Mr. White?"

"Wong."

"You mean White is wrong?"

"No. Wong is wight."

"Forgive me, young man, but how can wrong be right?"

"It isn't wong to be wight, but it is wight to be Wong."

I felt myself losing my composure hurriedly, but with great determination managed to keep myself contained. "Unless I am wrong, you are not White," I said.

"You are not wong. Wong is not white."

"No, wrong is obviously not right."

"Wight."

"What?"

"You are wight."

I took offense at this personal remark. "Just because my complexion is somewhat lacking in the blood-and-sun department, young man, is no excuse to call me 'white.'"

He shrugged. "Okay. You are wong."

I was indignant. "*You* are Wong!"

He seemed confused. "Both can't be wong," he muttered.

"Look. Are you certain you have the right house?"

"Yes. Wight house."

"I'm sorry, young man, but this house is brick, not white."

"House is not white."

"No. You are at the wrong house."

"Wong. This house is wight house . . . now it is Wong house."

My aggravation was beginning to overcome me. "Where are you from, young man?"

"Wight."

"You mean the Isle of Wight?"

"Isle of Wight is Wong isle."

"Then which isle is right?"

"The Wong one."

I felt like screaming, and was about to shut the door, but an inner sense of prudence prevailed.

"If you are Mr. Wong, please hold up one finger," I said. "If you are Mr. White, hold up two. If you are neither, hold up none."

He held up one—an inaptly chosen one. I ushered him in the door.

"You travel light, don't you?" I said.

"Oh, yes. Wong wight."

"Forget it. Your room is the first right door in the west wing. You may also use the rest room if you like."

He nodded. "First wight door in west wing. May use the west—"

"No, not the first *white* door. The white door is the wrong one."

He nodded. "White door Wong one."

"And the rest room is in the east."

"West is in the east."

"I'll show you," I said exasperatedly. "Then you can come down and cook Mr. Overlock's ducklings."

"Cook duck wings."

Intervening at this most crucial juncture in the well-being of our visitor came the Master, who with a few simple words instructed the cook where to go, what to do, and when and how to do it. The cook nodded in complete comprehension, and gesturing to me, said to the Master "Dim some." Mr. Overlock nodded dryly, and dismissed him. He then ushered me to the kitchen.

"Is that the cake you baked, Grave?" he asked, pointing to the big pink wonder.

"Yes it is, sir, but I have not quite finished frosting it yet. I have yet to ice 'Happy Birthday, Grave' on it."

"I'll take it as it is," he said, and picked it up, platter and all. "When my mice and I have finished it, I will ring, and you may come up and remove the platter."

With that, he took it to his room.

I barely had time to mourn the loss of my beautiful birthday cake when the front door bell rang again. Oathing with no little passion under my breath, I went to receive the summons, expecting, at least, an easier time with what now had either to be attorney Nottingham White or the anonymous plumber.

I opened the door, and saw a well-dressed gentleman standing outside, holding a case.

"Mr. White?" I asked.

"My name is Not White. I have come to see the suer."

"Yes, sir."

Pondering how well-fettered, right down to their tool-cases, plumbers were becoming, I took him out onto the grounds to where a removable iron grating gave access to the sewer conduit below, and told him to go down it. What I could not comprehend was why he showed such outrage at this, or why, after he had informed Mr. Overlock, the Master had me spend the remaining majority of my seventy-sixth birthday down that selfsame shaft.

I was released just in time to change for our trip to the gambling-house. Things were about to get worse.

MR. OVERLOCK'S gaming establishment, Parlour d'Overluck, was elegant, ornate, and dignified. It made no flashy pretenses; here you would lose, unless inordinately lucky. It resembled more of a distinguished bank than a social parlor, and indeed it existed to hold earnings, loan some out once in a while, and be repaid with interest. Its patrons were expected to keep their voices down, eat and drink with restraint, and graciously lose all that they brought with them, including, perhaps, identity. And such is the nature of the cow which will be milked in the morning that the regulars lined up dutifully and paid the Master for their daily round of displeasure without fail.

Mr. Overlock himself, of course, rarely played, it all being his own money anyway. However, the odd occasion had been known to exist upon which he would turn a hand, and the fact that he always came away the victor baffled me. I could understand his mastery of chess, and other strictly mental pursuits. But how does one "outthink" chance?

I was about to be given a lesson. We entered, and the Master surveyed the assemblage. Postures became more erect, expressions more subtle, as the gamblers beheld his onset. Proper behavior enveloped the throng like rain on pigs, all except for one individual seated at a card table, holding his sweaty head in his hands and groaning loudly. Mr. Overlock approached this individual.

"Sagramore 'Odds' Bodkin?" he asked.

The gambler looked up, or rather down, at the Master, with an expression of blunt surprise.

"Yes. How did you know?"

"I didn't, which is why I asked. I take it that you are losing."

The harried but little-haired Bodkin ran a hand through what remained of his mane, a crop which appeared to have been manually uprooted a tuft at a time.

"Yeah," he grunted.

"You are engaged in losing at an activity which you are quite obviously poor at," said the Master. "Why indulge in a practice at which you do not possess skill?"

"I do got skill, is why," replied the gambler defensively. "I just don't got it today."

"You are confusing skill with luck," said the Master. "Skill is consistent; luck is not."

"Yeah, well, skill takes a little luck."

"Wrong. Skill is learned, and by acquiring it, one can appear to possess luck. Without skill, one can appear not to."

Mr. Bodkin looked frustrated, and tapped his fingers on the table loudly. "Look, sir, I told you I got skill at this. But all the skill in the world won't help without a little good fortune!"

"Perhaps so," said Mr. Overlock, "but the reverse is also true, and, I suspect, more applicable in your case. We will put this to the test. The game I propose is twenty-one. So that neither of us can be taken to possess more or less 'luck' than the other, we will share each hand, but place separate bets. These will be kept hidden from the other. We will both be staked with an equal bank of, shall we say, two hundred silver radcliffes. We will play for one hour, or until one or both of us has eliminated his bank. I guarantee that at that time, I will have a bank of higher value than yours."

"And who's to provide this 'bank'?" inquired Mr. Bodkin.

"I am, of course," said Mr. Overlock, reaching up and taking four hundred silver radcliffes in chips from the dealer. The dealer said nothing.

"And what happens to the winnings?"

"You may keep whatever you have left."

Mr. Bodkin smiled. "I accept," he said.

"Naturally," said the Master. "Grave, find two partitions, so that each of us may see our mutual hand, but not each other's wager."

"Er…yes, sir," I replied. I glanced around, and found myself stymied in this regard. Nothing in the place seemed suitable for the purpose. "Excuse me, sir, but do you have a suggestion?"

"I suggest your death, you driveling wart," he snapped. "Give me your shoes."

I reluctantly disengaged my footwear and handed it glumly to him. He took one of the shoes and rapped me on the head with it. Then he placed each on the table so that bets could discreetly be made to the side of each one, out of sight of each opponent's adversary. The cards would be dealt between the shoes, where both could see them.

"Wait, Mr. Overlock," said Mr. Bodkin. "Who's to decide when to hit?"

"We'll play by house rules, never hitting a seventeen or higher, always hitting an eleven or lower, and only hitting twelve through sixteen when the dealer shows a two through a six. Agreed?"

"Whatever you say."

"Let us commence."

And with that, I proceeded to watch (with increasingly cold feet) a succession of rounds which saw the Master a consistent victor over his opponent, who broke on the first contest, came two-thirds shy of Mr. Overlock's total in the second, and gave up with a quarter-pfennig left in the third.

"You must be able to see through the cards!" he exploded.

"Ass," said Mr. Overlock. "Since we are playing by preset rules, it would not make any difference if I could see through the cards or not."

"Then how?"

"A greater portion of small-value cards remaining in the deck will favor the house," replied the Master. "If one subtracts all played cards from remaining ones, one may calculate what degree of an advantage either the player or the house will possess on the following hand. One must then either reduce or increase the amount of one's wager from its predetermined base amount by the same percentage that either favors or disfavors the house at that time."

"Ah, bullfrogs," snarled Mr. Bodkin. "That's just a lot of talk."

"Would you care for another round, to test that statement?" said Mr. Overlock. "This time using your own funds?"

Mr. Bodkin appeared to ponder the proposal unenthusiastically. "No," he said.

"Then would you like to play alone, this time employing my method?"

"I couldn't learn that thing in years."

"Then you must admit that to win consistently at this pursuit requires skill, that you do not possess it, and that skill can be learned, but you cannot learn it. Hence, my original question: why do you spend long hours at a pastime for which you do not possess the ability to do anything but fail at?"

"Because it's fun," muttered Mr. Bodkin.

"You are drawn and pale," said Mr. Overlock. "You pull at your hair. You blame others for your failures. Failing more often than you succeed, your miseries must duly outweigh your pleasures at this practice by a considerable margin. You cannot possibly call it 'fun.' Rethink your response."

"To what?"

Mr. Overlock appeared to flare slightly. "Do not provoke me too strongly, gambler. Why do you play this game?"

Odds Bodkin shrugged emptily. "Because…" He paused, then seemed to receive an inspiration. "Because the poker tables was full! And that's where my real skill is . . . poker!"

Mr. Overlock glanced over at the nearest poker table. "There is a vacant chair available. Prove your statement."

They walked over to the table in question, but I was too lost in thought to follow. Mr. Overlock's method at twenty-one had intrigued me no end. Was it possible, I wondered, to master the Master's technique and possibly win enough money to free myself from his employ at last? I stood daydreaming at the table, my garters quietly slipping down to my ankles.

"Grave!"

"Yes, sir!" I snapped out of it, only to see him approaching me with his riding-crop. "I'm coming, sir, I…just wanted to retrieve my shoes."

"Leave them," he snapped, giving me a buffet in the solar plexus. "And stay with me. I may require further services."

I wondered if he might want my trousers next, but, swallowing the stars induced by his casual assault and bidding my one pair of shoes goodbye, merely followed in his wake.

"Does it really work, sir?" I suddenly heard myself say.

He turned at me menacingly. "Does what work?"

"Your …system, sir."

He paused before answering. "Over time," he replied. "However, poor runs do occur."

"Then how did you know you would prevail so consistently over Mr. Bodkin tonight, sir?"

"I simply wagered extremely small amounts. I knew that this cretin, in his anxiousness to best me, would overrisk himself too often. I merely maintained a reserved betting pattern and never strayed too far from my initial unit size. If you had been paying attention, you would have noticed this. Let's see if you can attend the better at poker."

"Yes, sir." I furrowed my brow and stared intently at the game now unfolding in front of me.

The Master gave me a kick in the backside. "I said attend the bettor, Grave—he wants a drink."

"Oh. Yes, sir."

Procuring the "gentleman" in question his desired intoxicant, I was able to appraise the motley assortment of ruffians gathered at the poker table with some clarity. One was a large, single-eyed specimen whose sole absent feature was held, dicelike, in his hand; another, bald but for a snaky rope of braided hair erupting from the base of his neck, was staring at me with a hateful expression; a third sat stone-faced, a huge gape frozen in place upon his boyish façade; and lastly, our subject, who seated himself amongst the others with a fey giggle and proceeded to showily light an oversized cigar that looked and smelled like the missing part of a gelding.

The dealer himself was rather odd as well, for he had no nose, and seemed to suck in air through his ears. This gave him a kind of accordion-like effect, and when he spoke it did not surprise me that he sounded like one as well.

"How much will the gentleman require?" he wheezed, letting out a long exhalation.

"Credit him five hundred radcliffes," said the Master.

"Yes, sir," said the dealer, sending the units disking toward Bodkin. These he followed with one hole card and a face-up card. When everyone had the same, Bodkin's face-up card was seen to be highest.

"Would the gentleman care to open?"

"He would," replied Mr. Overlock.

"Very well," said the dealer. "The game is five-card stud. How much would the gentleman care to open with?"

Bodkin smirkily tossed in 100r, and all declined to join. Looking momentarily sheepish, he regained his smug demeanor quickly and said, "Well, I guess I won that round."

The dealer frowned, and passed out another pair of cards to everyone. He looked around for the high card. "Would Captain Quint be inclined to open at an amount more suitable to our other players?" he asked.

Quint, of the beroped nape, said "Ar," and proceeded to toss in ten chad. The rest followed suit, and the dealer flailed out more cards. Light wagering ensued with each successive card, until, with five cards, Quint showed two nines, the gaper two kings, and Bodkin two aces. The Eye had bowed out. Stakes remained moderate.

Bodkin looked at his hole card, carefully examined each of his opponents' exposed cards, and did some counting on his fingers. Then he laughed excitedly and threw everything he had into the pot. All folded.

Bodkin revealed his ace and scooped in the winnings. He looked at Mr. Overlock proudly and said "See?" to which the Master shook his head in obvious disgust. Bodkin looked baffled at this, and mouthed the word "What?" to Mr. Overlock. The Master then said to the dealer, "Discontinue his credit."

Bodkin looked like a scolded child, and looked closely at his winnings. Then, his face became illuminated and he said "Oh!" while the dealer shuffled and distributed the next set of hands. This time, the Eye opened.

Around the table came the remaining cards, and when the dust settled, the Eye held a threesome and Bodkin two pair. The Eye put forth a feeler. Bodkin glanced at his fifth card.

"Darn," he said, scowling. "Oh, well. It wouldn't be a game if no one played. I'll see yours and raise you ten."

The Eye folded instantly.

Bodkin took the pot and seemed totally befogged as to why Mr. Overlock was looking at he, the winner of his first hands, in such a disapproving way.

The next set gave the Mouth a chance to open—not that it wasn't already—and again disks flew. No one received much this time, making the possibility of a one-pair win genuine. In this respect, Bodkin looked once more to have the advantage, card-wise. His exposed cards were the three face cards and a nine. None of the others showed a ten-value card. The Captain folded. Bodkin, the Eye and the Mouth played.

Bodkin entered conservatively, and the Eye called. Then the Mouth raised the stakes by a small amount. Bodkin gazed intently at him, but the Mouth was like a still-photograph of a goldfish, and betrayed nothing. Bodkin looked at the Mouth's exposed cards, glanced at his own hole card, smiled, and made a big raise.

The Eye saw this, and made a raise this time. Bodkin flinched. The Mouth then increased the wager yet more.

Bodkin again looked at his card, smirked, and eyed the Mouth. "Trying to bluff me, are you? Well, two can play at that." He saw the Mouth's bet.

The Eye calmly met the wager as well, and upped it again. The Mouth met the new amount.

Bodkin squirmed, looking once more at his card. "You can't beat me unless I'm bluffing, either of you. I don't know what makes you think I'm bluffing. Would a bluffer do this?" He met the pot again, and this time raised it by twenty.

The Eye saw Bodkin's raise, and raised it again. The Mouth met it.

Bodkin looked at the Master. "Can I have some more credit, Mr. Overlock?"

"Never," replied the Master.

"But if I can't match their wagers, I'll forfeit what I've already put in!"

"Then you had best fold while you still have something to wager with."

"But I can win this hand!"

"No, you can't."

Bodkin grimaced, and poutingly folded. The Eye met the Mouth's wager, and won with a single pair of eights.

"Tell me why I couldn't win," insisted Bodkin.

"All of your cards being higher than your opponents', to have had a pair would have made you the guaranteed winner," said Mr. Overlock. "Yet you failed to increase this gentleman's wager after accusing him of bluffing. You had no reason to merely match his bet and risk concluding the round."

"That'n the fact that yer the most arse-obvious bluffer I've ever seen, even with me eye in me hand," chuckled the winner. "Sorry, Yawp," he said, addressing the Mouth. "I knew you was playin' his bluff, but I also knew you had nothin' higher than a seven."

The Mouth turned his face toward the Eye and said "Eat me" without moving his lips.

I deduced that Mr. Overlock was losing interest in Mr. Bodkin by his body language (he farted loudly). Anticipating that we would be leaving shortly, I let my eyes wander about and noticed the approach of a new figure to the table. He was a big, well-decked man with a smiling exterior, but with a distant glint of iron in his eye. By his expert tailoring, gold buttons and diamond cufflinks, I took him to be rich.

"What's this?" he said, transmitting effortlessly. "A contest of wiles, is it? My, it does look fun. Would there be room for a harmless old philanthropist to sit in and learn?"

"Harmless!" laughed the Eye, both eyes widening. "Buck, you're about as harmless as a knife in the chest. Go away."

The newcomer took a long rod out of a scabbard which clung to his belt. It was sharp, golden, and had three gems in the hilt. He hooked a chair from a neighboring table with it and seated himself between the Mouth and Bodkin.

"A solid gold poker," he announced. "Apt, what? I won it playing tiggywig with a coal magnate this afternoon."

"Go away! Go away!" shouted the others.

"Who is this, and why do they protest?" asked Mr. Overlock of the dealer.

"This is Mr. Bucknard 'Deer' Hart, sir," replied the dealer. "He is the club ace . . . one of the best gamblers in the region. Mr. Hart, our esteemed owner, Mr. Overlock."

Mr. Hart stood, doffed his cap, and bowed before the Master. It was then that I noticed how Mr. Hart had gotten his nickname, Deer; he had two small antlers growing out of the sides of his head.

"And his servant," added the dealer.

Hart snorted.

"This table's at capacity," grumbled the captain. "Ain't legal to let him in."

"Those are informal rules only, sir," said the dealer. "Considering his credentials and substantial level of credit here at the club, I feel that it is most definitely within the gentleman's rights to join."

"Quite," said Mr. Hart, tossing forth a small fortune in exchange for units. "And let that be a lesson to you, Jules," he added, sticking his tongue out at Captain Quint.

"Yes, Deer," said the Captain.

"The game, for the benefit of our newcomer, is five-card stud," announced the dealer. "The house will distribute the cards, one hole and four up, with wagering during each round until all participants call. The game will end with the final call of the fifth round or when all fold but one. Good luck, gentlemen."

Cards flew, and each received their "hole" cards. These were followed by the first of the visible cards held by all. At this stage, the layout was as such: Bodkin K♣; Quint 3♣; Eye Q♦; Mouth 3♦; Hart 2♠. The dealer announced that Bodkin had the high card, and the value it possessed. Bodkin took a germ's-eye peek at his hole card and then looked rapidly back up at the others, presumably to judge whether any had seen what it was. No one was paying attention to him. Bodkin scratched his chin and laid out five sovereigns. His adversaries met this. Another round of cards issued forth from the dealer's nimble fingers. This time Bodkin showed K♣ K♦, Quint 3♣ 9♥, Eye Q♦ Q♥, Mouth 3♦ 4♥, and Hart 2♠ 5♠. All showed promise except Quint, a fact stated as much by the dealer, and all threw ten more tokens into the pot to see the next set. This brought the picture to: Bodkin K♣ K♦ K♠; Quint 3♣ 9♦ 4♥; Eye Q♦ Q♥ 5♣; Mouth 3♦ 4♥ A♠; and Hart 2♠ 5♠ 7♠. Bodkin peeked at his hole card once again, and, eyeing the Master, placed out another restrained wager. All called, none raised. Bodkin looked at the others with a suspicious-looking squint, and murmured something like "Can't take it" before drawing in another engineful of smoke from his cigar. Quint sneezed, and grinned as Bodkin hurriedly protected his hole card from the blast. Hart stretched, and the Mouth stared at his cards in such a way as to suggest either gasping incredulity or yawning boredom, depending on how one read him.

The dealer, observing with us the interesting layout, delivered the last set with flair. First, he shuffled the deck one-handed, then he delivered the first card with a behind-the-back pass, and the next he blew from the deck into an upturned position beside its recipient's first two. He was balancing the deck on the back of his hand, about to deal to Quint, when Quint said "I'd like to get out of here by midnight, asshole. You deal mine the normal way, or I'll use your hand to unconstipate myself." The dealer regained his reserve.

Bodkin: K♣ K♦ K♠ 8♥ Hole
Quint: 3♣ 9♦ 4♥ Q♥ Hole
Eye: Q♦ Q♥ 5♣ 6♣ Hole
Mouth: 3♦ 4♥ A♠ 2♥ Hole
Hart: 2♠ 5♠ 7♠ 9♠ Hole

"Three, possible four of a kind; possible pair; one pair, possible two, possible threesome; possible straight; possible flush," said the dealer, surveying the scenario.

Detecting, perhaps, another threat to his supply limit, Bodkin opened modestly with ten.

"Seen it," said Quint readily, and with a look at the dealer, blew a stack of his chips neatly alongside the pile, adding ten more.

The Eye called, then looked at the Mouth. "It's up to you, Yawp," he smiled.

"Thirty radcliffes," said the Mouth, his words floating out of their portal. He threw in the lucre.

A slight sound of general remark oozed up. The stakes had now become rather serious, and it was now a contest of nerve as well as skill. What had begun as a rather casual pastime now threatened to fray the purse strings of the less wealthy four at the table.

"I am impressed," said Hart, tapping his nipples. "I see, indeed, that I am in for some spirited play. What the hell! Let us add another twenty to the collection."

One by one, he stacked his disks upon Quint's. Quint stared at them glaringly, and they fell off.

Bodkin alternately smiled, frowned, shrugged and sweated. His remaining funds were not substantial enough to withstand several hands of this nature, unless he won. However, he had a daunting display. Whatever the hole card was he repeatedly peeked at, it did not induce him to stop. He threw his seventy into the stew. Quint met it, and added ten.

The Eye held his other peeper over his cards, and then looked at his hole card with it. Then he set both down, and folded.

The Mouth, looking aghast, surprised or just thirsty, brought his wager up to those of the others, and looked probingly at Hart. Hart, looking like a stuffed deer's head, betrayed nothing. The Mouth now added a cautious five.

Hart saw it and unhesitatingly did the same, while Bodkin quaveringly tossed in an equal amount. Then Bodkin said "Wait!" and, in a deeper tone, "I'll raise it ten more."

The center of the table now resembled a pile of dirt—pay dirt. I couldn't help but drool at the sight of such immediate money, when my most recent remuneration had been a shoelace I had found which the Master had permitted me to keep. I found myself wondering if, given the initial capital, I couldn't master some of the lessons I had borne witness to that evening. Pondering this, I watched Quint up the stakes yet again.

The pot now well exceeded the hundred mark, and chips around the table were uniformly dwindling. Still, the players continued to add, until, with Hart the wagerer-to-be and Quint the last to raise, the pot stood at two-hundred eighty, with twenty yet to meet, and Bodkin in possession of only thirty more chips.

Hart looked at Bodkin in a gently pitying manner, like one watching a live lobster boil. "I take it you have no further credit at this establishment?" he asked.

"No, but I have a house," grumbled Bodkin.

"Got a little something left to take home to the wife?"

"Huh? She'll live."

Hart seemed to ponder for a moment, then met the outstanding twenty. Then he turned to Bodkin and quietly said "Excuse me, sir, but you are more knowledgeable than I. What do you do when you wish to meet your opponent's bet without raising it?"

"Hm?" said Bodkin. "Why, I call."

"The gentleman calls," said the dealer. "Show your cards."

"What? Wait!" shouted Bodkin. "I didn't—"

"The gentleman *calls*," repeated the dealer firmly, sweeping twenty units from Bodkin's pile into the pot with a stick. "Show your cards."

The hole cards were exposed, and the results were these:

Bodkin: K♣ K♦ K♠ 8♥ 10♠

Quint: 3♣ 9♦ 4♥ Q♠ K♥

Mouth: 3♦ 4♥ A♠ 2♥ A♣

Hart: 2♠ 5♠ 7♠ 9♠ J♠

Hart had won with a flush.

It seemed to take a moment for the loss to sink into the others. The Mouth crumpled up his hole card and tossed it on the ground. Quint said "Piss," then kind of laughed as he took a swig from his bottle of Old Shite. Bodkin turned red with anger.

"How can you have taken that chance?" he demanded. "I could have had four kings!"

"You were bluffing," said Hart, stretching. "Cap'n Quint had the fourth king. See?"

"Yes, but how did you know that?"

"Because you had him beaten with three of a kind. Why would he stay in the game, let alone increase the stakes?"

"Because he was bluffing, or assumed I was."

"That had nothing to do with it. No matter what his hole card was, you had him beaten. Even Winky here had a better hand."

"Then why did he stay in the game, at all?"

"Because he knew you had only three of a kind and that either of we other two had hands which may have beaten you. He was counting on both of us bluffing you into folding, then beating us with as little as one or no pair. The fourth king, as a matter of fact, would have been the high card."

"Would anyone care to purchase additional increments?" inquired the dealer.

He was met with scowls as the party, save Hart, rose and proceeded to disband. All were apparently unwilling to continue playing at the same table as Hart, had any the money to continue doing so if desired.

Bodkin got up and approached Mr. Overlock. "As you can see, it took the best to beat me," he said. "How about tomorrow?"

"Tomorrow I have an appointment with your wife," replied Mr. Overlock.

"Please don't go!" implored Hart of the departing players. "Won't someone teach me another lesson?"

None accepted, and each wafted away into the nethers of the club. Hart sighed and collected his winnings. Mr. Overlock summoned me to take him home.

Then a crash sounded, and the lights went out.

Wondering if the smoke of Bodkin's cigar had rendered me blind, I felt around for Mr. Overlock. A stubby fist to my genitals confirmed my find. As I looked at the stars now dancing in the darkness, I could feel the buffets of several others running around in a similar state, and knew it was not me. A chaotic din began to fill the air. The lights had emanated from a centralized chandelier, and I knew it must have fallen from the ceiling. As I thought this, a sudden eruption of four terrifying bellows sounded forth, and another form barged into me. It thrust something into my hand and disattached itself. As I gathered my stunned senses, I felt myself tripped, and fell down.

"Oh, excuse me, sir," I said, feeling the bulk of another individual already lying on the floor beneath me. I sat up, and just as I did so, lights burned back to life.

The dealer, his stick in hand, was twisting the knobs on some of the unlit gas lights lining the walls, and the place was full of standing individuals, save myself and the gentleman on the floor in front of me. I felt the tension of the place suddenly reintensify as everyone, seemingly, turned in my direction. It was then that I realized that the prone gentleman, still holding his winning poker hand, was Bucknard Hart, that one of his horns was broken and that his chest was covered with blood. I looked at the Master helplessly.

"What has happened?" gasped the dealer, running in our direction.

Mr. Overlock looked down at the body, and then to me. "It would appear that Mr. Hart has been killed."

"But how?"

"He has been stabbed in the chest," said the Master, adding, with a cold look at the object in my hand, "with what I would surmise to be a sharp, gold, studded poker. The one being held by Grave."

THE KEEP WHICH awaited me, the Catacombs of Onwall, was a place where the living went to become the living dead. Having already attained that state myself, one would think it to have had a home from home feel, which it in some ways did. The quarters to which I was assigned, a cell some five levels down, was not much smaller than my cubicle at the manor, nor much better lit. What did degrade it from that level, and indeed from the sewer where I had spent the afternoon, was the remarkably uncirculated fecality of it, the cockroach population, and the company. For I had a cellmate.

Something resembling a human pastry sat in a corner, a shoeless, shirtless mass of man covered with cuts. As the cell door slammed behind me, I regarded him with nervousness.

"You're wondering," he rumbled, "how a titan of my stature maintains such a godly girth under such prohibitive circumstances. Aren't you? Aren't you?"

"Er—yes, sir," I stumbled out.

"Well, you are too inquisitive, firstly," he said, "which is demerit number one. As for how, observe yonder roach dining upon the remainder of yesterday's toenail."

I watched the insect hungrily devouring the matter.

"Watch."

He proceeded to nab the cockroach between his toes, then picked it up and popped it into his mouth. I could hear it crunch.

"The cycle of life," he burped.

32

I felt a queasiness creep upon me in a manner not dissimilar to one of the zigzagging roaches. I had never quite learned to appreciate Mr. Overlock's style of consumption, but compared to my cellmate he was like a cow compared to cud. The human slug finished his meal, then gazed at me intently.

"I am called Antenor, after the manipulator," he announced. "I pull strings, I control actions. They bury me here from fear. Now I shall ask you the riddle of the spheres. When does the moon shine brightest?"

"Excuse me, sir?"

"When does it shine brightest?" he repeated. "The answer is—after it waxes! Why does it have so many craters? Because when it wanes, it pores. Why is moon cheese never eaten? Because it can't be separated from the milky whey! Ha-ha-ha. You wish more?"

"Uh . . ."

"Good. Why did the onion make the chef cry? Because it lacked appeal. What did the blind vet say when the colt whinnied in his ear? 'You sound like you're a little horse.' Why did the schoolmaster paddle Oliver Twist? Because the boy had asked for some oar."

He laughed hysterically at all of this, while I stood there wondering whether I should attempt to smile, shout for a guard or try a cockroach.

"You're a pansy, aren't you?" he suddenly said.

"I beg your pardon, sir?"

"I was not speaking to you!" he thundered. "I was speaking to the flower in your lapel."

I had a withered old carnation in my buttonhole.

"You are, aren't you? I have a flower, myself." He reached into a flesh pocket and pulled out a mushroom, one with a little mean face carved on it. "I grew him here. His name is Gus. He's fun, Gus."

He looked at me for a second, then burst out laughing again. "You're a lifeless one, you are," he said. "The most lifeless I've had since the one who strangled himself to death. Perhaps I should give you life. Sit on my lap and be my ventriloquist's dummy."

Alarm now definitely setting in, I desperately groped for a topic with which to occupy my companion. The most obvious one occurred to me first.

"Do you gamble, sir?" I asked.

He looked thoughtful. "Time itself is a gamble," he said. "One that I have had the misfortune of winning much of."

"Could you teach me?" I asked.

"Teach you to gamble?" he laughed. "Of course! As one who has studied under Tyche herself, I can sum it all up in a simple sentence: if you can master the act of giving away something of value for nothing, you have mastered gambling."

"But successfully?" I probed.

"Ah," he said, "that is the real question, isn't it? And it is one which does possess an answer." He leaned forward. "Remember this, for in all things it is the same. Observe the past to predict the future. If there are exposed cards, they can no longer be dealt. If there are discards, discount them. If a race has been won, it can be again, but one must prepare as though never having raced before. Who were the winner's opponents, for instance, and what have they learned in defeat? What were the conditions, and how have they changed? Look back and you may look forward. That is the key to gambling."

So saying, he reached a hand under himself and pulled out a decrepit set of dirty cards. "I play with myself," he explained. "It's a complete deck except for nines—I don't like nines. I will play you if you make it worth my while. What do you do?"

"Why, I am a gentleman's gentleman, sir," I replied. "Personal servant to Mr. Milo Overlock. Do you require any mending?"

"Not unless you can sew up one of these cuts," he grunted. "We have a little fight now and again."

I looked around. "'We,' sir?"

"Me."

I cleared my throat. "I'm afraid I am limited in such capacities, sir."

"I'll tell you what," he said. "When I am free, I want to set forth upon the world a dignified, civilized gentleman. I want to shine, to sparkle, to induce the instinctive admiration of all who behold me. In short, I want to be bathed. If I instruct you in the art of the wager, will you agree to bathe me upon event of my release?"

I disguised my horror in a cautionary question. "What was your crime?"

"High treason. I sold the queen's recipe for basted puffin flippers to some yellow from Wight."

I relaxed. Such a crime, I knew, could but carry the most unrestricted of sentences.

"I agree, sir."

"Very well. We will use dead cockroaches for chips. Our first lesson: gin rummy."

And so the night progressed. By morning (or what I supposed to be morning) I had lost about ninety percent of my hands and was ready to collapse.

"You may sleep now," the winner said. "Your lesson is complete."

"But sir, I thought you were going to teach me to win," I protested.

"Indeed I did," he replied. "You have lost nearly every hand. To win, do exactly the opposite of what you did tonight, and you'll succeed."

"The opposite?" I said. "I was trying to use the past to predict the future."

"Yes, but so was I. Hence, I canceled you out."

"Then shouldn't we have tied?" I asked.

"When two opponents employ the same strategy, the more experienced tends to win. Take my advice—play with an idiot."

My already exhausted mind swimming with all of this, I closed my eyes and tried to sleep. This was not aided in the fact that Antenor chose that moment to enter into a shrill argument with himself—something about eggs, I believe. My head was pounding, but after awhile my cellmate apparently decided to give himself the silent treatment, and in great relief I adjusted my position on the stone floor and stuck my thumb in my mouth. I was just blacking out when suddenly the cell door was yanked open and I was pulled by the lapels out into the passageway. Focusing blearily, I perceived Mr. Overlock's stout form standing there alongside a cellkeep of considerable development. I wondered if my gallows had already been prepared for me.

"Home, Grave," said the Master, slapping the thumb from my lips. "I require breakfast."

My brain sluggishly rotated. "Where's the cook?" came out of my now-unclogged mouth.

"He is cooking, you damned drone. It is your duty to serve. And you will address me with 'sir' or I will have your skin stewed and your viscera used for vegetables."

"Yes, sir."

We started for the surface, myself saying little though wondering much. Among my swirling uncertainties was whether the place I was leaving or the place to which I was returning was the better. I wasn't even certain I was out for good.

"So I will be returning after breakfast, sir?" I ventured.

He sighed, about as loudly as one can. "I am not going to come fetch you six times a day for my meals, Grave. I was willing to dispense with your services long enough to complete my objective, but that has been reached, however abruptly. I wanted you to languish here in presumed guilt to give the true malefactor a sense of security, and to test his recklessness. My profile of the assailant has been detailed enormously overnight, as he apparently struck again quite shortly after the gaming establishment closed. The dealer, he of the olfactory absence, was found bludgeoned to death near his home in the small hours. The weapon, as before, was left at the scene—this time a spade, with which the victim had been pummeled no fewer than five times."

"Good Lord, sir," I gasped.

"Quite. Two victims in one night, assuming one offender. Knowing your presumed guilt, it can only be concluded that the attacker is inviting attention."

"Then why did he put the first weapon into my hand, sir?" I asked.

"A temporary ruse, that you be arrested, the crowd dismissed and his freedom to strike at his second victim assured. It also ridded him of the weapon, which might have been discovered on his person if a search had been instigated."

"The weapon he took from Mr. Hart, sir?"

"Yes."

"Which he used to bring down the chandelier with?"

"No. He used the darkness brought about by the chandelier's collapse to extract the weapon and strike his victim. The chain suspending the chandelier had been secured by a hook on a wall, behind a curtain at the opposite end of the room. The chandelier being composed of several small oil lamps, the arrangement allowed for easy lowering and refueling of the fixture. Whoever struck it down would have had difficulty assailing the victim immediately afterward."

"A conspiracy, sir?"

"Or a lone operator who reacts quickly to opportunities which serve his ends."

"He seems reckless, sir."

"Because he struck so soon after implicating you? He knew you would only stay here as long as I wished it. He was undoubtedly aware that I knew of your innocence."

I mused, in my dazed way, at how another victim had given his life so that the Master, aware of my innocence, could profile his adversary.

"There was also another clue of sorts left at the scene," continued Mr. Overlock. "Five cards, as before. The jack of hearts, a four of spades which was cut in half, an overturned ace of hearts, a two of clubs, and a joker."

"But what does it mean, sir?"

"I will study them over duck wings. I am intrigued by a new dish suggested to me this morning by the cook, and I wish you to learn it. Carry me to the coach."

I WATCHED OUR cook carefully as he prepared the Master's meal, a glint of knowing suspicion in my eye. My cellmate's revelations had given me an insight into my coherency-challenged cohort's methods which now convinced me that his reference to wings at our meeting had been no accident, and which I now planned to use as my ace in the hole, so to speak. I knew upon entering the kitchen that he had been to the butcher's already, for some distinctly unusual "wings" were on display upon the counter, and he was coating them with breading. So this was his secret to great "duck wings." They weren't "duck wings" at all, but basted puffin flippers! And I was to endure tutelage from this chartreuse charlatan? Indeed not, I told myself. I knew his secret, and would decline his instruction. When the Master became ready to test my new skills, I would produce the most magnificent "duck wings" of all time. And meanwhile, I could engage my fellow hireling in an art to which I now felt ready to claim "teacher" status myself—the art of the wager.

"I understand you, eh, Easterners enjoy a little subversion now and again," I said.

"Wok," he replied.

I looked around for a wok, then remembered that we didn't have one.

"Sorry, we haven't one," I said. "Now then, I'm told that playing-cards were invented in the Orient."

"Wok at me."

I'd have been happy to throw a wok at him, had I one to do so with. I said as much, then asked him if he ever gambled.

"Wok! Wok!"

If this was his idea of puffin impersonation, I had little clue how to react except to hand him more meat. He tossed it down on the counter brusquely, then pointed at his eyes.

"Look at you?" I asked.

He nodded with a sigh.

"I'm sorry I don't speak Chinese," I puffed, "but I have no intention of observing your methods. I am quite convinced that I could produce your variety of duck without any training whatsoever, and I am prepared to prove that to Mr. Overlock. Meanwhile, let us spend what time we have in honest competition, shall we?"

I pulled out a deck of cards I had taken from the parlor bureau shortly after arriving home. The cook licked his lips.

"Shall we play?" I asked.

"Pray," he said.

"YESTERDAY, YOU ADVISED me to shut down my gaming establishment, lest someone be killed," said Mr. Overlock to Mrs. Bodkin sternly. "The following day, two are dead. How do you explain such remarkable timing?"

It was evening. We were in the sitting-room, the Master, Heavenly Bodkin and I. Mr. Overlock had scheduled his summons for the betting-parlor's peak hours in order to interview his subject (as he informed me) at a time her husband was most likely to be occupied. Despite the fact that I was the sitting-room's only standee, I was grateful to be away from the casino. I had entered heavily into debt with the cook that afternoon, and the very concept of gambling was sitting like a sandbag in my stomach.

"I told you the matter was urgent," said Mrs. Bodkin, still spirited but appearing somewhat shakier than the day before. "My fear has now been justified. Odds is guilty…you must take him."

Mr. Overlock looked her over. She appeared as attractive as ever in a low-cut gown and glistening earrings, but her expression had definitely become more pallid, and she fidgeted. "Yesterday your concern was for his protection," said the Master. "And now you want him taken?"

"For his own good," replied Mrs. Bodkin.

"If he is found guilty of yesterday's crimes, little good can come to him if taken. No, your motives are elsewhere. Perhaps you arranged the killings yourself, to implicate him? Easy to cast suspicion on one just beaten at cards by one victim, and dealt his losing hands by the other."

"I wasn't even present," she returned. "Not allowed, you know."

"I didn't say you committed the crimes personally," said Mr. Overlock. "But one such as you does possess a power capable of manipulating certain men—often the types attracted to the glamour of gaming circles. You are too primitively attractive to be without a companion, and my impression is that your husband is not it. Who, then?"

She pursed her lips and sat silent.

"I will not arrest your husband without proof of his guilt," said Mr. Overlock. "To win means nothing if one's opponent remains the superior player. No, he must be beaten. And until I beat mine—whether your husband or someone else—others lie open to victimization. I advise you to be forthright."

Mrs. Bodkin ran a hand through her hair. "When it comes to violence, I believe Odds a very capable player, Mr. Overlock. He has threatened it several times, and I don't think he was bluffing."

"Threatened whom? Yourself?"

"No, although I did feel it wise to tell him that my visitations with you were an effort to get you to extend him more credit, after remarks he says you made about an appointment with me."

"But he has never directly threatened you."

"No, but he has frequently expressed the desire to eliminate some of his tormentors at that club of yours—the ones who beat him regularly at cards. And now he has."

"You told me you feared him. I don't believe you do."

"I was embellishing, in order to prevent a crime."

"But lacking concern for his protection, how does doing so affect you?"

"Couldn't I just be concerned for the welfare of others?"

"No. You 'needed' me to close that club as much as you need me to arrest your husband now. There is a personal interest which you are not revealing."

"Fine then. Perhaps there is someone I have an interest in seeing spared. But his odds are getting longer, Mr. Overlock. He wants to keep gambling, because he can beat my husband. But kept losing, my husband is going to beat him like he did his dealer last night—five times with a spade, the newspaper said. Horrid."

"Who is he?"

She sighed. "Jack Ball. He's a sailor."

"No doubt," said Mr. Overlock dryly. "He played at the table last night?"

"Yes. He has the distinguishing feature of a single eye."

"What fleet has he served?"

"Well, he's a bargeman, actually. He works on Captain Quint's barge, the Shamrock, one of several formerly owned by the late Mr. Hart. They're all old shipmates from the days when the Blackhearts transported slaves and sold them to new world tradesmen. When the practice was eliminated, they became river bargemen. Mr. Hart discovered his talent for gambling, which made him wealthy, and the other two worked for him."

"And the dealer—a former shipmate, also?" the Master asked.

"Why, yes. How did you know?"

41

"They all have odd physical abnormalities."

"Yes. Caused by scurvy. Mr. Hart grew horns. Jack lost an eye, your dealer his nose and Quint his—well, let's just say there's no flap in his seat."

Mr. Overlock looked displeased. "You will not use such casual phrasing with me, female. Your association with sailors has left an influence upon your manner which marriage has obviously failed to rehabilitate. Your involvement began where—as a dockside entertainer? A dance hall hostess?"

"I served drinks," she replied stiffly.

"You served drinkers," said Mr. Overlock. "Your lover or your husband—who was first?"

"They were simultaneous," she stated crisply. "One for the money, the other for the show, you might say. Odds owned some boats which went through sometimes, then after meeting me, he settled here. To me, he was security. Jack was fun. Always joking, laughing—and what a patch. But now all he thinks about is gambling. And since gambling is illegal in Onwall outside of licensed casinos—the *one* licensed casino, I should say—whatever money Odds avoids losing to other players goes to you."

"Don't be absurd. Surely your—second mate, shall we say—pays for your companionship, with funds won from your husband. If the club is closed, what becomes of it?"

"I keep it. It's my money, you see. My portion of my husband's value. What Jack gives me rarely restores what I lose as Odds' worth decreases. If no one gambles, I can keep the money, and get something from Jack that wasn't mine to begin with. That's why Jack wants the club kept opened, because he can keep me with my own husband's money. He doesn't fear Odds, but telling him about our relationship would mean having to support me himself."

Mr. Overlock leaned back. "What makes you think this dalliance would last if your husband was no longer available to be duped?"

"I don't necessarily expect it to."

"I see. Considering that your affair, if exposed, could make a successful divorce settlement—wherever obtained—questionable, what shall we conclude? That your husband, no longer gambling, drops his threats against your lover? And your lover, encouraged by you—kills him?"

"That would not be necessary, Mr. Overlock. Not if you just put Odds away—for his own good, as I said."

Mr. Overlock may have smiled slightly. He leaned back, took out his pipe and began to smoke it, quietly regarding his visitor as he did so. "Those are lively earrings you are wearing, Mrs. Bodkin," he said. "I recognize them from the jeweled chandelier which collapsed last night. The work of your companion?"

Mrs. Bodkin squirmed a bit. "My intentions were as I told you, Mr. Overlock. To persuade you to see for yourself that Odds' environment is an unsettled one."

"Which is also why you painted him as something slightly more salvageable than the utterly inept gambler he truly is, and how you knew I'd find the evening interesting. How did you convince Ball to collapse it?"

"I told him I wanted some earrings made from its jewels, and that I'd leave him if he didn't get them. I didn't think anyone would notice where they'd come from."

"Your husband apparently didn't."

"I wasn't wearing them when I saw him today, and I didn't see him at all last night."

"He stays out often?"

"He usually requires the services of the pub next to your parlor after a night of gambling. Jack and the barge hands have to rise early and work, so they usually go to the pub before the parlor opens. Odds stays away from the bar when they're there. The Blackhearts are usually open and accepting to those they respect, but occasions arise when they'll get boisterous with any rival. Odds hasn't gotten to the respect stage yet."

"But they tolerate him at the tables because he loses."

"Right."

"Which is why they remained despite Hart's entry into the game last night."

"I assume so. Only a gambler as untalented as Odds would keep them at a table with one as good as Hart. Fortunately for them, Hart gambled all over, and there have been many times they could avoid playing at your club with him."

"Hart knew your husband?"

"Of course. He started using that innocent act of his to lure in novices, and it got to be so natural to him that he began using it all the time, even with gamblers he knew. Most of them knew better than to play him, but Odds thinks he can beat anyone."

"Thank you, Mrs. Bodkin," said Mr. Overlock. "You have fulfilled my requirement and engaged my interest sufficiently to draw this appointment to a close as it is."

"And you'll do something about my husband?" she asked.

"I will consider your request. You may leave."

With a look of subtle success on her face, Mrs. Bodkin nodded at the Master and rose.

"You may also leave the earrings," said Mr. Overlock.

Frowning, she removed the earrings, threw them at me, and made her own way to the door. I watched incredulously as she left.

"Sir, I—"

"What is it, Grave? You question her motives? While ambitious, they have no immediate bearing. Mr. Ball, her paramour, has every interest in keeping her husband in his present situation, and can therefore have played no part in any design linked to implicating him. As far as the chandelier is concerned, an outgoing individual such as Ball is described could, intentionally or not, have made his plan known to attentive others in the pub beforehand, especially if consuming heavily. Not that the murderer, if astute, required such foreknowledge to employ the plan's advantages."

"But could not Mrs. Bodkin be the murderer herself, sir?"

"No. Note her demeanor at the outset. Uneasy, as though she truly feared for her illegitimate swain's safety. The assailant in this case is almost brazenly self-announcing. He kills, despite the presence of an innocent proxy. He leaves intentional clues. He draws attention to his acts. His confidence and drive are of a different sort than hers, as I suspect are his motives. Her possession of the two earrings, which I will now relieve you of, lends credence to her professed involvement in the chandelier's collapse, the executor of which is unlikely to have been able to kill Hart. Even allowing that the implication of her husband was her intent, the abrupt second murder is both extemporaneous and illogical."

"Perhaps she wanted to frame Mr. Bodkin with the first murder, then committed the second in order to direct the blame away from me, and back to him," I said, feeling smart.

"Then why would she have had you framed you to begin with? Such an aim would have been better served if the assailant had merely dropped the weapon on the floor."

"Oh."

"This in addition to the fact that Mrs. Bodkin was not present at the time of the first murder."

"Oh."

"Get my coach ready, Grave. We go to the gaming-parlor."

"Oh, hell's witches," I muttered.

"What was that, Grave?"

"Er—all's well which is, sir," I fumbled.

"All is not well. And neither will you be unless you are ready to go in five minutes. Get the horses."

Grumbling internally, I went off and prepped the sullen nags, who, unaccustomed to so much activity, bit at me viciously and neighed without cease. Then I came back in and helped the Master into his overcoat, before doffing myself in the proper topper he insisted I drove about in. We set out, Death taking his seat in the carriage, and his three captives bearing him whither his whim fancied, in this case the Parlour d'Overluck again. As my fellow work beasts clumped toward it, conditions became evident that we were not the only souls so bound that evening, for a gathering of some note seemed to be forming out front.

I coaxed the horses along until we could get close to the congregation. Mr. Overlock bade me stop the coach, and I did so, coming to a stop somewhere near the gathering. I hurried down and opened the Master's door, whence he stepped forth in Napoleonic splendor, and the crowd, though he was behind it, turned as one and gasped at the sight of him.

"Mr. Milo Over—" I began.

"They are aware of my identity, Grave. Don't intrude."

Whatever the beguiling spectacle was which had entranced the throng, it was obviously no match for the sight of the Master. The rabble peered at him like needy little strays, and parted fluidly to allow him access to the attraction. He stepped forward with the air of one who knew what to expect, and I followed behind, my nose upturned.

It did not remain upturned for long, for as we closed in on the forefront of the building, one of the sheep stuck out a hoof, and I went tumbling to the turf. The crowd laughed raucously as I got up on my knees, grasped fruitlessly at my bounding riding-hat, and brushed the dirt from my tired attire. The Master looked at me like a sphinx eyeing the slave in charge of protuberances.

"You are an ass, Grave," he said in front of everyone. "Asses are less than horses. Hence, you will sleep in the stable tonight and the horses will use your room."

"Yes, sir," I said, swallowing sod.

"Now get up, or I shall see that your pathetic husk suffers the same treatment as the one now wearing your hat."

I got up, and saw what he was referring to. On the ground, at the egress to the alleyway between Mr. Overlock's casino and the neighboring pub, lay a body, face down. My hat had rolled to a stop on its head, and a knife was in its back. Mr. Overlock went up to it and kicked it over. It was the Eye, Jack Ball. Alongside the body was a short stack of five cards, the five of diamonds on top.

"Good," said the Master. "What I had anticipated has now occurred. Your 'murderess' can be dismissed of suspicion, Grave. The real key to these crimes is now ours."

I WAS DEAD TIRED by the time I crawled into the kitchen to put away Mr. Overlock's last dishes, in the wee hours after we'd finally returned. I hadn't slept in two days, and was feeling like a curdled egg. My mood had not been improved by having had to deposit the horses in my room on reentering, their neighs changing to distinct yeighs as I did so. They had immediately jumped onto my bed, collapsing it, and begun indulging themselves like yearlings, while I took a tattered blanket from one's back and exited the premises for final chores and stables beyond. By the time I had finished preparing, presenting and removing the Master's midnight snack, I was so tired I would have slept in the sewer, and it was with heavy foot that I slogged into the kitchen. Such was my rather indignant surprise when, upon illuminating the zone, I saw our cook sitting in a corner, wide awake and reading a copy of "Mr. Oo and Rinkypink" by candle.

Preternaturally annoyed, I went over, picked up the second volume he had sitting on the floor ("The Sex Ducks") and threw it in the trash. I wished it could have been him.

"Go to your room!" I demanded.

He stood up, smiling genially. Then the gangrenous leech took the book he was holding and slapped me on the backside with it.

"Yoip!" I exclaimed. "How dare you!"

"I hit you."

"What!"

"I hit you because you owed."

"You hit me because I'm old?"

"You owed but did not pay. So I hit you."

It penetrated. "I have every intention of paying any debt due you, young man. I was merely under the impression that our contest had not been completed."

He pulled out a deck of cards from nowhere.

"What? Not tonight, young man. I am going to sleep. And I suggest that, unless you plan to do the same, you do something more productive than reading trash. Tell me, have you done anything at all worthwhile today?"

"I swept and rewaxed."

I looked at the kitchen floor. It was filthy. "Liar!" I said.

He spanked me again.

"Stop that!" I yelped, grabbing a handy ladle and holding it between us. "Look, young man, I will be content to discuss this matter at another time, but right now I am tired. I am tired and I am going to go lie down."

"Why down?"

"Because I can't sleep standing up."

"Can't sweep standing up?"

"I'm leaving for the barn."

"Weaving for the barn?"

"I need to lay my head down."

"Weigh your head down?"

"Good night."

He shrugged, an impudent expression on his face. "You go now, you pay now."

"Excuse me?"

He rubbed his fingers together.

I cogitated. "Am I to understand that if I do not play you right now, you will insist upon collecting my debt?"

"Quite so."

"And if I refuse both?"

He grinned and pointed at the ceiling. "Tell boss."

When I was a child, someone told me that fairies lived in the grass. Out of some illicit impulse, I went out and stomped all over the lawn. I have been convinced ever afterward that my ultimate life as an insect has been their revenge.

"Very well," I grred, taking a seat at the kitchen table and motioning for cards. "I will play. But be prepared for a lesson in abject humility. Fierce is the spirit which rises from a Grave. Tonight, *I* will cast a spell." I waved my ladle like a fairy's wand.

"You bet," he said, and proceeded to stomp me.

BLEARY BEYOND belief was the state in which I served the Master his breakfast the next morning. The cook, having finished with breakfast and with me, had gone off to his slumber. I had retrieved the horses from my room, which, besides having been aswim with poop, had seen every fixture, furnishing and fragment chewed to the skeleton. I had managed to clean the quarters just in time for the Master's bell, and he now sat before me at the breakfast-table, staring at the latest set of cards and munching on the sinews of his morning wings with loud gurgles. I stood there in an almost disembodied trance with a fixed but unseeing stare at Mr. Overlock's face.

"Why are you looking at me as though I were some horrifying spectacle, Grave?" he said.

I snapped out of it. "Oh, pardon me, sir. I was daydreaming."

"Day is not the time for dreaming," he snapped. "Now, stand on one leg and count to one hundred. If you get even one number wrong, I will stab you in the knee with this fork."

"But sir, I—"

"Grave."

"One . . ."

By the time I had finished, my knee had been punctured more times than I could apparently count, and pain was shooting up me like fireworks lit off in my leg and bursting in my brain.

"Now drop your other leg."

I gratefully did.

"You will now find yourself more wakeful."

I thanked him, I think.

"Now observe the cards. 5♦, A♥, 2♥, K♥, K♣. Do these mean anything to you?"

"Not a damn thing," I didn't say.

"You will remember that they were preceded by the set left with the dealer's body—a jack of hearts, a four of spades cut in half, an overturned ace of hearts, a two of clubs and a joker."

"Yes, sir."

"The jack of hearts is one-eyed, as was the perished Jack Ball. An odd coincidence, or significant?"

I was stumped. "I don't know, sir. But if pertinent, what would the others mean?"

"Let us consider the sliced four of spades," he said, extracting one from the deck on the table and tearing it accordingly. "What does it resemble to you?"

"A two of spades with a four in the corner, sir."

"Your simplicity is creditable on this occasion. Now, what if I turn it over?"

I looked at the upside-down halved card and tried to be simplistic. "I think they look like two black hearts, sir."

"And what does the inverted four resemble?"

"A . . . well, a knife, sir."

"Jack Ball was a former member of the Blackhearts. He was killed with a knife."

I gaped. "And the overturned ace of hearts, sir?"

"He was stabbed in the back. It pierced his heart."

"But the two of clubs, sir?"

"He was killed between two clubs—his pub and the casino. And as for the joker, isn't that how Mrs. Bodkin described him in earlier times?"

"Remarkable, sir," I said. "But surely this may be coincidence. Were not those cards found on the dealer's corpse, rather than that of Mr. Ball?"

"Indeed, and that is the key. These cards are not clues to the crime which they accompany, but future crimes. Consider the clue left with Mr. Hart."

I pondered. "What clue, sir?"

"He was holding his poker hand when he died. Five spades. The dealer, killed later that night, was assaulted five times with a spade."

"Good heavens, sir. Can it be true?"

"I intend to prove it with the next set. Let us analyze it."

He laid out the five cards and peered intently at them.

"I have been ruminating upon these since first seeing them last night. There are several interpretations, of course, but let me tell you the conclusion I have formed the greatest confidence in. The hand was found stacked, with the top card being the five of diamonds. This card, I believe, refers to Captain Quint of the gambling circle, "quint" meaning five, and his first name Jules a homonym for jewels, or diamonds. He sits upon a series of hearts, followed by a club. I would interpret this as a metaphor for Hart's club, but the former Bucknard Hart did not own a club. He did, however, own barges, one of which—the Shamrock—is operated by Captain Quint. The shamrock is the symbol of the club card. Together, these cards seem to read Captain Quint on Hart's 'Shamrock.' One may infer that the next crime will take place on the barge. But will Quint be victim, or is he the killer? We must go there and find out."

"But when, sir?" I asked.

"The numbers on the last four cards may bear the answer. The five on the first card is clearly Quint, but these others must point to a time, or my deduction is entirely misdirected."

"Ace, two, king, king, sir? A time?"

"We must not expect the obvious, Grave. Our opponent is far too inventive for that. We must look further. Now, an ace may be one or eleven, and this is followed by a two. That leaves the kings. What do they mean to you?"

I thought and thought, but could think of nothing a king could possibly represent. Onwall did not even have one.

"I'm sorry, sir, but a king means nothing to me."

"Correct. A king means nothing. Zero. And that is the value we will assign to these. We now show ace, two, zero, zero. If this figure is a time, the ace can only be a one. One, two, zero, zero. Written, it says twelve o'clock."

"Noon, sir?"

"During the game two nights ago, Quint expressed a desire to get out by midnight. During inquiries last night, I discovered that he is very strict about this. He lives on the barge and returns to it around midnight every night, so as to receive adequate rest before starting work early the next day—a bargeman's practice as mentioned by Mrs. Bodkin."

"So you expect an ambush at that time, sir?"

"It is sensible to assume. It is, indeed, the one time most of Quint's acquaintances can know where to find him."

"How very convenient, sir. Shall I report this to the constabulary?"

"Of course not, Grave. It is we who will effect the capture."

"!!!!!!"

"What was that, Grave?"

"Nothing, sir."

"The river is a brief portion from here. Be ready to depart by ten-thirty."

"Yes, sir," I said.

"The rest of your day may be spent in education with the cook. These duck wings are irreproachable, and I will wish to test your development soon."

"Yes, sir."

This bit of assignment lacked the brittle effect he may have intended. Indeed, it filled me with the only little sense of victory I had had in some time. I waited the small eternity for the Master to finish, then took the dishes and made a beeline for the kitchen. The cook yet abed, I pored through the ice chest and various other places, wondering where he had stashed his magical meat.

"Pooh," I swore, not finding anything but duck anywhere. Then, still wanting a nap but energized by resolve, I grabbed my old overcoat hanging on the kitchen door-hook and bolted out of the home. Hopping on the rusty bicycle I used for these occasions, I wheeled my way to town and up to the butcher's shop.

"What'll it be?" said the butcher.

"Puffin!"

"Don't carry it."

"Nonsense! You're merely out of it. I know you've been selling it to Mr. Overlock's cook."

"Try the zoo, you deranged idiot."

I did.

"I want puffins," I said.

"Only pair died of old age yesterday. Why don't you?"

"Do you still have them?"

"On ice."

"Charge them to Mr. Overlock!"

And, puffins in tow, I dashed back. I had just put them in the icebox and retired to my room for a quick rest when the bell rang. The Master wanted his elevenses . . . and it was only ten. I got him his elevenses, waited for him to consume them, and took the dishes back to the kitchen.

"Stud!" shouted the cook.

"Huh?"

"Stud," he repeated.

"The horses are back in the stable," I replied stiffly.

He flourished the cards.

"No, no 'stud' now," I barked. "I am going to go back to my room now."

"No going back to womb now. Game, or cook tell boss."

I played with him for an hour, losing every hand. Then the bell rang.

"Yes, sir?"

"It is eleven, Grave."

And so on. About the only things I didn't do that day were sleep, win, and learn how to cook duck wings. The last of these was the only one I had chosen to forego. But my day, I knew, would come.

NIGHT, OF COURSE, had to come first. At ten-thirty the Master boarded the coach and I proceeded to conduct us to Onwall's river district, where goods were transported by barge to neighboring territories by way of the one major river. This river had no formal name, but it was said that an early traveler had once asked a native where water could be found in the area and the native had replied "The river runs nearby." The traveler took the name of the waterway to be the river Runs, which it was called ever afterward, with most people simply (and unfortunately) calling it the Runs.

"Are we there yet, Grave?" inquired the Master from within.

"The river runs nearby, sir," I replied, gazing forth at the nearby mass beyond. It curled through the dregs of the city and out to environs beyond. At Mr. Overlock's poke, I pulled up at a nearby warehouse, where I hitched the horses and opened the Master's door. After a brief look around, we proceeded to skulk into the fog.

"Ay there, rickets," said a figure emerging from a trash can. "What's the word from the other side?"

I regarded the oily being with fearful repugnance. "Good evening, sir," was all I felt capable of saying.

The figure stared at me in a discomforting way. "Ew look like me dead mother. Lend sonny a fiver, or I'll feed ew to me dog."

I could hear a distant mongrel howling in the depths of the can, like some otherworldly creature drifting between dimensions. Trembling, I pointed at Mr. Overlock. The figure's white eyes widened in the dark as they beheld him.

"I beg for mercy, sir," it said.

"Granted," said Mr. Overlock. "Now, tell us where to find the Shamrock, and vanish forever."

The figure pointed at a distant barge enshrouded by the fog, then promptly vanished away.

"Proceed, Grave, and no more socializing."

Not entirely satisfied by the apparition's easy dismissal, I made for the vessel in the mist. It was indeed a grim tub, one I could easily picture driving a man to the attractions of the gambling-hall. It sat on the soupy water, licked by lichen and looking distinctly at odds with the lucky symbol for which it had been named. What made me most uneasy about it, however, was my uncertainty as to whether the murderer we sought was upon it already, or if the victim was, or if I was the victim.

We crept up alongside and surveyed its ghostly exterior. The dark hulk stared soundlessly back.

"What do we do now, sir?" I asked.

"Board it, ass. The gangplank is already down."

"Eh—should it be, sir?"

"Aboard."

Shaking like an epileptic jellyfish, I quavered up the plank and on deck. Between the cold and my nerves, I had developed an uncontrollable shudder that ran from my head to my toes, and throughout every limb. I was trembling so much that I could barely help the Master aboard.

"You blasted invertebrate," he growled. "Get a hold of yourself or I will tie you to the anchor and toss it to the crabs."

He walked onto the deck and began poking about scrutinously. It was a rather simply designed scow, perhaps sixty feet from bow to stern, with both a towline and a rudder. The rear of the deck, where supplies were traditionally loaded, was open and spacious, and the damp surface betrayed no sign of footprints. The only internal quarters in immediate evidence was a meager middle cabin, its walls peeling and warped. A hatch lay near the bow. Apart from an errant bucket or two, a hawser curled in the stern, and the occasional fish bone, items were few, and all of them lacked obstructive qualities. It seemed clear that this open part of the boat, at least, was uninhabited.

"This appears to be the main level," said Mr. Overlock, "with one central wheelhouse and a bolted hatchway leading to lower quarters. Let us investigate the steering-compartment."

He took out a set of iron keys and went to the cabin door. After studying both the lock on the door and the keys for a few moments, he selected one of the keys and proceeded to open the portal.

"Where did you get those, sir?" I gasped.

"They were Hart's. I took them and the rest of his personal effects from the mortuary the morning after your arrest."

We stepped into the compartment, a typical barge bridge with charts, fixtures, and assorted paraphernalia suited to the trade. Tools for navigation were scattered about, a barometer was on display, and pieces of scrimshaw were in evidence. In a closet were some mops and buckets, and a set of nautical books was lined up in a case. I was not at all impressed, but the Master seemed unusually interested, especially with a large bottle he had found sitting on the floor.

"Does it have a message in it, sir?" I asked, intrigued.

"It has whiskey in it," he said. "What makes it useful is its glass. It may make an effective throwing-weapon."

"But—didn't you bring your gun, sir?"

"No. Fog is bad for its finish."

I gaped, feeling finished myself, when he handed me the bottle.

"Go outside and climb to the roof of this cabin, Grave. From there, you will be able to throw this item as a projectile to any point on the deck. I will keep watch here for anyone boarding the barge, and will tap the ceiling with a mop handle when I want you to hurl."

I felt quite up to this, though not with the bottle and possibly sooner than he wanted. Nevertheless, I took the smelly flask with a shiver, trying to keep it at the furthest length from my person as possible.

"Sir, shouldn't we search the rest of the barge? The killer may already be here, below deck or something."

"Only if he found a way to lock himself in from outside. Here is a step-ladder," he said, procuring one from the closet. "Pull it up after yourself once you get above."

Resigned (though not in the sense I wished), I received the lime-encrusted ladder and took it out into the mist. A light rain had begun to fall, lending an even clammier chill to the dismal evening. Restraining my bitter thoughts (lest Mr. Overlock somehow read them), I placed the ladder against the wet wall and climbed up it, squeaking in every joint.

Atop, I dutifully retracted the device and crouched down on the perilously slick surface to count my curses. The drizzle penetrated my thin outerwear and its droplets crawled down my skin like worms, while the mist became ever thicker and reduced visibility to mole level. I looked at the flagon of Old Shite in my hand and wondered if a nip of it might warm me up. It smelled like its name, but at the moment I was so cold that I would have sucked on a warm rag. I quakingly removed its cap, held my nose with one hand and lifted the bottle to my lips with the other. I sipped a drop, then slowly freed my nose.

Glurp.

An alarm began sounding in my brain, the kind that precedes diarrhea during a public address. Only it wasn't the calamity for which the present river had been inadvertently christened, but the upheaval of an offended ingestive tract. The elixir had tasted like a drop of concentrated sewage, and my stomach was revolting horrifically. What's more, the reaction seemed to drain away all of my limited blood supply, leaving me icecubic. Just then, the hum of a foul sea chanty met my ears and the gangplank creaked with the onset of a heavy body. Captain Quint was coming aboard—and he was not alone.

Shivering from fright and cold, and lurching with volcanic eruptions from within, I was barely able to steady myself enough to peer over the lip of the overhang. As I did, the vague shadows of two men were barely discernible below, sauntering up the forefront of the ship. They were talking intermittently, and the one that sounded like Quint was humming at intervals. The discourse appeared companionable.

"Good take tonight," said Quint. "(*Old man sailor, bend down low, wipe that poop deck, heave that ho…*) You've got 'em all bluffed down there. They think you're a gentleman. (*Buff that gangway, use your spit, shine that deck, you piece of*) It's getting late, though. Better be getting home to that lady of yours. I'll see you at the pub tomorrow."

"What makes you think she'll be waiting up?" muttered the other. The voice was familiar.

"Oh, she will be. She likes the way you kiss."

"Hmph. She enjoys sailors too much."

"That one's gone, though, now."

"Yes. I ended the affair the easy way."

"Har!" laughed Quint. "You should have been a Blackheart."

So saying, he ambled to the hatch, extracted his keys and began applying one to the lock. At this moment, I could vaguely see the other figure subtly pull an object from out of his coat. I could make out that it was reasonably big—not the typical sort of item one would be carrying in an inner coat pocket—and dark. I took it to be a stick of some description, though the fact that this was all a play of shadows left details scarce. I saw the figure raise it up and begin creeping up behind the bent Quint.

With dread in my heart, poison in my stomach and horror coursing through my bloodless skin, I anticipated the summons to come. Within instants, a thump rose imperiously up from beneath, and the moment had arrived. I stood up and reared back the bottle. Then, quaking spasmodically, I flailed it forth. The bottle spun through the air and soared deckward, where it landed with a blunt thunk and a crunch—on the head of Captain Quint.

The other figure paused suddenly. I heard the Master say "Stop or be killed" firmly from the deck below. The figure dropped its weapon and ran for the gangplank.

"Pursue, Grave!"

I grabbed the ladder and ran to the edge, where my foot struck a patch of wetness. In a howling instant, I remembered that I was wearing no shoes—I'd left them in the casino on the night of the poker game—and I went hurtling forward. Like an old puffin trying one last time to fly, I went whizzing off the roof, ladder in hand, and both it and I went driving into the deck below, impacting with a splintering, ferocious report. I heard our quarry's running steps recede from the gangplank and into the milky night.

Before passing out, I could just discern Mr. Overlock's approach. I saw him standing over me and muttering in a dark, quiet tone.

"A wart is an infection," he said. "It takes time to cure an infection. And time is what you'll have."

With these foreboding words floating in my ears, I vacated awareness.

DREAMS IN THE abstract shouted mercilessly in my mind as I plumbed the depths of an aching unconsciousness. It was as though all of my neurons were doing a fire dance around my bright burning brain, and my heart was tied to a stake in the middle of it, thumping fearfully. Around this was a crowd of pains, each of which was throwing pieces of splintered wood on the fire and laughing. This went on for a long miserable stretch until a voice suddenly penetrated the assemblage and said "Silence!" The little miseries stopped frolicking and sat down, the fire went into a slow burn, and I slowly floated to the surface. I found myself in what remained of my bed at the manor, and Mr. Overlock was standing next to it.

"Silence, Grave. You have been shouting in your sleep."

I focused in on the moment. "Sir, may I ask what has happened?"

"I have employed an idiot for a manservant."

"Who, sir?"

"One who has not yet begun to feel pain."

I shriveled, comprehending, then undulated on the bed. "Sir, have I been severely injured?"

"Not to an extent which will prevent you from preparing my breakfast."

"But the killer, sir—has he been captured?"

"The killer had been captured, until you provided him with his freedom. All he left was his weapon, an aptly-chosen shillelagh. We haven't even a clue to his next crime."

"But Captain Quint, sir. He can identify the criminal!"

"Captain Quint has died of injuries incurred from having had a glass bottle thrown at his head."

I gaped. "Sir, I—"

"Shut up, Grave. You would die far too soon in a prison, and I have no intention of seeing you receive so easy a punishment. Now, rise. I am going to test your education at the hands of my cook. It is your last chance to redeem yourself. And you had best do well, or I will change your name from Grave to Slave and make you his underling."

He departed. With little mental screams I lifted my anguished but unmercifully living body out of bed and forced it into its apparel. My moment, achingly timed though it was, had finally arrived.

I summoned all my willpower and shambled my way to the kitchen. Wincing at every movement but determined nevertheless, I extracted my secret ingredients from the icebox, assembled the breading materials and went to work, laughing internally in agonized triumph.

A short while later, they were ready, steaming succulently in a juicy pool of drippings. I would have eaten poison ivy first, but knew the Master's palate and saw in those wings the pinions of angels floating through his culinary dreams. The bell rang, and I lifted the salver with spectacular flair, strode into the dining-room and placed it before the Master with undisguised confidence, ready for the inevitable verdict.

I was unsettled for a moment by the sight of Mr. Overlock's mice sitting on the table. It also displeased me to note the presence of the cook, who was standing cross-armed to the Master's right and looking at me in an unpleasant way. Still, such detritus was unable to unman me in the face of my success. The Master had taken a fork, cut off a small piece of wing, and was now holding it momentously before his mouth.

Then he slowly lowered it to the level of the tabletop, and one of his mice came up to it and bit in.

It rendered me aghast that my splendid creation was to be tasted first by one of the Things, but not nearly as much as what happened next. The mouse spat the piece out on the tablecloth, looked at Mr. Overlock and let out a brief squeak.

"Thank you, Abernathy," said the Master, stroking the rodent's head. Then he turned his attention to me. "As I suspected. Basted puffin flippers. You have dared to present me with bile of this nature, in the moronic hope that I would somehow mistake it for duck?"

Now the cook chimed in, blathering in some foreign tongue and pointing at me.

"The cook tells me that you refused instruction in his art in order to repeatedly induce him to gamble."

I was shocked. "That isn't true, sir! Well, it isn't entirely true, sir. I did ask him to play the first time, but no more than that. I wanted to test your system. And I only refused cooking instruction because I had it on good authority that puffin wings were a recipe of the Queen's which this man had purchased illegally. His wings looked flat, like flippers."

The cook gibbered further in his ear.

"The wings he has been preparing have been deboned, and pressed," said the Master. "That is part of the secret process involved. Also, he had never been in this country before I summoned him, a fact I cannot err in knowing. And he has informed me that he did give you the opportunity to pay him his winnings and desist, but you desired the chance to win your losses back, a chance he gave to you. As a result, you are indebted to him virtually beyond hope."

"But sir, he cheats! I followed your advice, and that of my cellmate, but still I lost every single hand!"

"What was your cellmate's advice?"

"He told me to use the past to predict the future. It didn't work."

"Hm."

Mr. Overlock gazed at me. I did not know what to make of his stare, except that it was shared by his mice. Silence filled the air and I could feel the weird wheels of thought taking motion about me.

"Who was this cellmate of yours, Grave?"

"He called himself Antenor, sir. He was mad and untidy."

"Mad and untidy though he may have been, he was correct. One must use the past to predict the future."

"But I lost, sir."

"That is because gambling, however well practiced, must always involve luck. One cannot win without at least some degree of it. And you, Grave, are the unluckiest person in the world."

"Yes, sir."

"However, you have escaped the fate for which moments ago you were inevitably heading. For by relating your cellmate's advice, you have suggested to me a thought, one which I feel may possess the solution to the recent series of events which have preoccupied me. Get the cards and present them to me in the drawing-room. Wong, prepare for me a breakfast worth eating, then do the same for the mice. Time advances. Commence."

I hurriedly snared the nearest stack of ruin I could locate, and took it to the destination so ordered. Mr. Overlock sat down at a table and spread the cards widely, picking out several and setting the rest of the deck aside.

"What has been constant among these crimes, Grave—until you hastened our quarry's premature exit last night?"

"Er—offenses of his own perpetration, sir?"

"Cards. Cards were left at the scene of each crime, as a clue to the one to follow. One presumes that a set would have been left with Quint, had you not, as you observe, acted on the murderer's behalf. But there was one for which there had been no preceding clue —or had there? As your fellow inmate noted, one must look to the past to predict the future, an element our quarry has repeatedly employed. So where was the clue to the first victim, Mr. Bucknard Hart? I am now convinced that it lay in the final hand of the poker game we witnessed."

He took ten cards and placed them on the table in two rows of five. Silence ensued as both he and I stared intently at them.

After a moment he said "What do you see, Grave?"

"I see three kings, an eight and a ten, sir. I regret my shortcomings, but they suggest nothing to me but the fact that they caused Mr. Bodkin to lose the hand to Mr. Hart."

"I am not referring to those cards, Grave. I find these others far more revealing."

I directed my attention to the one-pair hand of the former Mr. Hart's other living adversary, the one I have referred to as the Mouth.

"Consider an individual so remote and uninvolved in these proceedings as to have perpetrated the biggest bluff of all," said Mr. Overlock. "One who, displeased by Hart's admittance to the game, sees in his very hand the symbols of his opponent's undoing. Another player's frivolous remark about a knife in the chest abets the perception. A moment of outwardly nondescript irritation masks a greater upheaval within, and in a moment the crime fantasized in the cards becomes reality. The victim dies still holding his winning poker hand, the sight of which acts as a springboard for our troubled subject's next act—the murder of the dealer who'd admitted Mr. Hart to the game to begin with, despite objections. From then on, murder becomes a game itself, a gamble, a series of bluffs and stakes with the ultimate goal of outwitting the opponent. For such a person, the game can never end, for in eluding capture he achieves his ultimate victory: a gratified ego. For he is now the ace."

He swept away Bodkin's hand and pointed at the Mouth's cards one by one.

"The three of diamonds—Hart was killed with a three-studded poker. The four of hearts—Hart was stabbed four times in his chest, shrieking each time. The ace of spades—it is called the death card. The two of hearts—read 'To Hart.' The ace of clubs—the losing hole card crumpled to the floor after the loss to the 'club ace,' Mr. Hart. Summary: A three-studded poker four times to the heart. Death to Hart, the ace of the club, crumpled on the floor. Killed by his own studded poker, the game for whose mastery he met his demise."

"Unbelievable, sir."

He swept up the cards and tossed them at me. "We have no further need for these, Grave. Now get me my flintlock and ready the coach. There are one or two more questions to be answered before we apprehend our man."

I readily obeyed, and, dizzy with the erratic occurrences of the morning, humbly and silently followed the Master's orders to the letter. We boarded the coach again, and even the horses seemed to sense an urgency in the air, for they responded with unusual adequacy. Mr. Overlock ordered me to the river district, and dismissing all natural reaction from my mind, I swiftly conveyed him thither.

THE ZONE, by day, was less a foreboding netherworld and more a refreshing representation of straightforward, unglamorous work. The riverfront dockhands and bargemen were bustling about laboriously, loading up their boats and hauling their wares downriver. Everyone was engaged in his business and seemed far removed from games and skullduggery. The Master told me to stop the coach and go to one of them, giving a description of the Mouth and asking where to find him. Obediently, I got off and walked down to a pier where a dockhand was flinging crates into the stern of a barge named Peacock.

In a few brief words, I described our adversary. Considering his description, I was in no way surprised that the dockhand recognized him immediately.

"He lives on the Flirt with his missus," said the hand, pointing to a distant vessel. "He ain't too popular on this scow, though. His wife's too pretty. Be careful who you talk to about him."

Grateful for his civil advice, I thanked him and turned back. It was a pleasure talking to a fellow wage-slave.

"Hey," he said.

"Yes?"

"Your fly's unbuttoned, penis-brain."

I stalked stoically back to the coach and related my pertinent finding to the Master. He snapped his fingers, and comprehending, I conducted us down-dock to where the name Flirt could be seen painted on the side of a vessel at port. We were there within moments, and I heard the click of Mr. Overlock's gun being cocked into position. I got down and opened his door.

The Flirt did not entice me. It lacked the charm such a wishful moniker implies. Nevertheless, it beckoned us up her gangplank like the river harlot, and like some male virgin reluctantly selected for seduction, I felt there was no turning back now. I escorted Mr. Overlock to the cabin door, knocked, and awaited destiny.

Destiny appeared in the form of the "pretty" bargewoman.

"Yeah?"

If this was indeed her, my concept of bargemen's tastes was suddenly clarified. For she was common if not ugly, ungainly if not graceless, and ample if not abundant. If this was the dock attraction, I could now see why the late Jack Ball had clung so consistently to Mrs. Bodkin in spite of her marital state.

"Are you the wife of the master of this vessel?" said Mr. Overlock.

"Yeah, I'm her. I'm Maw's wife."

Mr. Overlock looked at me. "Maw, madam?" I asked, sensing his thoughts.

"Yeah. Named after his yap, but also short for Maurice. Who's the gentleman—new wharf boss?"

"I am Milo Overlock," stated the Master. "And I have three questions. First, have you recently had an affair with a sailor?"

Concern entered into her face. "Wait a minute. If someone's sick around here, don't look at me. It's the water."

Mr. Overlock raised his gun to her face. "I repeat. Have you recently had an affair with a sailor?"

She wavered a bit, then put up one hand. "All right, boss, take it easy. I'll talk. You mean the guy on the Peacock, right? That's been over for days. Your daughter can have him."

"Question number two. How did the affair end?"

She smiled slowly. "I see. He's your son, right? Well, my husband didn't lay a finger on him. He did it the easy way—he beat me up. I haven't touched a sailor since."

"Question number three. What do you like about your husband's kisses?"

Indignation filled the bargewoman's face, and she put her hands on her hips. "See here, boss. Be fair—even I don't give a man's trade secrets to the competition."

Iron entered Mr. Overlock's eyes as he gazed down the barrel of his pistol. "One last time. What-do-you-like-about-your-husband's-kisses?"

Trembling, she said "He frenches."

"Thank you. And now stand quite still, and tell your husband to lower the firearm he is carrying."

It was then that I perceived the skulking form of the Mouth creeping up behind the bargewoman in the cabin, having emerged from what I now observed the open door of an inner corridor. How the Master, with his height, could have seen him I couldn't guess. Perhaps he'd looked between the bargewoman's legs.

"Good day, Mr. Overlock," said the Mouth. "I'm sorry, but I cannot lower my weapon under the circumstances."

"If you do not disarm immediately, I will shoot your wife," said Mr. Overlock.

"And if you do not lower your weapon, Mr. Overlock, I will shoot your manservant!" he replied. I saw him aim the gun at my eyes.

"Surely you realize that of the two eventualities, you possess the losing hand," said the Master.

"Hm," said the Mouth. "Indeed, you're right. However, if you shoot my wife, she will fall, and it will be a draw between the two of us."

"As you know, when two opponents employ a similar strategy, the more experienced tends to prevail. I trust that you are a more astute gambler than Mr. Bodkin, and will not underestimate your opponent."

"I'll call your bet, Mr. Overlock," said the Mouth. "As you see, I've got nothing to lose. Long odds or not, I might as well play the hand out."

"Very well," said the Master. "That being the case, may I suggest the other players fold their hands and leave the table?"

"Accepted," said the Mouth.

"Madam, stand over there behind Grave."

The bargewoman, looking shocked by it all, swatted aside my extended hand, moved out of the doorway and took her prescribed position to my stern. It seemed to me that, for a player who'd folded, I had been left in a rather vulnerable position. The gunman could now fire upon the Master or myself. I could see Mr. Overlock watching his opponent's firing hand fixedly.

"You may show your hand now, Mr. Overlock," said the Mouth.

"Before doing so, I must request that you forfeit this contest," said the Master.

"We've been over that. Nothing's changed."

"Yes, something has. Your wife is now out of harm's way. You must now consider two items before proceeding. Your life, and that of your wife."

"Explain that, Mr. Overlock. As you said, she is now out of the way."

"Yes. Which means that if I prevail, not only will you lose your life, but your wife will retain hers. She will be free to return to the arms of her enamored. How will it look to the dockhands if the 'greatest gambler' lost a stake like that?"

Mr. Overlock was right about his adversary's ego. The Mouth clearly twitched.

"I could shoot your man, and then her," he said.

"By the time you finish shooting Grave, I will have shot you," replied the Master.

"Good point," admitted the Mouth. "But it's all the same. If I go to prison, she leaves me anyway. I might as well take a shot."

"Not if we make, shall we say, a gentlemen's agreement? For instance, you surrender to me and I give you a few moments alone with her, to settle your affairs?"

"Ha! You think I'd believe you'd let me keep my gun long enough to 'settle affairs' with her?"

"Not your gun. But there is a shillelagh in my inner coat pocket which never did claim its final victim. You may consider it a means to settle your affairs the easy way."

"What's that!" exclaimed the bargeman's wife. "Me brained by that brainless gob? I'm getting off!"

She bolted for the gangplank, but Mr. Overlock stuck back his leg and she tripped face first onto the deck.

"Sit on her, Grave."

I jumped on the writhing, swearing, furious woman, still blocked from her husband's aim by the Master and now under me. She pummeled me in every known region, giving new dimensions of pain to my still-aching bones. However, I had no choice but to suffer her attack clingingly, for she was my last hope of fragmented vindication for my countless recent failures. Hence I clung, a rabbit on a tigress, and as each blow drove me into new vistas of agony, I thought of the vengeance of Milo Overlock, and it all seemed quite bearable by comparison.

"How would you like your wife to be doing that with another man—for pleasure?" said Mr. Overlock.

The Mouth's jaw, already drooping, sagged lower. A few moments of thought, and he nodded resignedly. "You're right, Mr. Overlock. I can't take the chance. The hand is yours."

He dropped his gun.

"Grave, stop raping that woman and pick up this man's weapon."

Who was raping whom was quite questionable at that point, but I stood up anyway. She gave me a last fierce kick to the onions, which caused me to spit forth the small bit of what was left in my stomach after my previous night's consumption. I stumbled away from her, while the Master kept her from running by means of his now redirected pistol. I grasped the Mouth's firearm.

"Keep it trained on her, Grave," said Mr. Overlock, pointing his gun back at the Mouth. "And now, a last question for my opponent. I deduce that Ball's intention of dropping the chandelier became known to you during the Blackhearts' regular pre-club gathering at the adjacent saloon. It is also quite clear to me what instigated your crimes later that evening, and what compelled them to continue. But what of an ultimate goal? Surely you did not intend to go on committing such acts indefinitely. A wise gambler knows when to quit."

"My goal was simple, Mr. Overlock. To keep the club open. I knew from Jack that Mrs. Bodkin wanted you to close it, and when you came down there I knew the possibility was becoming nearer to happening. For a bargeman like me, that's the only life there is. And I knew, from everything I'd heard about you, that you liked a contest of skill as much as anyone. I knew that as long as the bodies came, you'd be too intrigued to close the club. That was the center of it all, and a far too significant provider of clues for you to shut down before the mystery had been solved. As a matter of fact, I'd have stopped killing if you'd closed it. You'd never quit a game before it was over, and would have opened it again. All of this came to me as I watched the cards of that game. Some say the future can be read in the cards. When Hart was permitted to enter that game, I felt anger at first. Then I found insight."

"You seem to know your victims rather well, for one who is not a Blackheart," said Mr. Overlock. "Why did you center on them?"

"For that very reason—because I am not a Blackheart. Friendly rivals we may all be when it comes to drinking and gambling, but down here the Blackhearts band together. They work as a group to see that they receive the best jobs, the best trade, everything. Even Quint, who liked me a lot, gave me this jaw during a bar fight between Blackhearts and non-Blackhearts years ago. I'd have found more victims later on, but it was a pleasure to see the Blackhearts go first."

"If keeping the club open was your main priority, why did you not simply kill Mr. Bodkin and eliminate his wife's motivation to begin with?"

"Why would I kill the club's biggest loser?" said the Mouth. "The Blackhearts were good players, but Bodkin was worth money to me."

"Very well," said the Master. "Our game is now at an end."

"If I may have that shillelagh, then, Mr. Overlock, and a few moments with my wife, I will pay my debt."

"I'm sorry, but I do not have your shillelagh on my person," said the Master.

"What!"

"I was bluffing."

The Mouth gaped. "But you told me we had a gentlemen's agreement!"

"As Captain Quint observed, you are no gentleman. You merely bluffed others into believing so. I now call your bluff."

And with that, the Master shot him.

The bargewoman shrieked and ran to the fallen remains of her husband. For the next few minutes she carried on with general hysterics, while Mr. Overlock observed her with a cold eye.

"Contain your emotion, bargewoman," he said. "Does this not leave you free to continue your involvement with your Peacock, without fear of reprisals?"

She collected herself, and wiped her eyes. "Why, yes," she said. "Yes, it does."

"And by a simple strike to the jaw, can he not be made to kiss in a fashion similar to your husband?"

"Hm—yes," she said, standing up. "I suppose that's true." She chuckled.

"Then you may have your desire, and this boat as well. Lastly—is your paramour by any chance a Blackheart?"

"Yes he is. One of the last," she said.

"With a physical abnormality you can live with?"

"It's his best feature," she smiled.

"And does he gamble?"

"No," she said. "That's the one thing he doesn't do."

"Good," said Mr. Overlock. "That is why he wins."

I hobbled back to the coach and opened the Master's door for him. Between my pain and the immediate series of events, I was filled with a sickening feeling. Mr. Overlock must have read my expression.

"If you feel my action unwarranted, Grave, spare your derision. I gave him his chance, last night. I said 'stop or be killed.'"

Although this somehow failed to alter my emotion, I merely said "Yes, sir" and proceeded to drive him home.

IT WAS THE following day. I rose and made my way to the kitchen, to see if the cook had prepared the Master's duck wings.

But the cook was not there.

I went out to the dining-room, mystified, and found Mr. Overlock at the table, reading the morning's paper. Its headline read "Overlock Solves Card Killings." I walked quietly up to him.

"May I be of service, sir?" I said.

"Quite. You may prepare me breakfast. Duck eggs, poached."

"But sir, may I ask what has become of the cook?"

"I have released him from service. I have decided that teaching you is outside the capabilities of a normal man. I alone have any hope of it, which is why I keep you in my service. I never leave a challenge unfinished, and until you improve you will remain here. It takes time to cure an infection, Grave, and I anticipate that you will be with me for some while."

"I will try to improve, sir. I truly will."

"I'm afraid that recent circumstances have rendered the matter a moot point. You have accumulated a large debt with Wong, and this having happened while in my employ, I intend to see that it is repaid in full. Your entire salary will be sent to him until your debt is completely erased, and you will remain in my service until it is."

I swallowed hard. "That may be some while, sir."

"Indeed, Grave. For as punishment for your recent foolish actions, I am cutting your salary in half. I am being lenient with you because it was you who related to me the words which acted as a springboard for my solution to the recent crimes."

I didn't know a figure so small as that of my "salary" could actually be cut in half. His so-called lenience overwhelmed me.

"And as a reward for being the originator of that self-same observation which led to the solution, I have had your former cellmate Antenor released."

It's funny how being in the position Antenor was in before being given his release sounded better to me than the "lenient" punishment which I'd received. But times such as these cannot be adequately assimilated, for appropriate words have not been coined to describe them. I merely bowed formally, and returned to the kitchen to make the Master's breakfast. A new day had begun.

A knock sounded at the kitchen door. I opened it. Hardly believing my eyes, I saw Antenor standing on the other side.

"Greetings, my friend. This is the servant's entrance, is it not? I remember you telling me you worked for Mr. Milo Overlock. I want my bath."

2

Chapter Two
Milo Overlock's Salt

I sat in the water closet, testing the plumbing. The plumbing was working uncommonly well, and this I attributed to the fact that for the first time in a year, I was relaxed. My vacation, those two annual days of unrestricted, unconstricted (and unpaid, but who cares) bliss, were upon me. And I was feeling as young as seventy.

As eternal manservant to that icon of ego, demigod of duck and prefect of perfect Mr. Milo Overlock, I found any chance for freedom to be a cause for rejoicing. So why did I remain at all, after such long agonies of time? Because Mr. Overlock had not yet "dismissed" me, seeming to realize that continued employment was punishment enough for my varied deficiencies. The one indulgence he afforded me were two days off per year, during which I usually scouted out cemetery plots for myself, in dreamy anticipation of the future. Those two days began on the morrow, and I set about dusting the already-flawless neo-Gothic manor with a spring in my joints that defied their arthritic state, and counted the seconds until my release.

The bell rang. Even this was not enough to shatter my sanguine nerves at the moment, for I knew that the Master's coffee was merely too black, or too milked, or too much of whatever he had asked for to begin with; or possibly the book he was reading (which he had had me read first, for recommendation) was too startling, or too tame, or too whatever I had said it was. But it didn't matter. Attempting to contain the spring in my step (for the Master wanted quick service, but a quiet approach), I glided up the staircase and into Mr. Overlock's bedchamber, feeling like a newborn calf.

"Grave," said the Master in a cold, even tone, "I have decided to cancel your vacation."

The calf died at birth.

"My salt-mining operation has been experiencing an uncommon degree of worker deaths, which in turn has resulted in worker departure. I can't very well threaten them with a fate no more severe than that which they are fleeing, and as a result the operation is suffering. We must go and investigate. Prepare yourself to leave immediately."

I stood there utterly aghast. For one thing, it was nearly midnight; for another, I was well aware that Mr. Overlock's mining operation existed solely to supply him with the salt which he used himself, of which we had countless barrels filling several acres of cellar space. I attempted to salvage the sinking ship of my weekend by appealing to his practical side.

"But sir, wouldn't it be more convenient to leave at daybreak?" I asked, hoping he might forget the whole thing by then.

"It would not, Grave. The operation is on the other side of the Vast Mountains, and the journey will take a day and a half. I will sleep in the carriage. You will manage the horses."

"But sir, would you not find sleeping difficult under such conditions?"

"Not if you handle the reins properly. I will expect no bumps, a nice even speed, and no stops."

Considering that the Master's horses were as old as I and that the road through the Vast Mountains was a dry creek bed, I wondered at the feasibility of this command, but softened at the thought that Mr. Overlock's admonishments along the way might be the only things available to keep me awake at the reins. Despondent, I acquiesced with a grim "Very good, sir."

"Attend to my mice."

It was then that I noticed Mr. Overlock's trained white mice crawling around on his bedsheets. Mr. Overlock snapped his fingers, and they immediately formed a perfect, orderly line. I took the platinum-lined box they used as a domicile from the floor beside the bed, and dwelling sourly on the fact that my own room was an airless cranny with walls of plywood, delicately attempted to pick each one up and place it within its quarters. They nipped ferociously at my fingers until I yelped with pain, whereupon the Master snapped again and each became the model of perfect decorum. The Master smiled approvingly.

"At present, I am training them to attack," he said.

"Yes, sir."

I took the vile little snake snacks and stepped, bleeding, to the door.

"By the way, Grave," said Mr. Overlock as I walked across the threshold, "this coffee is too cold. Grind me another cupful and be ready to leave in ten minutes."

That much later, Mr. Overlock, cup in hand, was sitting in the carriage, while I, hatless and beltless but otherwise properly bedecked, held the reins, and we were off. As I alternately listened to Mr. Overlock berate me for going too fast and spilling his coffee, or grumbling that at this rate we'd be there by Armageddon, I thought dreamily of those lovely cool cemetery plots and how but for the briefest of hours I could have been sampling one right then. At that moment, I felt Mr. Overlock stick his hand through the transom and poke my back with a pin, and I jumped like one of the horses might have countless years earlier.

"Don't daydream, Grave."

I don't know how long it took us to get there (traumatic amnesia has completely blocked out the period from my mind), but we did arrive, at a sort of hilly wasteland dotted with mines and tracks on the other edge of the forested extreme of the mountains we had just passed from. The complex, which included a worker's barracks, a refinery, mill, foundry and smokestacks, had a deserted feeling, and we proceeded with haste to the quarters of the foreman, a brick shack in the centrality of the encampment.

I was shocked that, at the moment of my opening the Master's door, the foreman himself burst out of his shack, led by a pack of black, slavering dogs who immediately surrounded me and began to growl with savage bloodlust.

The foreman, a dusty bearded fellow who looked like a gorilla's rump with eyes, whistled, and his treacherous canines ceased growling and merely stared at me with frozen glares of hate. Summoning back my voice, I managed to stammer out "Uh—Mr. Milo Overlock," and the Master strode forth.

The foreman seemed quite overcome by such a visit. "Mr. Overlock, we are honored by your unexpected presence here. Allow me to say that we will extend—"

"Quite," said Mr. Overlock, extracting a small notebook from his coat pocket and consulting it. "You are Dreyfus Montague Cupton, foreman of this operation?"

"Er—yes, sir. You hired me, if you recall."

"And where is your assistant, Miles Underkey?"

"He is inside. Let me show you."

They proceeded inward, leaving the dogs with me. As these were perfectly still at the moment, I too stood still and waited. Beckoned, however, by the Master's "Grave!" I suffered myself to outrun the curs to the door, where the considerate foreman came to wave them off, almost in time to prevent injury. I limped into a room filled with ropes, lamps and other mining equipment, as well as Miles Underkey, who bore a remarkable resemblance to the Master himself. He was squat and rather stately. He even smoked the Master's tobacco.

"Underkey," said Mr. Overlock sharply, "I am well aware that you effected to look like me in order to win my favor and secure your position here, but you have failed to prove to me any similarity in competence. Why have we been losing staff?"

"Blame your bloody foreman," said Underkey, with remarkably defiant attitude. "The miners are supposed to be extracting salt, not digging graves—but with the security we have here, it's all the same thing. It's been happening on the lowest level of our newest mine, the Overlock, between the Milo Mine and the Master Mine. We've gone down and found the bodies, mangled to the bone. The lucky ones who've come up say it's monsters. Dreyfus' dogs are supposed to be the protection here, but they won't move a muscle down in the hole. For dogs, they give great impersonations of pussies."

"Don't blame my girls," snapped the foreman, looking hurt. "Up until a month ago, we never had a single death or mishap here."

"Could one of the workers be the cause?" asked Mr. Overlock.

"I doubt it," said the foreman. "These bitches eat studs and spit out nails. No employee could frighten them."

"An outsider, then?"

"He'd have to get in on foot if he was to go unnoticed, and that'd mean going through the woods, which are swarming with wolves."

"Hm." Mr. Overlock seemed to ponder for a moment, then said "Show me the maps."

Underkey proceeded to a desk, from which he extracted several maps of the complex, showing the many intricate shafts that had been created to procure Mr. Overlock's salt. Mr. Overlock studied them carefully, particularly the one which detailed the mine which had proven the source of the trouble.

"These maps are the first things to have interested me since I arrived," he said. "Who drew them?"

"I did, cap'n," said Underkey, with some pride.

"Is there any other way into the mine in question?"

"Only a fissure leading from a small cave out in the forest."

"Could an intruder be using that cave?"

"Presumably, sir, but like Dreyfus said, he'd have to be able to get past the wolves."

Mr. Overlock was silent for a moment, then said, "Grave and I will go to the mine."

Before my heart could resume beating, he turned to me and told me to dress appropriately and to procure the proper equipment.

Flutteringly, I inquired, "What will you be requiring to wear, sir?"

"I am going as I am. You will lead the way and inform me what to expect."

I saw those lovely cemetery plots in my mind and regretted that I would not be likely to procure one before meeting my demise. Knowing Mr. Overlock, he would have me cremated and my ashes disposed of in the water closet.

"Commence, Grave."

And so it was that momentarily I found myself, an elderly valet of frail figure and reserved habit, donned in denim and a steel headpiece, carrying a lantern and leading Milo Overlock, decked in his best tweed suit, into the lift which descended into the bottommost layer of Overlock Mine.

It smelled salty and damp, with a vague carrion-like flavor. It was very dark, and my lantern seemed to cut into about one foot of it, revealing only more darkness beyond. Mr. Overlock prodded me to move forward, and reluctantly stepping forth, I led the way into the abyss.

I wandered slowly for a bit, thinking how other valets only had to mix their masters' drinks and press their masters' underwear; a state I could expect only in heaven. Every time I slowed down, the Master's cane was there in my back, spurring me forward and deeper into the hole, where the air got danker and more unbreathable by the moment, and was assisted toward this goal by the Master's incessant smoking and deadening brand.

We had gone on for some time when the Master said "You're hesitating, Grave."

"I'm sorry, sir."

"You really are the most inadequate of servants."

"I apologize for my shortcomings, sir. It is merely that I heard some noises in the passage before us, sir."

"Good," said Mr. Overlock. "Let us proceed to investigate."

"But sir," I protested, "it may prove dangerous. I would not wish to be remiss in my duty to protect you."

"I trust that you will not," said the Master severely. "Advance."

Sighing and commending myself to God, I stepped forward several paces, Mr. Overlock remaining a safe distance behind me. Then suddenly my lantern caught a glint of blood-red eyes in the dark, a multitude of horrific growls filled the air and in the space of an old man's scream the cave was filled with the hugest, most hideous wolves I had ever seen.

"Grave!" said Mr. Overlock, but I had already guessed his requirement. And such was my training, my blind commitment, and my precognizance of fates worse than death, that I willingly threw all my effort into protecting the Master at once. I rushed at the wolves, attempting to push them further from Mr. Overlock, and they in turn rushed at me. I kicked and grabbed and flailed my arms helplessly, as various parts of my body which I had not felt in years came alive under the bites of the lupine helldragons. With a vague but not totally satisfying sense that I had adequately fulfilled the duties of my post before expiring, I soon gave up the struggle and awaited my fate. It was then that I heard a snap of fingers, and the wolves immediately desisted and formed a straight, orderly line.

Mr. Overlock came and stood over me. "You fool, Grave. If you would have waited and listened, you'd know that these are my wolves. I trained them."

He helped me up, clearly disgusted by my headstrong reaction. As I stood there dripping gore, he patted the wolves' heads one by one. I awaited an explanation, but instead he took my lantern and began to lead the wolves back through the shaft. When I realized that he was not going to wait for me, I pushed my bones back into their sockets and hobbled after him.

"But sir, I don't understand!" I said when I had caught up.

"Of course you don't, Grave. I trained these wolves to guard the boundary of this operation when I first purchased it. They will kill anyone but myself."

"Pardon me for inquiring, sir, but how did they get down here?"

"Someone has managed to train them to do so, and has used the small cave in the woods to get them here. When I was examining the area prior to purchasing the property, one of my mice discovered the cave. It was covered up. I investigated it further and found that it contained gold deposits. I trained the wolves to guard the wooded area. As I knew it would, the mining operation has finally intersected with the vein, and my test of employee loyalty has shown me who I can and cannot trust to continue with the operation."

My eyes were opened, at least figuratively. "Then the person who trained the wolves used them to discourage mining in this area, so that he could keep the gold discovery to himself?"

"Correct."

We returned to the lift (with the wolves) and ascended to the surface. The warm sun felt delicious as it turned my wounds to scabs. I decided that I would never go underground again (unless, of course, Mr. Overlock ordered me to). Mr. Overlock proceeded straight to the foreman's shack, and opened the door.

"Mr. Cupton and Mr. Underkey, please come out here immediately."

The foreman and his assistant emerged, and appeared shocked by the sight of the wolves, which glared back menacingly but stood well-behaved beside Mr. Overlock, awaiting the snap of his fingers.

"Mr. Cupton, where are your dogs?" Mr. Overlock inquired.

"Er—in the kennel, sir."

I had guessed it. Only a man who could train dogs like that would have been able to master the training of wolves. His dogs being afraid of the wolves, he had naturally put them away prior to releasing the wolves into the cave after Mr. Overlock and myself.

"Good," said Mr. Overlock. "And now, I wish you to go and procure restraints for Mr. Underkey until the constabulary arrives. He is guilty of setting these wolves loose in the mines."

Mr. Underkey was quite aghast, as was I. "What the bloody hell?" were his words and my thoughts.

"By your own admission, you were the person who drew the maps," said Mr. Overlock. "To have learned of the cave in the woods, you must have been able to move safely among the wolves. You mapped it so that if I or anyone else were to accidentally discover it, its exploration would seem unnecessary. Your resemblance to me and the tobacco you smoke convinced the wolves, though I'd hoped better of them." He glared at the wolves, and they wilted.

"You can't prove that," snapped Underkey. "I had a gun with me when I discovered that cave."

"Mr. Cupton, please go and obtain the restraints while my manservant and I apply a little test to Mr. Underkey."

The foreman did so, while I gulped at the sudden reintroduction of my presence.

"Mr. Underkey, stand by Grave over there."

Underkey, looking as red as one of Mr. Overlock's underdone ducks, paused reluctantly, then stalked angrily over to me, barging me with his shoulder.

"Now then," said Mr. Overlock, "let us see which of you these wolves consider 'enemy' and which they consider 'friend.'"

And without waiting for me to finish even one screech, he snapped his fingers.

Suffice it to say that the wolves had no greater friend in the world than Mr. Underkey, and no greater enemy than me. Which having proved Mr. Overlock's point, he eventually snapped his fingers again, and I was unfortunately allowed to live. The upshot was that the salt-mining operation became a gold-mining operation, Mr. Dreyfus Montague Cupton got a raise and stayed on to supervise it, Mr. Miles Underkey (whose real name was Embeth Weems, and who may have been a girl) went to prison, and I, despite remaining at my slave's wage, got my two-day vacation, albeit one spent in a hospital. Unfortunately, two days was not nearly enough time for my broken bones to set, and when I was summoned back to Mr. Overlock he found my service unacceptably slow.

I suppose, when I think about it, that the elaborate degrees Mr. Overlock had gone to in order to "test" employee trustworthiness after discovering the gold vein, and the resulting loss of workers, were rather extreme, but then, gold is the very salt of life to Mr. Milo Overlock.

3

Chapter Three
Milo Overlock's Dinner Party

"**A**RE you fearless, imperturbable, desperate for employment, suicidal, a masochist or insane?"

I asked this of the applicant, knowing that to endure employment with Milo Overlock, he would have to be one or more of the above. As Mr. Overlock's oldest employee (qualification: insane) I was compelled to do the hiring of the help. And when the help invariably failed to impress the Master, it was I who was blamed. So I always began with this pre-screening inquiry.

It was the week of Mr. Overlock's annual dinner party, an affair to which he always provided some central "surprise" element, for the challenge of his guests and the amusement of himself. I personally dreaded the experience like few others, being perpetually in the dark about what his hellish surprise was, and to what extent it would involve me (which it always did). But being that misery loves company, I applied myself to the task of procuring others of my hapless ilk for the trial ahead, envying them that theirs were but temporary captivities, and not the lifelong servitude of the condemned. With many a vindictive simper, I selected the ones I disliked most and began training them for their tasks.

"Now then," I began, lining the lessers abreast in the kitchen and effecting my most lordly manner, "to begin with, be aware that I seek perfection. Mr. Overlock is accustomed to this, and I will not tolerate less in others than I have achieved in myself. It is not unattainable. You must simply observe my actions at all times. Do this and you too will reach the pinnacle of professional attainment that after years of hard work I have managed to—"

The bell rang, somewhere above. I thought a hard oath, annoyed at this imperious interruption of one of my priceless moments of bluster. With a dignified "One moment, please," I excused myself and, walking slowly until free of all eyes, gamboled anxiously up the flights and into Mr. Overlock's bedchamber.

He had already started up from his bed, and was bearing an expression of extreme impatience. It did not help matters that I'd rather abruptly barged in, and he appeared momentarily startled. It was such moments as this, with my heart beating like a claustrophobic prisoner on the walls of my chest, that made me dream devout dreams of death; however, I was not about to court death openly just then. I bowed obsequiously, and, I fancy, whimpered.

"Grave." said Mr. Overlock slowly, turning to a bureau and looking through one of its drawers, "there are times when I feel that you would be well-served by a riding-crop."

I cringed as I saw him extract one. "I—I beg your pardon, sir," I said, combating the impulse to kneel, "I was training ten of your newest employees."

He approached me. "Training my new employees?" he said. "Grave, you are not even qualified to train a thought. On what grounds do you presume to train others?"

He flexed the crop in his hand, and I begged God that I wouldn't be ordered to bend over. "Er—by example, sir. I hold myself up as a model of inadequacy to which all must be careful to avoid."

He stared at me, then nodded briefly. This answer appeared to satisfy him, and although he maintained his hold on his riding-crop, he returned to his bed.

"Grave, have you prepared the unmarked invitations to be sent?" he asked.

"Yes, sir," I lied.

"Good. You will address them to the names on this paper." He handed me the parchment from his bed-table.

I stepped forward and received the list, giving it a cursory review. What it contained surprised me greatly.

"Forgive me, sir, but each name on this list belongs to one of your enemies. Business rivals, political adversaries, those who have everything to gain by your downfall. Hardly the type of guests one would invite to a dinner-party."

"I am well aware of the content of the list, Grave. And it is precisely as I intend." He chuckled, quietly and dryly. "These names are necessary to my plans this year."

I shuddered, but felt hopeful that he was at last prepared to take me into his confidence on the matter. "Then—may I ask what those plans are, sir?" I ventured.

"No you may not," he snapped. "Simply see to it that each arrives."

"But sir, will it not be difficult to persuade your enemies to accept such an invitation?"

"It will not. No one refuses an invitation to one of my social gatherings… it is one of Onwall's highest honors. And who more readily courts entry to an opposing camp than one's opponent? See to it, Grave."

"Yes, sir." Hopeful that I had finally been assigned a task I could manage, I sauntered to the door.

"Oh, and one more thing."

"Yes, sir?" I said, frisking back to his bedside.

"Bend over."

The night of the event arrived, if one might label an "event" an affair that consists of merely five guests. I remembered far more elaborate gatherings when I once buttled for the Queen, until Mr. Overlock demanded her staff of her. I am the last survivor of the group, and it seems to me strange that one would hire on an extra ten employees to serve five guests who are destined for an unpleasant time anyway. However, I distributed duties as best as I could, assigning as individual departments the wine, the pantry, the cooking, dishwashing, serving, table decoration, door, floor and chairs. My own was a higher level of service altogether, for as the Master always wanted me close at hand, I was delegated the honorable title of "human napkin" or facial blotter, and was to stand close to the table with a ready eye to each guest's mouth for the moment that drool or gustatory detritus exhibited itself, and immediately eliminate it with my ready sleeve. To test my performance in this capacity, the Master allowed no napkins of any sort on the table for anyone, and I felt that if I could get through the night without a snap or a "Hey, boy" directed at me, I could breathe easily.

Momentarily, my well-trained doorman led in a bald, burly pumpkin of a man with piano-key teeth who was announced as Vice Premier Bagbottle, and I grimaced as he waddled up to me.

"What's for dinner tonight, ass?" he asked.

"No, sir. Duck," I replied, and he kicked me.

This Vice Premier was the one figure in the monarchy which Mr. Overlock didn't own, and it was rumored that he was seeking to gain control of the country for himself by paying those in Mr. Overlock's pocket even more for their allegiances than Mr. Overlock himself. He was accumulating wealth to this end through contributions from hostile territories, territories that stood to gain the most if the Vice Premier took over. He didn't as yet have the necessary funds, but it was believed he was close.

Next there followed Wartford Dent, the diminutive, complexion-challenged speculator who was the only other man to deal in real estate of any sort in the country. It was said that should the Vice Premier take over, Milo Overlock would be driven out and his properties sold to the highest bidder. Dent meant to be this bidder.

Next came Lady Tabitha Wynx, the downy noble whose favors had been the downfall of many a social climber. Her nest, an imposing mansion which rivaled the size of Mr. Overlock's, was rumored to have been financed with the hush money of several stately heads, for Lady Wynx was fickle, attractive, and discreet by arrangement. She was as self-serving as the Master himself, and was said to have set her sights on Wartford Dent.

We were now graced by the presence of Freequoth Flagmask, editor and operator of the only Onwall newspaper that dared to criticize Milo Overlock. The Master had won countless suits against it for libel (even though I had yet to read an untruthful article) and it could little stand another. However, a scandal which could be proven regarding Mr. Overlock stood to hold immense value to Flagmask. He sat at the far end of the table and watched everything closely.

Lastly there arrived Ellery Upcobb, chief constable. He seemed a nice kind of fellow to me, clean-cut, unpretentious and very devoted to the law. But he had fined me for driving the carriage recklessly the prior week and had delayed Mr. Overlock's arrival at the opera. And while I had been the one to pay the fine, the delay had rankled with the Master…

"Good evening," said Mr. Overlock, standing and eyeing the assemblage. "Congratulations on being the five chosen recipients of an invitation to the Annual Overlock Dinner. Grave, the soup."

I hastened off to alert the server, who brought out the first course: duck-blood soup with a plop of creamed alligator floating like an island on top. It was served hot, prompt, and spill-free. The boy had promise, if he continued to apply himself to my teaching.

"I am wondering," said Bagbottle at this point, "why you, Milo Overlock, who opposes everything which each of his guests stands for, chose this particular group to so honor on this occasion."

"Officiously asked," replied Mr. Overlock. "And the answer is one which should follow naturally…I invited each of you in order to see you destroyed."

A general tone of indignation rose up. I had to rush to the mouths of those who had already sipped the soup.

"You are threatening to destroy us all at this dinner, then?" asked Flagmask with fire in his eyes. "I will have to make a note of that, in case we find arsenic in our wine."

"A typical misquote," said the Master. "I said that I invited each of you in order to see you destroyed. It is you who will destroy yourselves."

Another indignant reaction.

"Does this little man presume to tell us that we came here to eat ourselves to death, or something?" sneered Lady Wynx. "His food isn't that good—in fact, I find this soup revolting."

"Forgive me," said Mr. Overlock. "It is my practice to eat duck for dinner. Grave will see that you receive something tasteless."

"How do you mean, we will destroy ourselves?" inquired Wartford Dent, his pimples about to burst. "We are united. You are our common enemy."

"Correction, I am your uncommon enemy. One who circles about, so that when you shoot at him, you hit your own man. I encourage you to be wary tonight, my adversaries. For within this house you will find everything you require to bring about my downfall, but prove incautious and you will bring about your own. With that, a toast: Eat well, for tomorrow you die."

This brought about a general rumbling, and not one lifted glass. Constable Upcobb seemed to see it his duty to take charge.

"Now, now, folks, don't get restless. I'm sure Mr. Overlock is just teasing you. He knows that he is just as much a subject of the law as any of the rest of us."

"I know nothing of the kind," said Mr. Overlock with an iron glare, then said to me "Grave, the duck."

I went far enough away from Mr. Overlock to be able to snap my fingers unstartlingly. As I did, the server came out and began to distribute the duck. I'm not sure what the guests thought of it, after the tone Mr. Overlock had set for the meal, but they sucked it down dutifully, and with barely a word for the remainder of the feast, followed it with stewed oranges, steamed smelt, cocks' combs and eye candy.

The meal over with barely another utterance save a grunt, Mr. Overlock grinned a steely grin and stood. "My servant Grave will now escort you on an exclusive tour of my home. Grave?"

Unprepared as I was for this, I gathered my senses together, brushed my dribbling sleeves and said, "Uh, yes. This way, if you please," and hastily pieced together in my mind a rough order in which to take them round the house. The fact that they each stared at me with molten hatred did not aid my composure much, but Mr. Overlock, standing to the rear of the assemblage with an unaccountable look of quiet triumph on his face, spurred me to my task without delay. I proceeded with a dignified safari through the Master's mansion, stopping at each room to give its history (and being stopped, one sentence into each, by Mr. Overlock's "That's enough, Grave") until we came upon the collection-room, into which I had assumed Mr. Overlock would not wish his guests escorted.

"Stop here, Grave. I wish to give my guests a view of my collectibles."

"But there's no door," said Bagbottle incredulously. "Just a shelf lined with antique books."

"In actuality, it is a sliding panel, the combination of which is activated by applying pressure to different places within the mansion. Open it, Grave."

"You mean you allow your manservant the combination to your valuables?" asked Lady Wynx.

"Trust Grave? You must be joking. I have been activating the combination as I have followed the tour around the house. That is why I chose to remain to the rear. Grave, the panel will now slide open."

"Yes, sir."

Putting my seventy-five years of accumulated strength into the task, I wheezed and grunted and slowly managed to slide the book-laden panel open, while Mr. Overlock's guests (including the muscular Police Chief Upcobb) looked impatiently on. When I finally completed the task, and the sight of the collection-room was upon all, a sudden interest filled the congregation and they flowed into the room before I could utter a word of introduction.

The collection-room was composed of two parts, one being the body of the chamber where Mr. Overlock's objet d'art was displayed, and the prominent walk-in safe in which he kept his money. His collection of material valuables was quite impressive, and among the many items which elicited reaction were some Shakespeare rough drafts ("all the world's a page, and all the men and women merely paragraphs…"), the Venus de Milo's arms, the Golden Fleece and a painting of the Mona Lisa laughing hysterically. I attempted a discussion of each, but no one was paying attention, so I thankfully blended into the background and awaited the denouement.

"As one collector to another, I must offer my admiration," said Wartford Dent. "However, your method of security baffles me somewhat. This room is all but impenetrable from outside. How, then, is one to prevent being locked within?"

"There is nothing to keep a person locked inside," answered Mr. Overlock. "The room is impenetrable from without, but there are no hindrances to exiting. The same applies to my walk-in safe, the facade of which you see on the east wall. Anyone inside may easily come out, but from outside it is inaccessible. Unless, of course, one has the combination, and I alone am in its possession."

"May we—may we have a look inside it?" asked Freequoth Flagmask, a little bit of printer's ink drooling from his moue.

"No," said Mr. Overlock. "Such a sight would be, perhaps, too much of a temptation to a gathering so well positioned to gain by my loss. This little introduction was merely my way of whetting your appetites, so to speak. Grave, conduct our guests to their rooms for the night. I will again take up the rear, to insure that they all leave safely."

I proceeded to lead the guests to their respective rooms, grateful that the distasteful evening was drawing to a close at last. When all were packed into their shrines accordingly, and I was done procuring for Lady Wynx her extra soap, Upcobb his dime thriller, Wartford Dent his face cream, Freequoth Flagmask his sleeping mask and Bagbottle his bottle, I took a few minutes alone in the water closet before being summoned by Mr. Overlock's bell at the climactic moment. After attending to his countless little needs, I then proceeded to the kitchen, where I could at last do a summing-up with the servants with proper expanse, pomp and fulsomeness.

Having dismissed them to their quarters some time later, and feeling a rare satisfaction, I proceeded with candle and cup in hand to my own remote room, thinking that I might do a little milk-and-cracker dunking before fading off. I had just shimmied into my nightgown and was slowly slipping the first biscuit into the lacteal brew when the house alarm began blaring with a force and raucousness that made me spill the entire concoction over the length and breadth of my gown. Jumping up and shoving my quaking feet into their heelless slippers, I ran from my cubicle and went bounding toward Mr. Overlock's wing of the manor.

As I scurried through the passages, I passed by several of the roused guests making aggrieved appearances in their doorways. Receiving their various what-the-hells with brief "Sorry, sirs" and "Shortly, madams," I kept up my pace for the Master's suite, until suddenly he appeared in the hall in front of me and I skidded to a stop, bumping him slightly.

"You confounded idiot, Grave," was his remark. "Go into my bedroom at once and disengage that alarm."

Although I knew he had just emerged from there, I made no comment but to dash puplike for the sanctum, there to pull the cord next to Mr. Overlock's bed which silenced the device. When I emerged again, he was admonishing the present guests and ordering them assembled at once in the drawing-room. With huffs of outrage, the chastised visitors began withdrawing to their rooms to dress, and I toe-ran up to Mr. Overlock to ask instruction.

"See that the guests are gathered immediately, Grave, while I inspect the collection-room. And get dressed. You look like an androgynous ghost."

"Yes, sir."

A short while later, after being called every name imaginable by the guests I had been instructed to escort downstairs, I stood in the drawing-room, properly dressed, awaiting the entrance of the Master.

He strode in, carrying two bulky-looking burlap bags labeled "Draft Row Building Supplies." He set them on a table.

"What is the meaning of this outrage?" exploded Vice Premier Bagbottle. "First, we are pulled from our slumbers in a most startling, horrible way, then we are ordered about as though we were prisoners in this castle!"

"Yes, Overlock," shot in Flagmask, yanking a notebook and pen from his pocket. "What's the story here? How dare you push around loyal subjects of the Queen?"

"Silence," said Mr. Overlock stonily. "As for being temporary prisoners here, you are. As for being loyal subjects of the Queen, you are not."

Ellery Upcobb shoved his badge in. "Now hold on here, Mr. Overlock. If there's to be any prisoner-taking, it'll be by authority of the police. On what grounds do you propose to detain us?"

"On the grounds that I have had money stolen from my walk-in safe. The bags in question were sitting on a pressure-plate, atop a dais. I found one of these bags of dry mortar sitting in their place. The other was on the floor, having apparently fallen off. That is what triggered the alarm. There is no telling when the crime occurred. It could have taken place any time between the tour and the sounding of the alarm."

All looked thoughtful. "Then how can we tell what happened?" asked Upcobb with confusion. "A search?"

"Indeed," said Mr. Overlock. "Grave, instruct the servants to examine every portion of each guest's room. Then return here."

"Yes, sir."

"Wait a minute," said Lady Wynx. "Who's to say that a servant didn't do it?"

"My photo-security system may enlighten us on that count," replied Mr. Overlock. "Go, Grave."

I galloped off to instruct the servants, relieved that I had retained them through the next day's breakfast. I gave them hurried, unelaborated instruction, asked them if they had seen any of the guests after dinner (they hadn't), then returned with haste to the drawing-room. There I found Mr. Overlock holding up a small photograph.

There is, of course, no need to expound upon Mr. Overlock's proficiency at photography. Even in those days of plate-based primitivism, he had a camera which could take photographs with an exposure time of only thirty seconds. It sat in a nondescript corner of the collection-room facing a well-illuminated antique clock. Little though it was known, sliding open the panel door caused a discreet cord to be pulled which activated the camera, causing it to take a thirty-second exposure of the clock. By developing the still, Mr. Overlock could find out when the door had been opened, and he had evidently been developing the image while I had been escorting the guests.

"Observe the clock," he said. "The door was ajar at 10:45. Grave, when did you begin addressing the servants?"

"Why, earlier than that, sir."

"And you were still addressing them at 10:45?"

"Decidedly later than that, sir."

"Then that absolves the servants, who in turn absolve Grave. They can't have been in both places at once."

There was a silence, as everyone looked from one to another. Then Flagmask popped in with, "Shouldn't everyone let it be known just what they were doing at 10:45?"

"Why, we were sleeping, of course," said Lady Wynx with contempt. "How could it be proven otherwise?"

"Perhaps it cannot, and perhaps we should not begin there," said Mr. Overlock. "Instead, let's center on, shall we say, the concrete. These mortar bags from 'Draft Row Building Supplies.' Can anyone identify that company?"

A nervous silence appeared to ensue.

"No one? How odd. I would have guessed that if our diligent chief here were to make inquiries, he would find at least two stockholders in a company called Draft Row."

Vice Premier Bagbottle squirmed, then murmured "It's his company," pointing at Wartford Dent.

All eyes looked at Dent, whose eyes, in turn, glared angrily at Bagbottle.

"Draft Row is an anagram for Wartford," said the Vice Premier. "I'm sorry, my boy. I will do what I can for you, but I cannot invite scandal."

"You fat, dictatorial blob," growled Dent angrily. "How dare you attempt to implicate me?"

"They would have found out anyway."

"Then let them find out how I got it in here! Look at me. Where could I have hidden it? The only person in this room with enough baggage to smuggle in those kinds of bags is you, Vice Premier."

The Vice Premier turned the color of a riper pumpkin, but seemed to maintain his composure. "The clothes I wear provide room for my person, and nothing more."

"Really?" sneered Dent. "And how do we know it isn't padded? I think the police chief here would be well-advised to check."

Ellery Upcobb seemed torn between his duty and his security. Recalling to mind the devotion to service that had carried him to fine even Mr. Overlock, I guessed on the former, and was correct.

"I would be obliged if you would join me in the next room, sir," said Upcobb respectfully.

The Vice Premier stood up, smoldering. "I shall make you pay for this indignity," he told Dent as he proceeded for the door leading into the adjoining parlor. "Meanwhile," he added at the portal, "please be so kind as to inform Mr. Overlock why you were in Lady Wynx's room all evening long."

Lady Wynx gasped loudly. "How dare he make such a remark! And in front of a newspaperman, too! Wartford, tell them that there is no truth whatsoever in it!"

"There's no truth whatsoever in it," said Dent.

At this point, one of the servants, the dishwasher, came down carrying two large bags of what looked like the Master's money. He handed them to me and I almost fell over from the weight.

"I found these under the bed in the Blue Room," he said.

The room of Wartford Dent.

Dent gasped at the evidence. "Someone must have planted them in my room. I'm being framed."

"If you were in your room the entire time, you would have seen anyone making such an attempt," said Mr. Overlock. "Did you?"

Dent gulped, then looked at the floor in a shamefaced manner. "I couldn't have," he said. "I *was* in Lady Wynx's room."

The dowager blanched at this confession, as the newsman scribbled furiously. "You squat toad," she hissed. "My stock in your company is up for grabs tomorrow."

"Very well, Your Ladyship," retorted Dent. "Now that I've deprived you of your opportunity to sell me your silence, please tell us where you went for the five minutes you left me alone at just about the time in question?"

"Like I told you, I went to use the water closet," she growled. "An evening with you rather brings that on."

"And who can verify that? You knew that my room was empty. It was your perfect opportunity to frame me."

The lady seemed momentarily ruffled. "Well, I …I went to the water closet nearest my room, which was on the other side of Mr. Overlock's bedroom. I opened his door by mistake. Perhaps he saw me?"

"I did," confirmed the Master.

"And did you see him?" asked Flagmask suspiciously.

"Why, yes. He was in his bed."

"Then that proves Mr. Overlock didn't do all this himself, as a frame-up," murmured Flagmask. "Someone really did steal that money."

At this point, Upcobb returned with the indignant-looking Vice Premier. "He needs as much space for himself as his clothes will provide," said the police chief. "What's been happening here?"

He was briefly brought up to date by Flagmask.

"So what do you propose we do now, Mr. Overlock?" asked the constable.

"Let us review," said the Master. "The money was found in the room of Wartford Dent, but both Lady Wynx and Vice Premier Bagbottle claim that he was in Lady Wynx's room this evening. Vice Premier, how did you know that Mr. Dent was in Lady Wynx's room?"

"Her door squeaks," grunted the Premier. "I thought it might be mice. I looked out and saw him going in."

"How many times did you hear the door squeak this evening?"

"Um…two other times. I thought the house was infested."

"Two other times," murmured the Master. "My count as well, as she came and went from the washroom. Therefore, Wynx and Dent have alibis, as do I. The money was planted in Dent's room by someone who knew he was absent from it."

All looked at Bagbottle.

"Vice Premier, you have admitted that you knew," said Mr. Overlock.

Bagbottle went from pumpkin pie to blueberry. "That is far from saying that I am the only one who knew, Mr. Overlock! What about our grope-happy constable here? Or that gossip columnist?"

Mr. Overlock nodded seriously. "True," he said. "We must consider that they, too, could have known of the tryst. Indeed, our only recourse is to seek further evidence, which is best gained by an examination of the scene itself. Shall we repair to the collection-room?"

All reluctantly assented, and momentarily we were back in the collection-room peering about. This time the rare artifacts and priceless papers were uninteresting to all. It was the common, the atypically typical that sought audience there, and it was to this end that Constable Upcobb and the Master now applied themselves.

"Constable, what do you make of that?" said Mr. Overlock, pointing.

All looked at the floor near the safe. A large puddle of auburn liquid was amassed there.

Upcobb bent down and sniffed. "A liquor of some kind," he said.

"Grave," said Mr. Overlock, "can you identify this spirit?"

I'm bound to say I wasn't overjoyed at being reintroduced to affairs, and certainly not as a liquor expert, but I dutifully stepped forward and applied a practiced snout.

"It is Fluffingham and Puttney's, sir," I stated as soon as fume struck nostril. "A brandy."

"And did you provide any of our guests with this elixir at any time this evening?"

"Why, yes, sir."

"Who, Grave?"

"The—the Vice Premier."

"Anyone else?"

"No, sir."

"Could anyone have taken it from the kitchen?"

"Impossible, sir. I was in the kitchen at 10:45, addressing the servants. They had been on duty the entire evening, and would have seen anyone entering the kitchen."

All were silent for a moment. Then the constable said, "I've heard enough. Mr. Overlock, would you like me to arrest Vice Premier Bagbottle?"

"You may do as you please," said Mr. Overlock.

"Then, Vice Premier, I arrest you for attempted burglary," said Upcobb. "I would be obliged if you would accompany me at this time."

I need not relate the outbursts that the Vice Premier now issued forth. Suffice it to say that he threatened the constable with every vengeance imaginable and likewise affronted his heretofore benefactor Wartford Dent. He wrapped up his tirade by calling the lady several names only pirates use and telling Flagmask that if one word of it appeared in the papers, he would use those papers to line Flagmask's prison cell. Then Upcobb, begging a premature departure from the occasion, escorted the Premier to and out the door, and into their bleaker futures.

After they left, a strange mix of relief and newfound uneasiness settled on the air. I meekly offered to sop up the mess, and utilized my own handkerchief toward this end. The guests remaining filed slowly outward, and seemed uncertain whether to return to their rooms or bid a hasty retreat. Mr. Overlock made it simple for them.

"As for the rest of you, you may leave the premises. I have been entertained enough for one evening."

Lady Wynx stood before him regally. "Mr. Overlock, our parting is one I feel strangely capable of bearing."

With one last searing look at Wartford Dent—and a fearful one at Flagmask—she flowed out the door.

"Well, Mr. Overlock," said Dent, "your little dinner party has managed to set me back financially, politically and romantically. And I didn't commit a single crime. Congratulations."

"Dismissed," repeated Mr. Overlock.

With a smirk, Wartford Dent also retreated from our lives.

"Well, Mr. Overlock, you've certainly provided me with a story," smiled Flagmask. "Not the one I wanted, but still a story."

"Grave," said the Master, "have another decanter of that brandy placed in my room. I seemed to have spilled a small snifterful while procuring the photograph."

The newsman gaped, and was without speech for a moment. "You mean…you mean that brandy was yours?"

"Quite."

"And you had the Vice Premier arrested on that evidence? Mr. Overlock, you just provided me with the kind of story I wanted. A die-hard frame-up of Bagbottle coupled with false arrest. When this story breaks tomorrow, you'll be ruined. And there's nothing you can do about it."

"Do as you choose."

"You bet I will. You'll see the story as soon as this old geezer brings you your first breakfast in the morning. Toodle-oo, Milo. Look alive, Grave."

And he was off.

Trained to suppress my desire to question the Master's motives as I was, I nevertheless found this peculiar course of events baffling.

"Stop squirming, Grave. I know that you are desperate for enlightenment."

"I am, sir."

"And the pathetic thing is that you are the only one other than myself with enough facts to deduce the truth of the situation."

My absent expression must have been enough to suggest to him my regrettable need for further elucidation. He stooped to the task.

"Tonight my every aim was achieved. Our political and business adversaries, all of whom are dependent upon each other for crucial support, are now antagonists. Without their unity, none can prevail, and I am free of their collective threat. As soon as it becomes known that the Vice Premier has been falsely arrested, he will use his power to see that Constable Upcobb will never practice law-enforcement again, a state of affairs to be desired after the constable abused his authority last week at my expense. And I will finally have an ironclad libel suit which will destroy Flagmask's tabloid."

"Indeed, sir?"

"Quite. He means to have it printed that I had Bagbottle falsely arrested. At no time, however, did I claim that the brandy was the Vice Premier's, and when asked by the constable if I wanted the Vice Premier arrested, I merely said 'Do as you please.' Excluding Flagmask, four witnesses—yourself included—can attest to the fact that Constable Upcobb acted of his own accord in the matter. And as for attempting to frame anyone, Lady Wynx can substantiate the fact that I was in my room at the time that all of this took place. When Flagmask prints information to the contrary, he will be immediately crushed."

I considered this bizarre chain of facts in a daze, realizing finally what the theme to Mr. Overlock's party had been. But how had it been accomplished? And how did it involve (as it always did) me? His unsolicited response confirmed that mind-reading may also have rested among the Master's accomplishments.

"Grave, can you account for all of the servants that you hired for this dinner-party?"

"Why yes, sir. I was addressing them this evening in the kitchen. All were accounted for—the wine, the pantry, the cook, the dishwasher, the server, the table decorator, the door, the floor and the chairs."

"That's nine employees, Grave. Didn't you tell me you'd hired ten?"

You know that feeling when what's left of your heart gets the impulse to head for the hills and makes a beeline for your mouth, but you defeat it at the aperture and instead it gives up and takes a dive into your stomach acid? Such was the sensation which fell upon me now, mixed with vomit.

"I dispatched the tenth servant to hide within the safe all evening, then to activate the alarm at the given time," said Mr. Overlock. "I procured the mortar and arranged the implanted money bags well in advance. The servant has fulfilled his duties perfectly, and will be recompensed beyond his wildest dreams. You, however, failed to detect the absence of the tenth servant. As a measure of security, that is abominable, Grave. You will be punished accordingly. Now return to your quarters."

The party was over. Mr. Overlock's enemies were dispensed with. The servants all went on their way, happily rewarded and wondering what I had made such a fuss about. I, in turn, spent the next week on my hands and knees, scrubbing the floor of the entire mansion with my toothbrush. Mr. Overlock came to inspect my progress every fifteen minutes on the dot, and I regret to say, his riding-crop was always with him.

4

Chapter Four
Milo Overlock On Deck

THE wind was blowing coldly, the customs line had been long, and our quarters, once we got on board, were naturally too small. Milo Overlock was taking a holiday at sea, and I was there to shoulder the blame for every forthcoming inadequacy.

"Stop wheezing, Grave," he said, "and get my trunks unpacked. It's disgraceful enough that I had to wait for you to be searched in customs, but you couldn't even get my baggage up the gangplank without requesting help from a porter. Must I order the entire crew to ignore you before you learn to carry out your duties on your own?"

"I'm sorry, sir," I faltered out, swallowing blood.

"That won't do. Now unpack and see that these quarters are expanded."

"Expanded, sir?"

"Immediately."

With a sudden hello from an ulcer of which I had been unaware, I nodded hopelessly and proceeded with my task. Then I had an inspiration, and while Mr. Overlock went out to inspect the deck, had some ship personnel remove some of the incidental furnishings from the cabin, resulting in a much more "expanded" appearance.

"Look, sir," I beamed, when the Master returned. "I've had them increase the size of your quarters."

"Do you equate the removal of some incidental furnishings with increased dimensional capacity?" snapped Mr. Overlock sharply. "Don't take me for a fool, Grave. I shall simply utilize your adjoining quarters as well. You shall sleep with the crew."

"Yes, sir."

I unhappily made my way to the ship's personnel deck, only to find that there was no excess room for my accommodation. I was informed, however, that I could sleep in a lifeboat. I went to inspect the available ones, climbing in to test their discomfort levels, and was confronted by an angry purser, who, convinced I was a stowaway and ignoring my every explanation, arrested me and put me in the ship's brig. It was there that I spent the next two hours, listening to my heart tick away the Master's teatime, and wishing, as I so often do, that I was stone cold dead.

A click of the lock indicated that my freedom was imminent. The officer, looking as though he still didn't trust me as far as he could fling the anchor, stated that Mr. Overlock had attended to my release, and that I was to proceed to his quarters immediately. Wondering whether I couldn't just whither away in my cell for the rest of the voyage, but spurred by my keeper's impatient snap, I forlornly made my way from the ship's brig, and, after getting lost several times between the boiler room and bilge pump, finally saw light again and landed once more in the warm, wide quarters of Mr. Overlock.

I stood there emanating servile readiness, and he eyed me darkly.

"You're a dog, Grave," he said. "Bark like one."

I contained myself for a moment before this unforeseen request, then hesitantly put forth an undignified "woof."

"On all fours, Grave."

Some wonder why I bear it, but the fact is that were I ever to leave Mr. Overlock's service, he would see to it that I never received employment again, anywhere. This fact stood painfully before my eyes as I crouched to hand and knee, and barked about like a bloodless mongrel in anxious need of a cat to eat.

"Rise."

I rose, attempting to reassume my detached attitude of before.

"Your ineptitude begins to verge upon the intolerable, Grave. One more failure to bring me my tea on schedule will cost you dearly. As it is, I am suspending your pay for the week."

I suddenly wished I had that cat.

"Now, there is a group of highly respected scientists aboard who have invited me to inspect a new species of sea-life they have discovered. You will wheel me there immediately."

He sat down in the cushioned wheelchair that had been provided for his pleasure during the trip, and motioned doorward. Arthritically, I bent to my task, and in moments we were at the cabin (which was, of course, on the uppermost deck) and I was knocking, audibly but ever so unstartlingly, upon the door.

"Who's there?"

I looked about, surprised, then saw one of those pipe things that ship personnel use to communicate through. It was attached to the door, and the voice had come through it.

"Mr. Overlock, sir," I answered.

"What?"

"Mr. Overlock, sir."

"Fist your old warlock's cur?"

Some other vague voice from deeper inside the room said something indistinguishable at this point, and the door was gratifyingly opened. On the other side stood a huge man, bearing the garb and detachment of my ilk. Recognizing a brother in servitude, if a broader and possibly less educated one, I mustered up a pleasant expression. Congeniality is never misplaced.

"Excuse me, sir," I said. "Mr. Milo Overlock requests the pleasure of an audience with the eminent gentlemen of science who have, we believe, made an unprecedented discovery beneath the great sea's depths. If indeed this discovery portends, as we foresee—"

"Shut up," the behemoth interrupted.

"Huh?"

"Shut up or I'll kill you."

He grunted this out like a drunkard, his eyes glazed and vacant. This had not been the voice at the speaking-tube, I noticed—I took that to have been the unsympathetic-looking ancient with the ear horn next to him. There being little one can say in response to the statement given, I "shut up" accordingly, and directed a helpless glance toward Mr. Overlock, who appeared to lack compassion for my cause.

"Proceed, Grave," was all he said.

I looked back at the apelike gentleman and attempted to reason with him on a more common level.

"Excuse me, my fine fellow, but Mr. Overlock has been invited to view the new specimen your masters have on display within these quarters. With your kindly acquiescence—"

"I said shut up or I'll kill you. You unnerstand me, corpse?"

As kindly as I took this premature recognition of the state to which I most avidly aspired, I was compelled to correct him. Considering his command, though, I was uncertain as to the form of communication to use. Sign language I dismissed. Charades? Apelike noises?

"I hate to interrupt this chat with your intellectual peer, Grave, but I find the hall somewhat lacking in fascination. Now wheel me into the room."

Caught between a rock and a very hard place, I felt something like a starfish preparing to battle a squid. I turned to the old doorman.

"Sir, may I—"

"What? Learn to speak up, gramps."

I gave up. Devoted to my duty as I was, I turned my attention back to the muscular cretin, kissed my bones goodbye, and—

"Apu, allow Mr. Overlock to enter."

God must have been inside the room, for these saving words could only have been issued from His lips. The gorilla did not move, however. It was only when a second voice uttered the same command that the creature rumbled and inched ever so slightly to the side. My access presenting itself, I proceeded to wheel Mr. Overlock awkwardly through the small space, bearing his venomous asides at every bump and squeeze. We found ourselves in the cabin at last, and if I thought I heard another murmur of "I'll kill you" as I passed Apu, it was nothing compared to the glares of hate which greeted me from the eminent scientists within the room, glares as hateful to me as their beams were adoring to Mr. Milo Overlock.

"Mr. Overlock," smiled the wormy tadpole I had mistaken for God a second ago, "allow me to introduce you to our assembly. Three of the finest scientists in the world today. Dr. Adipose 'Gill' Gilhooley, discoverer of the Upper and Lower Gilhooley Islands and several other historic firsts; Dr. Kip 'Kippers' Ipswich, Dr. Gilhooley's former assistant and now a prominent oceanographer in his own right; Dr. Si 'Cyclops' Simon, the blind brain surgeon who can see, they say, through his mouth; and lastly, myself, Seabert Coxswain, ship security and friend to all our better citizens."

He sneered at me, then proceeded to direct the Master's attention to a square container of liquid that sat on a table against one side of the room.

It seemed to be a twenty-liter aquarium full of red water, with a small piece of debris floating in it.

"Gentlemen, the Kippergill Cyclopoid," announced Coxswain grandly.

Mr. Overlock gazed at the container and I became aware that the "debris" was indeed an occupant, which upon focusing I perceived to be something like a seahorse coated in mattress-stuffing.

"As you see," said Dr. Gilhooley, "it thrives in blood. One part blood to two parts seawater is the most diluted solution it can survive in. That is why it was discovered in the shark-infested waters off the Upper Isle, I believe. It follows sharks and other predatory sea-beasts so as to be in constant supply of bloody water."

"You talk as if you were the filthy slug's daddy," growled Dr. Ipswich. "I am its rightful discoverer, you pompous bilge-wiper. Your island, my worm, remember?"

"I dispute both your claims," said Dr. Simon at this point, his mouth hanging open as he faced each of the others. "I own rights to the fish. My boat—my expedition. Ipswich accidentally catch creature while fishing for lunch. He no scientist. Gilhooley find island while lost in fog—he no scientist! I scientist."

Apparently something else had been sacrificed when he was born with his eyes in his mouth—a grasp of words, perhaps.

"As you can see," said Coxswain, "there is some doubt regarding the rightful owner of the creature. While it is clearly necessary to split the credit for the discovery, possession remains an unsettled point."

"And how do you propose to resolve the question?" inquired Mr. Overlock.

"I shall act as intermediary," said Coxswain. "Arguments for all sides will be considered, and by the end of the journey I will have made my decision. Meanwhile, the highest measures of security will be effected to protect the creature."

"I am curious as to what those measures are," said the Master.

"Well, for one thing, the aquarium is securely affixed. Apu, try to lift it."

Apu stood motionless, staring into space. Coxswain sighed, and said "Dr. Gilhooley, please instruct your servant to lift the aquarium."

"Apu," said Dr. Gilhooley, "please do as this gentleman wishes."

The man-beast approached the tank, and put his huge arms around it. I'm sure they touched on the other side. He grunted, and proceeded in his attempt to lift it. It creaked and groaned, but did not leave its base. Apu grew purple, and made ghastly noises, but it wouldn't give. "Get up," growled Apu. "Get up or I'll kill you!"

"Tell him to stop," said Dr. Ipswich. "He'll distress the Kippergill."

"Stop, Apu," said Dr. Gilhooley, and the caveman immediately ceased, returning to his detached attitude of before.

"However, that is but the simplest measure," said Coxswain. "I shall be glad to inform you further, Mr. Overlock, at a more discreet time—dinner, perhaps?"

"I am dining at the captain's table tonight," said Mr. Overlock. "If you hope to dine with me, you will need to secure an invitation."

"I will see what I can do," said Coxswain. "Until then."

With this, I wheeled the Master to the door, and we were free of the assemblage.

"Grave," said Mr. Overlock as I propelled him back toward his stateroom, "I do not trust ship food. Therefore, I have made arrangements for you to oversee my meal preparation tonight. See that it is perfect, or else."

I regret to say that this remark stopped me in my tracks for an instant, resulting in a barrage of effronteries from the Master, but I regained a modicum of composure swiftly enough to grimly complete the trip. I passed the afternoon in slavery, attending to Mr. Overlock's every conceivable wish, until the red hour struck, the inevitable arrived, and I repaired to the galley to "oversee" the Master's dinner.

I gained an impression of how things were going to go as soon as I entered. A fat, bald, cross-eyed man wearing nothing but a leotard and whose back-hair was copiously covered with flies, turned to me from the live duck he was beating to death with an axe-handle and said "Whuhthuhfugdoyouwant?" Things went downhill from there.

The first duck I brought to the table gained me but the most ferocious of the Master's glares. The second one he picked up and dropped on the floor in disgust, which I had then to clean up. By the fifth one, I decided to cook the duck myself from scratch, and tried to give the cook some instruction on the subject. Sadly, he was too busy chewing on something that had been crawling around in his leotard, and would not pay attention. When I turned the duck in, the Master said "One of the legs is acceptable," and commanded me to stand at his side throughout the meal, which by this time I was all too happy to do. He ate very slowly, and I waited to see if Seabert Coxswain would arrive. Coxswain arrived, but not until the other diners at the captain's table had vacated.

"Sorry, Mr. Overlock," he said. "The only available opening at your table tonight was for the second dinner hour. Now I can attend to your questions."

"How is the creature being protected?" asked Mr. Overlock. "Aside from having its aquarium bolted down?"

"Well, for one thing, there's our guard inside the room," said Coxswain. "You saw him. Old guy. His name is Lee, and he was an armed sentry at the Bastille in younger days."

"Is that all?" inquired the Master.

"Far from it," said Coxswain. "The door is locked from the inside, and the only means to open it is also from within. It is securely bolted by a steel bar, and the guard is under strict instruction not to open it without receiving a special password. As for the delivery of this password, we use the copper speaking-tube you may have seen when you first arrived at the door. This is a highly sensitive communication device now used on ships to convey messages quickly between officers and crew. It is often used in large households as well, to relay information between floors. As I alone know the password, it is foolproof."

"How does an individual as frail in appearance as your doorman manage the opening and closing of so secure a door?" asked Mr. Overlock.

"That's part of my insurance policy. You see, the steel lock, while impregnable, can be freed by the disengagement of a simple spring. However, the door containing the steel is weighty, and requires a healthy man to open. The guard, being old and decrepit, cannot, so he is unable to abduct the creature himself. He can merely spring the lock, and cannot leave his post until relieved by myself."

"How would you protect yourself from suspicion, should the creature be stolen?" asked the Master.

"That's what Lee is for."

"And could he not work with someone else?"

"Not without implicating himself."

"Impressive," said Mr. Overlock, and Seabert Coxswain will never know how great a compliment he had been paid.

Little more was said, the Master having received what information he desired, so Coxswain ordered and the two ate quietly for another hour or so. I stood, hungry and my feet aching, the entire time. I had just begun to dream of my funeral, rich with flowers and a nice roomy casket, when an alarm sounded and I felt my spine jump up through my cerebral cortex. Coxswain leapt up and shouted "That's the security bell. Someone may be after the Cyclopoid! Hurry, Mr. Overlock!"

He dashed off. Mr. Overlock calmly picked at a few vegetables, wiped his mouth on my hand, turned to me and said "Grave, wheel me to the scientists' deck…by way of my stateroom."

His new pleasure in being "wheeled" everywhere displeased me not a little, nor did the fact that the "scientists' deck" was up three flights, and nowhere near his stateroom. However, my broken arches somehow succeeded in the task, and I was only glad that I had been behind the Master and not in prodding position.

The door to the crime scene was open. Inside was Coxswain, pulling at his hair in distress, and Lee the doorman, hunched in a corner and looking unwell. The tank which had once contained the Kippergill Cyclopoid now contained nothing but bloody water.

"The creature has been stolen, I presume," said Mr. Overlock.

"Yes!" screamed Coxswain. "But how? This ass can't tell me a thing."

Mr. Overlock went over and examined Lee. "He has suffered a head injury," he said. "He is barely conscious. Get a handful of water."

Coxswain scooped some out of the tank.

"Throw it in his face."

Coxswain did. Lee stirred slightly.

"Who struck you?" said Mr. Overlock.

Lee opened his mouth, but nothing came out.

"Was it this man?" said Mr. Overlock, pointing at Coxswain.

Lee shook his head.

"Why did you ask him that?" demanded Coxswain.

"You've been alone with him since we parted," said Mr. Overlock. "While I don't believe you would have asked me to accompany you if you'd had designs on the creature, I thought it best to free you from suspicion before the doorman died."

"Then who did do it, Lee?" asked Coxswain.

Lee died.

"Damn," said Coxswain.

The Master looked around. "The door is not broken in," he observed. "The locking mechanism has been released."

"No one but you and I knew about that," said Coxswain. "I told you about an hour ago, and this happened within the hour. We were with each other the entire time."

"If no one knew about the security system, the intruder could only have hoped to break in the door," said Mr. Overlock.

"But the lock's made of adamantium steel!" protested Coxswain.

"A fact known only to yourself and the victim," said the Master. "This door does display signs of an attempted forced entry. I believe that the intruder either intentionally or unintentionally disengaged the lock mechanism during his efforts at breaking into the room."

"I wouldn't have believed it," grumbled Coxswain, pacing around the room agitatedly. "It was supposed to be invulnerable, and—excepting Lee—I was the only one who knew the password. I, who was with you when this happened."

"Tell me the password," said Mr. Overlock.

The security chief looked uncertain. Perhaps it was the fact that it made little difference now, perhaps it was the innate impossibility of denying one of the Master's commands, that made him open up. "Very well," he said. "I made it quite simple. The fish was discovered off the coast of the Upper Isle in the Gilhooley chain. Hence the password: Upper Isle, Gilhooley. Simple as that."

Mr. Overlock wheeled himself over to the tank. "Hm," he said. "As I surmised, you've bolted the tank to prevent its removal, but left the lid completely free. The intruder simply scooped out the creature in a container and departed with it."

"I'm ruined," slobbered the security chief. "Please, Mr. Overlock, help me to undo this terrible occurrence."

"I am not in the habit of abetting the incompetent," said the Master. "However, were I in your position, I would probably search the scientists' rooms. Beginning," he added meaningfully, "with Dr. Ipswich."

"Dr. Ipswich," murmured Coxswain in breathless worship. "Thank you, Mr. Overlock...thank you."

We repaired thither without hesitation. We found Dr. Ipswich reclining upon a chaise-longue, smoking opium and reading a copy of "Fanny Hill."

"How dare you intrude upon my privacy like this!" he cried as Coxswain burst in. "Please explain this intrusion!"

"Before you are granted an explanation, you must answer one question," said Mr. Overlock. "Where have you been since six o'clock?"

"Right here," said Ipswich.

"Nowhere else?"

"Nowhere else! Now what is the meaning of this?"

"Search his room," commanded the Master. "Grave, wheel me to the lavatory."

I wheeled Mr. Overlock to the water closet promptly, while Coxswain searched the outer room, Ipswich ranting the while.

"Grave, search his sleeping quarters while I investigate here," said Mr. Overlock. "Assist Coxswain in any way he thinks you can."

I acquiesced respectfully, and approached the young security chief, who was crawling around on his hands and knees, looking under the chaise-longue. "May I be of any service, sir?" I inquired.

He jumped up, looking at me as if to say that the best way I could serve him was to serve myself to the sharks, but all he said was "No you may NOT!" and resumed his hand-crawling.

I went then to inspect the bedding as the Master wished, but found myself impeded by Dr. Ipswich, who stepped in front of me and refused to let me pass.

"Forgive me, sir," I said, "but I have been requested by Mr. Overlock to remove the bedclothes."

"Any time some bone-bag Marley's ghost of a half-male handmaiden can go through my stuff'll be the day I wipe my ass with a harpoon gun," he sneered, and spat on my clavicle button.

I cleared my throat, if a trifle uneasily. His motives appeared rather suspicious, and I suddenly itched to search the bed. "Be that as it may, sir, I must insist that you allow me to inspect your sleeping quarters. My duty in this matter is quite clear."

He grunted with a little smile. "No problem, crab bait," he said, and reared his fist back with eye firmly planted upon my midriff.

I was saved by, of all people, the Master, who at this moment chose to call out from the washroom, "I have located the creature."

Coxswain emitted gasps of ecstasy, Ipswich expressions of disbelief and I a breath of relief as Mr. Overlock emerged, bearing a small vial containing a red liquid and the floating corpse of what appeared to be the Kippergill Cyclopoid.

Coxswain screamed "It's dead!"

"Quite," said Mr. Overlock.

Coxswain took the vial and looked at it very carefully. "Ipswich, you'll get the rope for this."

"But—but it isn't mine!" shouted Ipswich.

"I found it clasped to the underside of the washbasin pipe," said Mr. Overlock. "The creature has died—either of stress or of oxygen deprivation."

"I am not guilty!" shrieked Ipswich in fits, as Coxswain pocketed the flask and commenced applying hand-restraints to the furious doctor. "Someone must have planted it there!"

"By your own admission, you have been here since six o'clock," said Mr. Overlock. "The creature was stolen later than six. No one could have come in here to plant the creature without your seeing them."

"Then one of you must have done it while you were searching," he demanded. "It is the only explanation."

"Besides being insulting, you are inaccurate," said the Master. "We were all in the dining-room when the crime occurred, a fact to which the captain and several others can attest. We could not have obtained the creature in order to plant it now. In addition, the doorman himself absolved Coxswain before dying, eliminating the possibility of a conspiracy and betrayal between them."

"I've heard enough," said Coxswain. "The doctor is going to the ship's brig."

Ipswich raised quite a row at this, and in spite of my reassurances that the brig wasn't really all that bad, he was led away spewing derogatory expletives worthy of the ship's sailors, all of them directed, it seemed, at me.

I am grateful to report that the rest of the evening proved reasonably eventless. Mr. Overlock retired to his stateroom with a cognac and a book on symbolic logic, while I picked my weary way to my lifeboat. I made certain not to be witnessed this time, climbed under the tarp and in. There was about two inches of water in it, so I tried to figure out a way to sleep with my head and feet suspended above the basin on two separate seating planks. I was just beginning to master it by the time the sun rose and I was off to fetch Mr. Overlock's tea.

I crawled in like a starfish at low tide, bearing the Master's elixir. He was wide awake, of course, and preoccupied with untying a complexly-knotted piece of rope one-handed.

"You look pathetic, Grave," he said, immediately eradicating the knot and taking his teacup with the hand that had been so occupied. "I shall require your fullest alertness this morning, if we are to reacquire the Kippergill Cyclopoid and apprehend its abductor."

I must have wavered there for a moment, this news leaving me totally befogged. Had the previous evening been a dream? It couldn't have, as I hadn't gotten any sleep. I desperately fought to clear my brain.

"Don't look so absurdly stupid, Grave," snapped the Master. "What you saw yesterday was not the true creature. It was simply a dead seahorse to which mattress-stuffing had been affixed with waterproof glue. I brought it with me on this trip with the express intent of substituting it for the living item."

"But sir, how did it end up in the room of Dr. Ipswich?" I ventured to ask.

"Quite simply, Grave. I brought it with me when we went to search his room. That is why I had you take me to the scientists' deck by way of my stateroom—so that I could procure it beforehand."

"Then, if I may ask, sir, where is the real Kippergill?"

"With Dr. Gilhooley. He had his servant Apu steal it."

I must have appeared baffled.

"Attend, Grave. No one knew about the lock mechanism. Who best to send on a mission of sheer breaking and entering than a man of strength? Note that the door did bear marks of attempted force. Imagine the bestial and one-note Apu, frustrated in his efforts to break in the portal, alerting the attention of the half-deaf guard. He shouts into the speaking-tube, uttering in his anguish a variation on his favorite phrase: 'Open up...'"

"Or I'll kill you," I said, as much as I could for distaste.

"Correct. Assuming that Apu addressed his command to the doorman by name, the result sounds remarkably like a demand for access, followed by the password 'Upper Isle, Gilhooley.' Having inadvertently uttered the liberating phrase, he went in, subdued Lee, procured the sea-beast and took it to the only person for whom he has displayed a willingness to act—Dr. Gilhooley."

"Excuse me, sir," I said timidly, "but why did we not simply approach Dr. Gilhooley last night, rather than implicate Dr. Ipswich?"

"Because Gilhooley would have had the creature well hidden. By now, he has heard the news of the Ipswich arrest, and will no longer find it necessary to conceal the creature as thoroughly. Where yesterday it may have been anywhere on the ship, today it will assuredly be in his room. I took the liberty of relieving Mr. Coxswain of his keys last night during the disturbance. We will now go to Gilhooley's chamber and ambush him."

I disliked the sound of this intensely, especially considering the physical dissimilarities between Apu and myself. I hazarded the thought of pleading the matter with the Master when he said "Get me my flintlock-pistol," and then I knew there was no turning back. Resignedly, I extracted the weapon—which Mr. Overlock had somehow managed to pass through customs—from his luggage, and wheeled him off with it to the gates of my doom.

"Sir," I said as we set forth," forgive me for being so bold as to make the inquiry, but may I ask why you chose to implicate Dr. Ipswich as opposed to, say, the rather grotesque Dr. Simon?"

"Dr. Ipswich is Dr. Gilhooley's former assistant," said Mr. Overlock darkly. "And I despise servants who betray their masters." He paused to glare back at me. "Is that all the information you require, Grave?"

I swallowed. "Yes, sir."

"I am gratified. Accelerate."

With every step feeling like a wade in swamp-mud, I pushed the none-too-light Mr. Overlock to the door of the stateroom of Dr. Gilhooley, and foolishly asked if I might knock first.

"You may not," snapped the Master. "Here's the key. Open it."

With a dim throb in my blanching extremities, I turned the key in the lock and shoved the door open. I ran back and rushed Mr. Overlock through the doorway. I slammed the door shut. The scene was one which I will attempt to freeze in my mind and describe like a photograph.

There was Dr. Gilhooley, sitting on a chair and holding a large pear-shaped flask at arm's length, cackling victoriously. There was Apu, standing on his knuckles and facing us, his simian mouth hanging open in astonishment at our intrusion. Before me was the Master, calmly sitting with his flintlock cocked and aiming it variously at both of them. And there was I, cowering behind the wheelchair, hoping that the Second Coming would hurry up and come.

"If you please, Dr. Gilhooley, I will now relieve you of the Milogill Overpoid," said the Master.

"The—what?" cried Gilhooley.

"For you will either release the creature into my possession, or I will expose you to the ides of offended justice. Select."

Gilhooley squirmed for a moment. Then "Apu—attack!" he shouted.

Apu jumped forward, but was stilled by the aim of the Master's fine flintlock, which was aimed squarely at his eyes.

"It is time for you to change allegiances, Apu," intoned Mr. Overlock ominously. "Either betray your master or face condemnation for your part in this crime. Decide now."

Apu stood in mid-attack position for the space of about a minute. Then he slowly stood erect.

"What's the matter, Apu?" demanded Dr. Gilhooley. "I told you to attack!"

"Shut up," said Apu.

"What?"

"Shut up or I'll kill you."

Gilhooley was cornered. He was facing the Master's gun, Apu and the brig. Still he held the flask.

"Very well, Mr. Overlock," he said slowly, rising. "Very well."

He approached the Master, arm and flask extended. Mr. Overlock eyed him grimly. Then—he bolted! He ran right past me, threw the door open and ran out. I goggled in disbelief.

"Grave—pursue!" said the Master.

Flustered, I grabbed the handles of the wheelchair and obeyed. Out we sped into the corridor. I spotted the doctor in the hall ahead, making for the door which led to the outer deck of the ship. I trundled clumsily behind, spurred on by the dire fear of what would happen to me should I fail to keep pace with the brigand. Out into the light I directed the wheelchair, hastened by the Master's imperious usherings. The morning wind blew cold on the deck, making booming noises against the mainmast, and we were high on the forecastle of the ship. And there before us, as if by a miracle, stood Gilhooley, running no more but standing pressed against the railing and holding the flask with the Kippergill—or Milogill—over the sea. We closed in on him.

"Stop, Mr. Overlock," cried Dr. Gilhooley, waving about the flask. "If you don't drop your accusations against me, I'll drop this—and with it goes both your evidence and your prize. There are no witnesses here—make up your mind!"

Unlike Apu, Mr. Overlock did not pause before making his decision. He shot Dr. Gilhooley in the stomach, and both Dr. Gilhooley and fish fell into the sea.

I stood in shocked amazement, and gazed around. As the doctor had said, there were no witnesses about. I looked over the railing. Floating far below was the flask, with Dr. Gilhooley nearby, end-up on a billowing stain.

"Get the Milogill, Grave."

I turned in abject horror. "What! I mean—I beg your pardon, sir?"

"Retrieve it immediately," said the Master, reloading his flintlock. "But first, you must bleed. Should the creature have escaped its container, it will be attracted to the blood of Dr. Gilhooley's wound. I wish it to be attracted to yours."

And with that, he shot me. Stunned and quite awake with pain, I was not immediately able to recognize that it had been but a glancing blow, merely enough to remove the tip of one of my fingers. Then Mr. Overlock wheeled himself forward slightly and pushed me overboard.

Down I flailed, dripping juice, until the mile was up and I crashed into a brick wall of sheer ocean, gasping and gurgling and seeing a plethora of stars, galaxies and nebulae.

I bobbed up and down for a moment, feeling the grip of the ocean like a great hand pulling me into its briny depths. All feeling left my body and

I was desperately tempted to fight no more. Yet somehow in the midst of my death-struggle with the mighty, undulating hydrosphere I could see in my mind Milo Overlock, looking sternly at me and reminding me of my mission. In a vague, spluttering stupor I set sight on the flask which was somehow quite close to me; in a bleary, indefinable way I somehow saw that the rancid worm was still within it; and as I grasped it, sinking, something alerted me to the plop of a life preserver alighting nearby, which with my one unbloodied hand I managed to drape upon myself. Then I felt myself being lifted upward, slowly, my guts heaving with every lurch. I saw the ocean recede beneath me. I looked, and saw my hand still holding the flask. In moments, I found myself being pulled back onto the deck by Apu, holding my lifeline like a gorilla would cling to a vine. I panted, and coughed, and fell to the planks with unabashed indignity. I was alive.

"The flask, Grave."

Suddenly reminded of my position, I forced myself to rise and effect the proper posture of a gentleman's gentleman. I quietly adjusted my raiment, and handed Mr. Overlock the flask.

"Thank you, sir," I awkwardly fumbled out, "for saving my life."

"Nonsense, Grave," said Mr. Overlock. "It was for the Milogill."

He turned to Apu and said "You are dismissed. Wait in your quarters for further instruction."

Apu bowed, grunted, and retracted. A hopeful thought entered my mind.

"Sir, now that you have engaged the services of Mr. Apu, may I ask if it is your intention to release me from your employ?"

"Not at all, Grave. Apu will only remain in my service long enough to be relegated to my salt mines, where he will quietly vanish. As I said, I despise servants who betray their masters. As for this specimen, it will remain in my private collection until enough time has passed for it to be 'discovered,' by myself, in another corner of the world. Now please wheel me away from this distasteful site, and bind your finger. It is time to inform the captain that Dr. Gilhooley has committed suicide over his grief at the death of the former Kippergill."

And so passed the first two days of Mr. Overlock's happy holiday at sea. Just imagine, I thought to myself as I quietly wheeled the Master away, in only three more weeks we would be home.

5

Chapter Five
Merry Christmas, Milo Overlock

"**D**ECK the halls with boughs of holly, fa-la-la-la-la-la-la-la-la…." I stood watching the youthful carolers as they went through the old selection, dreaming of that long-ago day when I too had so occupied myself. The snow in Onwall had come up to our knee-breeches—it was always plenteous in winter—and to be sure, our voices had been quite inexperienced, but oh what a warm memory it was, full of tingle and hope and wonder and a future of many merry Christmases to come. I sighed a heavy sigh of nostalgia, and listened as the last ringing high note wished me a happy new year, thinking that life was really not so bad after all.

"Quite wonderfully done, my lads," I said, clapping very quietly. "Wonderfully done. Do you by any chance know "'E'en The Lowliest Ass, 'Twere Blest'?"

It so happened that they did, and they began to render it, with a more than usually understanding reassurance.

"Grave."

Right in the middle of the word "blest," the song stopped dead, and I wiped the dreamy smile off my face with anxious haste.

"Are those visitors bearing gifts?" asked Mr. Overlock from the parlor within.

"Eh—no, sir; indeed, I believe that they would favor an honorarium."

"Then shut the door. It is cold and I have no time for beggars."

With a sad shrug, I turned back to the carolers. "I'm sorry, children, but the Master does not—"

"I said shut the door, Grave."

I shut the door in the children's faces.

"Come in here, Grave," said Mr. Overlock.

I approached him.

"Don't let me catch you entertaining any more of these inbred local urchins on my time. Have you erected my tree yet?"

"I was just about to, sir."

"Proceed without delay."

You may think it odd that Mr. Overlock, quite the least sentimental being on the planet, would favor a Christmas tree, but he had me procure and decorate one, every year. Of course, every decoration was in some way a replication of himself, from the papier-mache Milo heads to the plaster Milo figurines to the wondrous, wide-winged Milo angel which stood atop the tree. But there was also the need for a suitable place to lay the myriad gifts which were sent to the Master every season, from every opportunist in every corner of the country, and a tree had limbs within which to secure some of the smaller ones. Hence my special seasonal task of seeking, then cutting, then storing, then lugging in the brutish branch-bearer and decorating it before Mr. Overlock's critical eyes.

The fact that it was, by demand, always three times his height and twice mine, did not render the affair much easier.

"Stop that infernal gasping, Grave. If the tree is too heavy for you, take a rest."

Rather surprised, I paused in my labor of carrying the six-foot-wide tree through the three-foot-wide door and asthmatically gulped in quarts of white-cold air.

"I mean of course that you should take a rest *after* you put up the tree, inept sluggard. Those who rest during work receive no pay."

I could make a case for those who did work without receiving pay, but I merely said "Yes, sir" and lifted my beneedled bundle anew, trying to keep my tortured grunts and outbursts of agony under control.

"I favor the window," said Mr. Overlock. "It will allow for added room within the parlor."

I proceeded to the window, speculating that with the number of gifts Mr. Overlock received piled everywhere, it would not matter if the tree was near the window or growing out of his armchair. However, I did not debate a point he knew all too well already. I merely consigned myself to the fact that I would be moving everything again the next day, and tried not to break the window (or my back) as I righted the tree.

"It is only three days until Christmas morning, Grave," said the Master. "Try not to spend two of them finishing this. The décor, if you please."

I readily acquired the boxes possessed of the miserable Milo merchandise and started strewing it about the limbs. I was not particularly aided in my alacrity by Mr. Overlock's decision to argue my chosen location for each and every bauble, nor by his ongoing criticism of how long I was taking. However, things seemed to be making a fitful progress by dinnertime, when the little brass bell alongside the front door tinkled, and I was alerted to the fact that someone was pulling on the ring outside.

"Pardon me, sir," I said, pausing in my trials. I went to the door and opened it. A huge, sinewy man who seemed composed strictly of knotted rope stood without, leaning on a very large parcel parked upon the doorstep.

"Delivery for Mr. Milo Overlock," he grunted.

"Thank you, my fine man," I said. "Could you please bring it into the parlor?"

He blinked. "Ain't my duty," he said.

I looked at the large box. I endeavored to lift it slightly, popping a blood vessel in my finger. "I'm sorry, sir, but I find myself unable to convey the package. Would you be so kind to assist me?"

He leaned forward with a growl. "Ain't – my – duty," he repeated. "Now up with the tips."

I pondered a moment his meaning, then grimaced with indignation. "Not the slightest compensation shall you receive, sir, until you help me to bring in this box."

He grabbed me by the lapel, and I was able to perceive that his hand was bigger than my head. His hot nose-breath, like the steam of a compost-heap on a summer's day, gathered like a film on my whiskers. "Gimme money," he demanded, and started fiddling in my trouser-pocket with his other hand.

I emitted all kinds of hideous gurgles as he burrowed about in there, until he suddenly ceased and I found Mr. Overlock standing beside me. The cretinous courier backed up in obsequious silence, and removed his hat humbly. Mr. Overlock held out his hand and the goblin meekly handed him the one treasure he had managed to rape from my pocket—a copper button. The Master dismissed him with a gesture, the ruffian beetled off, and I stood there emanating gratitude for Mr. Overlock's intervention. "You're insufferable, Grave," was all he said, depositing the button in his own pocket and returning to the parlor. "Now bring in the box."

I pondered hopelessly for a moment. Then, "May I request the cook's help, sir?" I asked.

"Provided that it neither delays nor devalues the dinner he is presently preparing," said Mr. Overlock.

I sprung to without delay. The cook, a yellow brigand acquired from an Eastern junk in exchange for a box of tea, had a way with duck, and was also quite wiry enough to bear the task of helping me tote in the weighty parcel quickly. We set it in the parlor near the tree, and I blotted my brow, feeling like a lumberjack with lumbar pains.

"It must weigh two hundred pounds, sir," I said. "Who could have sent it?"

"Perhaps if you looked at the delivery label, you would find out," he snapped.

"Oh. Yes, sir."

I found the packing slip and saw that it contained an inscription in verse. I read it aloud. "'From he who gives to him who takes, I hope this brings you lots of breaks. Signed, Oglethorpe Jones-Dupree, The Bricklayer.'"

Mr. Overlock appeared to ponder. "Hm," he said, "the man I commissioned to repair a wall at my mattress factory. The children had made a hole in it and were escaping, resulting in a labor shortage. Sadly, they found the new wall just as vulnerable, and I had to make an example of the bricklayer."

"Perhaps he seeks to make amends, sir," I suggested. "Perhaps the gift is a ton of new bricks, stronger and more durable ones."

"A ton is not two hundred pounds, Grave," said Mr. Overlock. "Sometimes there is less at hand than meets the eye."

The cook, meanwhile, proceeded to bring out the Master's duck, which was placed on a silver salver before him. Mr. Overlock inspected it coldly. "As I suspected—overdone. Procure a live one from the pond, Grave."

"But sir, that's the cook's duty!" I protested, gaping at the bleeding raw mallard.

"It was your incapability that resulted in its being overcooked," he shot back. "Now go get a fresh one and have the cook prepare it in the next ten minutes. And Grave," he added, "no shot damage. Capture it by hand."

There is nothing quite like wading, waistcoat-deep and formally attired, into an ice-cold duck pond on a black December evening and trying to nab one of the little feathered bagpipes by hand. Suffice it to say that after about an hour of frostbitten diversion attempting to quack deceptively enough to lure one to its doom, I started throwing rocks at the beasts, and to my complete surprise managed to kill a hen. I sloshed my way manorward and held my prize up proudly, only to find the Master in the kitchen, who informed me that I had taken too long, he'd wanted a drake, and that the duck was damaged beyond edibility. He further added that he'd already sent the cook to town for a duck, had had it prepared and eaten it, and that the duck I had slaughtered would instead be my dinner. He took it, chopped its head off with a cleaver, threw the body in the trash and the head at me. "Your dinner, Grave," he said, and sent me to bed still dripping.

It was while I was lying in my room, gnawing in caveman fashion on the duck-head, that my inspiration struck me. Every year I was expected to give Mr. Overlock a gift for Christmas, and it was a matter of much anxiety with me. For if Mr. Overlock did not approve of my gift, he not only withdrew the gift he had allegedly prepared for me, but penalized me as well—even going so far, on occasion, to reducing my yearly two-day vacation to one or none. To date, he had never approved of one of my gifts to him. It was becoming clear to me that material gifts, of the inexpensive kind I could afford or the painstaking handmade kind like some of those gracing the tree, were inadequate, and I was loathe to come up with an alternative. But as I crunched on the duck's brain, wondering what a duck thought and why, it suddenly occurred to me that what the Master liked most was to think, and that a gift which could provoke that process might well win his favor. I decided to give him a mystery for Christmas, one that he could solve and which would provide a big pay-off at the end. I would take and hide all of his presents on Christmas Eve, he would have to find them, and when he did I would surprise him by revealing that I had been behind it all. I could just imagine his beams of approval. "Grave," he would say, "not only are you the most efficient manservant the world has ever known, but the most brilliant as well. I love you." Then he would shower me with gold, and promote me to his associate, with servants of my own to diss unrelentingly. I was so delighted with the thought that I giggled and snuggled into my blankets with what was left of the duck's head on the pillow next to me, and actually got an hour or so of good sleep before the Master rang for his midnight snack.

The next day I could have walked on air. I even faced undaunted my anticipated task of relocating the tree and all the presents to yet another area of the parlor. And although the Master forbade me the cook's assistance this time and "supervised" me throughout, I did it all without the slightest problem or discomfort, and attributed this to my improved strength from all the recent lifting and my bracingly clever plan. When I was finished with the procedure, Mr. Overlock took a paper and pen and ordered me to read off the names of every person who had sent a gift, presumably to know just who and who not to make the new year memorable for. Even though this required me to re-lift most of the presents I had just transported for the second time, I didn't mind. For my gift was the lightest of all, and though it did not possess a tag to read, was bound to make the greatest impression.

Christmas Eve arrived in customary fashion. The Master sat in the large armchair in the parlor, smoking his pipe and drinking curried yap. I polished the pipes in the basement, waiting for bedtime with a tinge of uncommon excitement. I don't know what the cook was doing; I presume it had something to do with dark deeds and opium. Shortly the clock tolled the ten o'clock hour, and I came up to obtain a snack for the Master, which I brought to his room and placed on the table beside his bed.

Christmas Eve is the one night the Master prefers relatively uninterrupted by foodstuffs and such; he generally sleeps it away as one would a cold. Hence my procuration of what was usually his midnight snack two hours earlier. I turned down his bedclothes, closed the curtains and stood waiting quietly for his appearance. He arrived a few minutes late, holding a candle, whence I quickly extracted his night raiment and assisted him into it.

I rather expected a "Merry Christmas, Grave" or something similar, but all he said was "I want a toe rub," and I immediately bent down to administer the massage. I had just begun doing it when he suddenly protested that my hands were cold, and kicked me in the lip. I bowed, labia swelling, and began to withdraw. Then he said to me "Don't be a fool tonight, Grave" and blew out the candle.

I found this warning somewhat ominous, but my equilibrium returned as I closed the door. A fool was the *last* thing I was going to be tonight. I slipped off to my room, had a milk, and braced myself for my mission ahead. Then I opened my door, peeked about, saw that all was quiet, and set forth on my quest.

I have to admit I felt curiously giddy that night, like a boy of sixty. Creeping around in the dark on Christmas Eve, especially on that rarest of occasions when I was assured of some uninterrupted solitude, was enough to inspire in me quite a sense of the ethereal, and I danced about like a frost fairy, trying to keep the sound of my bones down to a chestnut-like crackle. And the surprising thing was that the presents felt, if anything, lighter than they had last been. I was amazed by what regular lifting and a positive outlook could do. I decided that, since I had the whole night, I would hide each in a different place around the house, and stretch Mr. Overlock's pleasure to its furthest point. I took the first available gift and headed toward the pantry, when I received the first sour note of the evening. The door to the pantry was locked.

This struck me as odd. Not that locking it was difficult, for one of the features of Mr. Overlock's mansion was that every door therein could be locked from the outside, rendering every room (if he wished) a prison. What made it odd was the twofold fact that although the Master kept the keys, he never went to the trouble of locking anything himself (he'd have me do it) and rarely wished anything locked but the collection-room anyway. I stood in somewhat bewildered silence for a moment, then shrugged, dismissed it from my mind and proceeded to my second choice, the smoking-room.

The smoking-room was locked, too. Now feeling provoked and baffled, I took the package back to the parlor and began skulking around the manor, trying every door. They were all locked, big rooms and small, from the library to the conservatory. Even the water closets were locked, rendering matters quite uncomfortable for any but He who possessed the key. I quietly tried Mr. Overlock's door; it too was locked, albeit from the inside, as the one room so equipped. Indeed every room in the house was locked except mine. I began to suck my thumb.

Then—bother, I thought. If my room was the only available one, I would put them all there. It would still be the last place the Master would look, and with any luck I would be able to relocate some of them while he searched around in the morning. I smiled, still enthused, and proceeded to transfer the hoard into my plywood sanctuary, where it piled up like ants on a low-rent hill. When I was done, I breathed a sigh of fatigue and plopped upon my hay-stuffed mattress, too tired to make the run to the duck pond which nature might otherwise have demanded. Curled up like a contented ox in its stable, I expelled a tired breath and proceeded to fall into a deep and lengthy slumber. I began dreaming that I was St. Nicholas surrounded by scores of adoring children, to whom I was distributing dozens of wondrous and individualized gifts. Then one of the youngsters began rapping on my head with a cane, demanding "I want my breakfast, Grave," and I awoke, the sun shining, my bladder burning, and the Master pounding on my door demanding his morning meal.

"Coming, sir," I cried out, hoping that he would not open the door and perceive the presents before he even knew they were missing. It was bad enough that I had failed to hear him ring—I attributed this to the incessant bells of my dream-sleigh—but trusted that the pleasure he would receive from my "cerebral gift" would obviate any drastic punishment. I scurried into my attire and trotted forth to the hall, hoping that I could use the water closet before the Master became too impatient. I ran to one, only to note that he was in it; then I ran across the house to another, finding it still locked. Defeated and desperate, I ran out to the duck pond, discovering to my dismay that snow had fallen in the night and the pond had frozen over. I kicked a hole in the ice, which was thin, and soaked my right leg up to the calf with green water that was slightly colder than the outermost moon of Neptune. I nonetheless produced a receptacle for my goal, and after contributing, galloped my way back into the manor by way of the kitchen. Blotting my sodden fatigues with a soft apple (no towel was available), I restored my presentability as best I could and made my way to the dining-room, where I was certain the Master awaited, riding-crop in hand.

Surprisingly, he wasn't there. He arrived a moment after I did, proving that Christmas Day is indeed the day for miracles.

"I'm sorry, sir, but your breakfast appears not to be prepared," I said. "The cook is nowhere to be found."

"He has been dismissed," stated Mr. Overlock briefly, surprising me. "You will attend to my breakfast. Duck eggs, Grave."

"Yes, sir."

I must say, of all the cooks that had come and gone under the Master's aegis over the years, I was not particularly heartbroken to see this one depart. However, I was rather confounded as to what transgression had won him his ticket back to the mysterious East. His last night's creation had not faced any serious rebuke from the Master, and he had not yet prepared breakfast. I could only presume that he had come in addled by exotic elements and possibly gotten a bit carried away with the cleaver. Whatever it had been, I was quite surprised to find the duck eggs whole in the ice box when I hobbled to it on my frostbitten leg.

I poached the orbs and presented them to the Master with the papers and a vase of flowers. He poked at the eggs a bit, buried himself in the papers and ignored me for the next half-hour, while I stood by with salt-shaker in hand. Then, without taking his eyes off the journal or laying his fork down, he swallowed a mouthful of yolk and said "Where are the presents, Grave?"

I gulped. The abruptness of his inquiry had startled me, giving rise to hopeful anticipation mingled with an unaccountable sense of foreboding. "What presents, sir?" I replied, rather weakly.

"Those items which individuals with ambitious agendas use this day as an excuse to present to their betters," he said. "They are missing."

"Are they, sir?" I said. "Quite a mystery."

"You stole them, Grave."

Choke. "Not at all, sir."

"Shall we inspect your room?"

"But sir…"

He rose and began promptly walking across the house. I followed, like a dog who has chewed his keeper's slippers, aware of the wrong spin my brilliant gift was perversely taking. My heart barking in my larynx, I realized that I could now but hope that Mr. Overlock would accept my explanation for events and still recognize the quality of my concept and the value of my intent. Then I told myself that if I believed that, I was a bigger horse's ass than even Mr. Overlock thought I was.

"Your bedchamber, Grave," said the Master as we arrived. The door was shut. Mr. Overlock extracted a key from his waistcoat pocket and inserted it in the keyhole. A spring was released, I could hear the bolt shoot back and to my great mystification realized that the door had been locked. Then, before I could protest further or offer a word of preparatory defense, he opened the door and the booty shone forth before him.

Except for the fact that upon closer inspection the "booty" wasn't booty at all, nor were things as I had left them. The boxes were all open, ripped up and scattered around, and there wasn't a sign of a single gift within any of them. I stood there, warm saliva crawling out of my open mouth.

"Where are the contents, Grave?" asked Mr. Overlock stonily.

"Sir," I spluttered, "I…I am quite at a loss."

"First you deny putting the boxes in here, then you pretend not to know what has become of their contents. You are a thief, Grave."

"No, sir! I…I merely wanted to give you a mystery as a gift, so I hid the boxes in my room last night. But I did not open them, I assure you, sir!"

"Your excuses are as weak as your intellect. You will be shackled and arrested, and may offer your assurances to the presiding judge before he condemns you to your dungeon."

I dropped to one knee before him. "Please, sir, don't have me arrested. Believe me, I am innocent—I merely wanted to please you!"

He gazed at me expressionlessly, like a dead tree. "Inside, Grave."

I stood up, hopeless. He motioned to my room. Shoulders slumped, I dragged my way within. All was lost. My only hope now was that I would eat better in prison—then I remembered that Mr. Overlock owned it. He would probably even be my judge.

"You will stay locked in this room until the constabulary arrives," said the Master icily. "They will then make a thorough investigation, and take you to your cell."

He closed the door and locked it. I was left with my shattered "cerebral gift," which now threatened to shatter me. I toed a few package remnants, but it was true. Not a single object existed within any of them, nor were there any about. Yet all the boxes had been intact when I arose, and even the fastest thief could not have stolen their contents in the amount of time since. Besides which, no one could have gotten to the front or kitchen doors without being seen from the dining-room, and all the rooms had been locked—including, mysteriously, this one. So where had the presents gone, and how?

I decided, halfheartedly, to make a slightly more complete review of my pathetic cubicle before the hands of justice arrived. My room had no window—just a closet, bed and bureau. I picked up all the boxes and looked amongst them with great scrutiny, but not even an errant price tag remained. Then I went to my closet. Depressingly bare, it contained several pairs of valet livery, a can of shoe polish and a keepsake box containing some shiny nails, a piece of wire and a good wine's cork; nothing else. I went then to inspect the bureau; however, but for undergarments and ties, the only thing new inside was a big spider, which bit me, but unfortunately was not poisonous.

It seemed in order to check under the bed next, so I stretched my backbone, crouched creakingly and peered. Then, with a shocking, sudden spring which made the spider's bite seem like a kiss from a wood nymph, something barreled out at me from under the bed, knocked me backwards, and stood panting, wolf-like, in a corner of the room. I was certain I had unleashed some monster from the depths of the earth, and grasped my chest in agony. My heart was like a hummingbird's, and seemed only to be warming up for its best effort. I hazarded myself to look, and saw that the hideous creature which had claimed my last few years was indeed a man, heavy with three days' growth and ill-bathed, standing in the corner like a wrestler about to commence a round. His sinewy hands flexed open and shut, he glared at me with meat lust, and his hot breath came out in stinky steam. I tried to scream but my voice was floating around in my lower extremities at the moment, rendering my utterances kind of a dry oink. I forced myself to rise, and stood confronting the villain, willing as much composure upon myself as possible.

"One side, ghost," he growled, breaking the ice. "Ain't no one gonna find me here."

I swallowed. "Who—" squeak "—are you?"

"Someone your boss out there ruined. One word from him and not one potential client in the country hires me. My wife leaves me, and even the soup kitchens won't let me in. I live by the docks, drinking sewer water and eating whatever I can catch crawling in the mud. And why? Because those kids got past my wall. Not that they actually got through it. They dug under it. But I got the blame."

It was then that I realized I was speaking to Mr. Oglethorpe Jones-Dupree, the Bricklayer.

"I figure Mr. Overlock takes in more presents at Christmas than the Queen's male masseuse. But I can't steal 'em—he'd have 'em found before I could carry a tenth of 'em two hundred yards. However, if I can ruin 'em, he gets a Christmas he always remembers—the day he lost everything like I lost everything!"

I'm bound to say that I sympathized with the brute, in spite of his cowardly demeanor in the face of adversity.

"But I ain't waiting for no peeler to find me in here when they come looking for you," he said. "I'm busting out that door."

Sympathetic to his cause though I was, my duties as valet were nevertheless regrettably clear, not to mention that this ruffian was my only alibi.

"I shall be compelled to detain you, sir," I said.

He nodded with a churlish grin, and began circling about the room. He looked like a dog but he walked like a cat, and I was a very, very old mouse. I started to recoil, but held my ground, determined to die in the performance of my duty. My eye then fell upon a cheap blue vase which sat upon the bureau, and I grabbed it, feeling that I might use it as a weapon.

"I discourage you from advancing further, sir," I said, brandishing the pot. "Else I shall find it necessary to strike you."

My high-toned advice apparently failed to strike a responsive chord in him, for he immediately lunged forward. I bellowed, and threw the vase into the air. He caught it as I crouched before him, blubbering for my life. This, too, appeared not to meet with its desired end, for he cracked the pottery upon my skull, everything wavered for a moment, then the world quietly vanished from my view.

A space of time seemed to pass before I could see anything at all. Then a sweet music filled my ears, and slowly my surroundings became illuminated. A blue sky extended as far as I could see in all directions, and this was filled with big, fluffy white clouds. I was floating among them, and feeling as if every ailment I had ever had was miraculously healed. Then, some comforting, familiar voices seemed to beckon me on to the biggest cloud of all, and I flew there, finding a huge golden gate resting thereon and beyond it the most glorious sights and sounds imaginable. I glided up to the gate and was met my a great old man in flowing white robes, holding a silver set of keys in one hand, and a huge book in the other.

"Greetings, my son," he said. "Do you seek to pass through the pearly gates?"

"Yes, sir, oh yes, sir!" I cried, thinking how great Christmas Day must be in heaven.

"And what is your name, my son?"

"Grave, sir. Of long and loyal servitude."

"Grave…" he murmured, thumbing through his big book. "Oh, yes. Here we are." He looked for a moment, as I quivered with anticipation, gaping with joy at the wonders that awaited me. Then he pursed his lips. "Hm," he said, closing his book. "I'm sorry, Grave, but you may not enter."

I goggled in shock. "But sir, I have been faithful and trustworthy my whole life!"

"Oh, I know that. But you see, Mr. Overlock has not given his permission yet."

I gaped, but before I could utter a word, I was whisked backward like a blade of grass in a wind-tunnel, the vision vanished from my sight, and all became black once more. Then my aches and pains returned plus some, my eyes slowly opened and I focused upon what appeared to be my room.

There was a red stain on the floor where my head rested, but everything else was normal. I forced myself to rise. My door was open, and the house seemed very quiet. Struggling to remain on my feet, I hobbled out of the room and into the hall. No life was about, and in spite of my pain I felt very curious. I walked around the house, finding nothing and no one, till I passed by the panel to the collection-room, which was usually kept sealed.

It was wide open, and within stood Mr. Overlock, admiring an assortment of unfamiliar treasures I could only presume to be his Christmas presents.

"Ah, Grave," he said. "Assist me in cataloguing these gifts."

I limped in, befogged.

"From Eggremont Phipps, the dental surgeon: King Solomon's mouth."

There it was, sitting in a jar of water, lips and all.

"From H.G.W., a time machine. See that it is dusted."

There it was, resting in a corner, looking like it had been there awhile.

"From our Queen, a proclamation guaranteeing me her next heir."

"Excuse me, sir," I interrupted, "but may I ask what has become of Mr. Jones-Dupree?"

"He was apprehended up the street by the constabulary shortly after freeing himself from your quarters and exiting the house."

"But sir, these presents. I thought he had destroyed them."

"Not at all, Grave. You recall the day that the two hundred pound present arrived, which you could not move without the aid of the cook? The next day you moved it all by yourself without difficulty. An inanimate object does not spontaneously lose weight, and two hundred pounds is often the weight of a man. Suspecting an intruder, I locked every door in the manor that night but yours, and with the aid of the cook, placed all of the gifts in this impenetrable collection-room. After extracting every gift from its container, I had the cook repackage the empty boxes and place them back beneath the tree."

"But sir, how did you know the empty boxes were in my room on Christmas morning?"

"I knew by the fact that your name was not among the givers when I had you list them that you did not plan a conventional gift this Christmas. I knew that the boxes had to be in your room or stolen, because on Christmas Eve, as on the night before, every room was locked but yours. Theft was not the motive, for if it had been, the thief could have attempted it on either of the two nights prior to Christmas Eve. No, the intruder meant to *destroy* the presents, and on the night before the holiday."

"May I ask how you knew that I had moved the boxes?" I inquired.

"I knew that you had put the boxes in your room, because if the intruder had put them there you would have seen them in the morning and reported the oddity. If you had meant to steal the presents, you would not have left the evidence scattered publicly about your room. I knew that it was merely due to some misguided idiocy that you had taken the boxes."

"Sir," I asked meekly, "if you knew I was innocent, why did you lock me in my room?"

"Before coming to breakfast, I locked your bedchamber to prevent the exit of the intruder, but no evidence existed as yet to implicate him. After giving him time to tear through the boxes—which of course he could not have done at night without waking you—I opened the door in order to ascertain that my theory was correct. Seeing that it was, I accused you of the crime in order to present to him a viable reason for my locking you in the room. I knew that he was likely to be able to break through your door, and that any suspicion of an intruder's guilt, rather than your own, might prompt him to depart before the constabulary could arrive. I trusted in your presence to detain him long enough for his capture by the authorities, whom I had already notified. It did."

Bedraggled though I was, I could not help but feel a little gratified that my suffering had at least led to the apprehension of a criminal. "Then—I have given adequate service, sir?" I asked.

"Quite the contrary, Grave. By your absurd decision to move the boxes from the parlor to your room in order to produce what you call a 'mystery,' you obviated my original plan to capture the intruder. I had the cook stand guard outside all night on Christmas Eve in order to waylay the villain when he exited after his futile carnage. It was the cook I had alert the constabulary the next morning when I realized that you had bungled my plans. Because he provided such excellent service in the face of your ineptitude, I decided to give him the Christmas gift I had originally planned to give you."

I gulped. "And that was, sir?"

"Retirement. With a house in the country and a steady pension for life. Instead, you will be both my valet *and* my cook from now on, saving me the money of hiring two servants and in turn supporting the ex-cook's pension."

I do not have the words to describe what I felt on hearing this, nor did I then. Perhaps such words have never been written. All I said was, "Then may I get you your dinner now, sir?"

"Quite. Fresh duck tripes, quickly."

"Yes, sir."

I turned to go. "Oh," I said, turning back. "Merry Christmas, sir."

"It is no longer Christmas, Grave. You have been unconscious for two days. I hope you enjoyed your next year's vacation."

The next day I tried the time machine, but it didn't work.

6

Chapter Six
Milo Overlock On Safari

THE affair began in proper, I believe, as we drove home from the cannery. Mr. Overlock was in a dangerously grim state, and it bothered me not a little. His salmon canning business was being plagued by a labor shortage, as the staff was growing older, bigger, and increasingly able to overpower the guards. Every bump brought vitriolic asides from the Master as we rode along in the carriage; I offered some levity in the form of "It's not what's in the can, sir, but how well it goes down," and he stabbed me in the kidney with his fountain pen. He then demanded that I alter course—he wanted to observe some rare antiques—and we were off to the home of Vandemere Bibbons and his wife, Agony.

I could never understand why the Master chose to spend time there. It was quite clear that he despised Bibbons and viewed him as a rival who dared possess several prized collectibles which the Master clearly coveted.

Bibbons never parted with anything in his collection, so bargaining was useless, and he was, in addition, a smirky, arrogant aristocrat with a weepy wife of repellingly immense proportions. But Mr. Overlock had me take him there often, and I was forced to spend ungodly minutes gazing upon atrocious pieces of history's stool which someone had once called art and which had been fetching millions ever since.

Bibbons was as drippingly, and artificially, welcoming as always.

"Mr. Overlock! Come in, come in, come in. You simply must see my new pieces. Guess what I just procured—King Tut's nipples! I have them resting in vinegar in a cool, dark place. Shall we repair to my den?"

"Some tea, Grave," said the Master, quietly helping himself to a chair.

"You prefer me to bring some things out to you, then?" said Bibbons with a cocksure air. "Quite wise. It'll be best to take this sitting down."

I went to concoct Mr. Overlock's tea—a curious mix of oolong, white wine, butterflies' wings and hashish—and returned to find him sitting at the dining table, looking blankly at a swirling white gas in a clear jar, as Bibbons jumped up and down excitedly, insisting that he had captured Great Caesar's ghost.

A sudden, ringing scream almost made me part with mine, and the entire upper floor was suddenly alive with blistering cries of intense torture. Holding my tongue as I am so trained to do, I gaped at the Master and his host, and was appalled to see them carrying on their dull business as though nothing whatsoever was going on. But the outcries continued, with many a horrible "Help!" thrown in, and I fidgeted with fear. Finally, one of Bibbons' eyes looked at me, while the other continued to rest on his objet dreck, and he smirked. Mr. Overlock continued to sit emotionlessly where he was.

"Don't wet your pants, Gravy," said Bibbons. "It's only Ag, giving sump to another bloody infant. If it's mine, I'll shove the next one out myself."

"But sir, hadn't I best fetch the doctor?" I asked urgently.

"For what he'd charge, I could get Van Gogh's other ear," he spat, and the conversation ended.

Mr. Overlock's attention seemed drawn to a dark object which was sitting on a glass display stand in a corner of a nearby windowsill. It appeared to be a rock, and upon it was engraved, in capital letters, the word "Harmless."

"Interested in my harmless rock?" grinned Bibbons. He went and procured it. "What do you make of it?"

Mr. Overlock examined it carefully. "Basanite, with a greenish tint caused by a common underground algae, engraved in a bold style in which all the letters meet, and chiseled from a broader source with a pike awl. I would hazard it is one of the missing pieces of the Riddle of Ganymede."

"Quite right," said Bibbons. "One of the last two that have not yet been restored. I paid the wretch well who managed to chip out this one. But it is an extremely rare acquisition, coming from one of the deepest regions of the Dark Lands. It originated in an underground vault leading to countless miles of catacombs excavated by the slaves of eccentric explorer Atwater Ganymede."

"Catacombs to which he added traps," added Mr. Overlock.

"Indeed," said Bibbons. "To solve the riddle would gain its decipherer an understanding of the labyrinth's true path, and possible access to its ultimate prize—the Ganymede fortune. However, the riddle was carved directly into a wall, and chipping it out, not to mention the journey to it, is difficult."

"And without the wall in which to insert the piece, it cannot be authenticated," said the Master.

"No it can't," said Bibbons, frowning. He took the piece and replaced it on the windowsill. "I am nevertheless satisfied that it is genuine."

They continued to prattle on over their tiresome toys while I stood agitatedly listening to Agony's screams until with time the outbursts mercifully subsided and were replaced by her sobs and the mewling of the newborn, which had an ugly bellow falling somewhere between the growl of a wolf and the grunt of a bilge-pump. Bibbons set his latest article aside and seemed to sigh. "I suppose I had best go up and see the little pus blob." He turned and walked toward the staircase. "You want to see it, Mr. Overlock?"

"I am here to view antiquities," said Mr. Overlock. "Your children are far from rare."

"You're telling me."

Bibbons ascended, and the Master and I were alone in the parlor.

"May I refill your teacup, sir?" I asked, anxious that I might leave temporarily as well.

"No, Grave. I will go upstairs, and you will steal the Ganymede stone."

I felt like a blood clot had just burst in my urethra.

"If you are discovered, you alone shall shoulder the blame. I shall take no longer than one minute. Proceed."

He rose and advanced to the stair. Stunned by his sudden command, I fumbled anxiously into action, and tripped over the chair he had backed up into my path, cutting my lip on the table-top. Panicking, I crawled over the table and reached wildly out for the loathsome rock, grabbing it and knocking its glass stand to the floor, where it shattered. I slid off the table toward the windowsill, hit my nose on it, and came to earth on the fragmented glass, which pierced my shoe and shot up my arch. I howled in pain, and hastily stuck the rock into my mouth to muffle it. I hobbled, trailing blood from the hole in my shoe, back into the body of the room. I stuck my finger up the hole and pried the glass shard out of my bone, which was like uncorking a bottle of wine. The wound flowed copiously while I tried holding the Master's teacup under it; then I had the bright idea of stuffing one of my white gloves in it. This stayed the current for the moment, and meanwhile I realized that I had the rock in my mouth and no place to hide it. Then the carriage crossed my mind. I would run out and hide the stone under the seat, and quickly return. It was then that I heard footsteps on the staircase, and realized that I had no time for the operation so outlined. Desperately, I shoved the rock down my trousers into the focal crux, and Mr. Overlock descended, well under a minute, with Mr. Bibbons just behind. I stood there, slightly contorted with testicular pain, thinking that "harmless" was not the word I would have inscribed on the rock, as my host and the Master stared at me with palpable disgust.

"I—I tried to pour you some wine, sir, and spilled some," I faltered out, hoping that this would cover both the blood and the glass.

"Then you will have to make restitution," said Mr. Overlock stonily. "Give Mr. Bibbons your day's wage."

I frowned, for it had been the first day in some while that I had even received a wage. I reached in my pocket and pulled out three gold coins, which I then deposited in Mr. Bibbons' hand. One of his eyes seemed fixated on my crotch, while the other kept glancing (I could swear) at the windowsill.

"Sorry, Grave," he said. "I have an eye for old rocks." He sniggered, dislodged his gaze and turned to the Master. "Leaving so soon, Mr. Overlock?"

"Quite."

"Hope you got all you wanted from the visit."

"We shall see."

"Until we meet again, then. May it be soon."

"It will be."

With that, the merry little visit concluded and we returned to the carriage, Mr. Overlock pausing before entering to stick his hairy hand down my pants and yank the rock out full force. I managed to hold my tongue, but I was certain the muffled scream could be heard coming out my ears. We hastened back to the manor and the Master immediately enclosed himself in the library, while I pranced forth to the water closet in order to mollify my screaming bollocks with unguent. I took my trousers down and began lotioning the war zone in slow strokes, and was settling into a relaxing stupor in which women were beginning to take shape, when the vile bell rang raucously and I dropped the lotion jar on my one good foot.

I tottered out, walking gingerly without bending either knee, and hurried to the library, where the Master sat in a large cushioned armchair perusing a book on the Dark Lands.

"On your knees, Grave."

I immediately kneeled before him, wondering if his next wish was for me to serve as an ottoman.

"I want a foot massage."

I wanted a foot, period, but I began administering the rub anyway.

"As Mr. Bibbons accurately related, Atwater Ganymede was an explorer who amassed amazing wealth pillaging the resources of the little-traveled Dark Lands. When he grew old, he became eccentric, and had his hundreds of slaves begin excavating an underground maze of immense proportions. Throughout these passages he included a multitude of deadly traps, like bottomless pits and crushing walls, all to protect the fortune he had hidden somewhere within. No one who has attempted to navigate the labyrinth has ever returned, despite the riddle engraved on the wall of the aperture. The stone carving you so ineptly pilfered is one piece of that riddle."

"But sir, did I not understand Mr. Bibbons to say that there was another missing piece of the same conundrum?"

"Indeed, Grave. It is in my possession."

I gaped. "But sir, this is remarkable!"

"No it isn't. The riddle itself is not the vital item. The piece I possess, for instance, contains but the simple three-letter word 'its.'"

I pondered, putting the two words together in my mind. "'It's harmless,'" I murmured, confused. "I thought you said the caves were quite the opposite, sir."

"'Its' in this case does not contain an apostrophe, you matchless simpleton. The riddle in its entirety reads 'Put together, its words will

146

show / The only harmless way to go.' The answer to which is, of course, a map. A map containing worded directions. It is the map which is the vital missing clue."

"But sir, where can the map be found?"

He held up a tube made of mithril which had been sitting inconspicuously at his side. He uncorked it, and pulled out a scrolled piece of paper. He unrolled it and held it up. The parchment appeared to have been ripped up several times, and the fragments reglued together. On it were several words reading "First right, second left, down the shaft," etc, which seemed to indicate some definite path through an array of tunnels.

"Amazing, sir," was all I could say.

"Procure the ship tickets, Grave. We set forth immediately to begin our safari through the Dark Lands."

Possessed of the Master's flintlock, some fresh linens, a canteen and an ample supply of tobacco, we set forth upon a quest which I could only hope to be a bad dream. Being that my worst nightmares were always better than my best realities, I knew that such was not the case. The truth of this became clear when, on the very day we boarded the ship, we encountered Vandemere Bibbons, sitting in a deck chair and drinking iced geneva with a smug expression on his face.

"Mr. Overlock and his water boy, I presume," he said. "Now, don't tell me. You're off on safari, aren't you? The very same idea I had. Originally I thought I'd go and authenticate the Riddle shard like you suggested, but you know, it disappeared. Right after you left. I suppose under most conditions I'd believe it stolen. But no thief would dare attempt such a thing, seeing that he'd hang if caught. Isn't that right, Grave?"

I couldn't answer. Lunch had risen above my larynx.

"But let's not talk about that right now. I'm off to the Dark Lands to bag myself an elephant. What do you say we make a friendly competition out of it, Mr. Overlock? See who can bag an elephant first?"

Mr. Overlock was inexpressive. "The greater feat would be to see who can bag an elephant second," he said.

"Oh yeah? Why's that?"

"He'd have to survive longer."

This seemed to silence Bibbons for a moment, long enough for us to part from him without enduring any further conversation. We adjourned to the Master's cabin, and I began to unpack the huge trunk that I had been dragging since leaving the coach at the wharf.

"You'd best put on the accoutrements you will be wearing on the safari, Grave," said Mr. Overlock. "I trust you remembered to pack suitable apparel as I ordered."

My heart fell, like the arches of my still-aching feet. I had presumed the "suitable apparel" he had ordered to be for himself, and had acquired, accordingly, khaki shorts, a vest, leopard-skin boots and a pith helmet. Not only was the asinine garb unspeakably unsuitable for a gentleman's gentleman, it was in the Master's size—nearly one half my own in length, twice in width.

"And you had best learn to stop dragging that trunk around," he added. "You will be carrying it on your back throughout the safari."

The appropriate note for the voyage being therefore struck, the rest of the sea journey did not fail in keeping form. It rained continuously the entire time, which pleased me in the fact that it helped me to avoid running into Mr. Bibbons, but less so in regard to the fact that I had to sleep every night in the crow's nest (the only available space). After several days of this jollity, we docked at the mouth of the mighty Throat and spent our first evening in a festering village called, in translation, Bloody Flux. There I spent the evening at war with an assortment of insects ranging in size from bumblebees to barn owls, all of which seemingly desperate for my ash-white, grumeless stalks, and utterly uninterested in any part of my full-bodied Master.

The second day on land was even more unbearable. First I had to struggle into my safari vest and shorts, which hung like wide-mouth bags but which were hardly long enough to conceal my navel or my more ivyish pubes. The pith helmet was so small it looked like a pinwheel beanie on my head, and the leopard-skin boots were so ridiculous that the fact that my ten toes poked through the fur seemed an improvement. I humbly presented myself in the Master's room and was assessed of my appearance in a well-considered summary review.

"You look like an ass, Grave."

"Then may I change back into my usual uniform, sir?" I asked hopefully.

"No. You ordered those vestments, you will bear the burden of their absurdity. Now before we leave, I want you to fill our supply trunk with at least three additional gallons of water and all of the provisions I have listed here. You will find them at the trading post next door."

He gave me the list. "Yes, sir," I said respectfully. "Excuse me, sir, but would it be appropriate for me to address you as 'bwana' throughout this expedition?"

"If you do, I will have you disemboweled," he hissed. "Proceed."

I went outside to the "trading post" lugging our ungodly vestibule of supplies, and found it to be nothing more than a teepee with a few cases of hardtack and a gorilla's head or two. What's worse, the gentleman in charge, a swarthy midget wearing a necklace of knives, not only did not speak the Queen's Tongue, but seemed at a loss rendering his own tongue as well. Then I realized by his disjointed mumblings that he had no tongue, a fact that did not stop him from gibbering incessantly, and I merely helped myself as best I could. Then I tossed the ratling a shiny rock, hauled the goods out of the tent and dumped them arduously in the trunk. I finished, turned, and to my surprise saw Mr. Overlock standing directly behind me. I adjusted my fatigues, bowed reverently, and hoped he hadn't heard the things I had been muttering about him under my breath while packing the trunk.

"The proprietor says you paid for these goods with a rock, Grave," he intoned coldly, and I perceived the halfling, standing in the Master's shadow, brandishing one of his neck-knives.

"I'm sorry, sir," I said, then I felt in my pocket and realized that I had not been given any money for the provisions. "Sir, I—"

"Give him one of your boots."

"Excuse me, sir?"

"Don't make me repeat myself, Grave. Give him one of your boots."

I yanked off one of the skins and tossed it at the little spectre.

"Now, lift the trunk on your back and strap it on with this rope," commanded Mr. Overlock, flinging a rope at me.

I stared at the box, assessing it. It was so heavy it was making a six-inch deep imprint on the ground.

"Lift it, Grave."

I squatted before the trunk, reached back and yanked upward.

"Ugh!" I screamed, a disk slipping.

"You infernal convalescent," snarled the Master. He snapped his fingers and the midget immediately picked up the trunk, slapped it on my back and strapped it in place. I felt like a worm carrying an anvil.

"Here's a paper fan," said Mr. Overlock, handing me the object. "You will breeze me with it while carrying me on your shoulders."

"What!" I cried. It's not that I had expected the Master to do any walking of his own on this "safari," but I had anticipated a pantheon of proper niggers to bear at least some of my lesser burdens. Now I realized that I was to be the sole "bhisti," and that not even an animal was to accompany us.

"The track is quite easily followed at first," said Mr. Overlock. "We follow the Throat upstream for ten miles, then make our way inland through raw jungle for another five, cross a twenty-acre veldt and camp tonight on the shore of the Lesser Gut."

"Ahem—did you say 'camp tonight,' sir?" I panted out.

"Quite. Unless you waste any more time and we must travel after nightfall as well. Bend."

Camel-like, I leaned forward and took the added bulk of the Master up onto my shoulder bones. He made the trunk feel like gauze.

"Now rise, Grave," he commanded, and I attempted to straighten myself.

"I…I can't, sir."

"What?"

"I can't straighten up, sir. I'm trying as best as I can."

"Oh, you are, are you?" he growled, and snapped. The demonic dwarf then reappeared, whipped out one of his knives, and gave it to me in the fundament with the kind of glee I could only suppose him to save for nights when they served snake dinners. I cried out horribly, but the Master was in a great position for stuffing his hand in my mouth, and I stood up abruptly. His aim having been achieved, Mr. Overlock then prodded my sides as he would any beast of burden, and we were off on our expedition. I wish I could say it was enlightening, but lightness had nothing to do with it.

The day was a hot and weary one. After the first mile or so, a kind of insensate numbness set in, and I performed as in a kind of automatic trance, with my only impulse being to make the legs go. From time to time they too threatened not to operate, but the Master was there to help, and using his pen knife, was able to keep enough artificial nerve stimulus provided to keep his shambling machine moving. We followed the aptly named Throat for a time, its bilious disgorge making its way from the stomach of the earth to the depository of the sea; then turning inward, plowed through untrammeled vegetation for a spell, the Master directing while I hacked with one hand and breezed him with the other. By the time we reached the wide veldt, I was desperate for water, and suggested opening the trunk for the canteens. Mr. Overlock informed me that he was already supplied, and produced from his waistcoat pocket a little gold whiskey-flask, whose contents he proceeded to imbibe.

"But sir, what am I to drink?" I pleaded, a yellow crust beginning to form around my lips.

"Being that you are unable to stand up unaided with this trunk on your back, we cannot risk taking it down to open it," he said. "You will have to wait until we cross this grassland; then you may drink from the Gut."

The veldt was dotted with unpleasant animals, to be sure, but none were willing, it appeared, to dare an effrontery upon the Master. I slugged across the endless plain as daylight waned, and reached the Lesser Gut just in time for the last light to fade, causing me to sludge right into it. Mr. Overlock having remained above water, his denunciations were less caustic than they might have been, and I must say the water felt rather good on my flaming footpads. I turned around, walked up the shore, and lowered the Master earthward. I felt as Atlas might have felt if he'd chucked the earth sunward and made a beeline for one of Arcadia's better bath houses. Striking a match, I dislodged the trunk, opened it and fired up a lantern. I secured a folding chair for the Master, provided him with a pipe, and stood brokenly awaiting instruction.

"Your feet, Grave."

"My feet, sir?"

"Look at them."

I gazed down, and perceived the problem. They were covered with leeches.

"Hold still, and I will pry them off with my pen-knife."

"Quite unnecessary, I do assure you, sir!"

"Silence, Grave."

I held my breath as he began to administer his act of kindness. Although my feet were too numb to feel the leeches, they were quite able to feel the Master's blade, and I bellowed as he removed the beasts, each one receiving a thick chunk of my flesh as a souvenir.

"Quiet, Grave. You will attract the notice of our neighbors."

I jumped. Was it lions, bats, crocodiles?

"Note the illumination to the south. Smell the distant smoke. Hear the vague sounds of natives singing. The expedition party of our shadowy friend, Mr. Bibbons."

"Mr. Bibbons, sir?" I gasped. "But how did he find us?"

"A blind and deaf cripple could follow you, Grave. He is after the map he knows we must possess. I am therefore entrusting it to you. Keep it safe."

He handed me the tube, which I cringingly accepted. Then he returned to his seat, filled his pipe and took another drink from his flask. Then he demanded his duck dinner.

"Your…what, sir?"

"My duck dinner, Grave. Prepare it. Then you may drink."

"But sir, I didn't pack any duck. It would have spoiled."

"Duck bills don't spoil."

"No sir, but—"

"You will make me a soup out of duck bills, the ones I brought."

"The ones you brought, sir?"

"Yes. You don't believe that I would trust your intelligence to furnish such an item?"

"I rejoice in your foresight, sir."

"Do not feel that you're in the clear yet, Grave. I brought enough for tonight only. Tomorrow you will have to procure them on your own."

"But sir," I protested, "ducks are not native to this country."

"Then you will hunt duck-billed platypi, if necessary. Dismissed."

Downhearted, I took the beaks and conjured up some soup, not daring to think how I would make it last the rest of the trip. I provided it to Mr. Overlock, who swallowed it down to the last drop and then informed me that I might now drink. Grinning widely for the first time in my life, I ran for the river, got down on my knees and lapped it up like a dog in an alley corner. I stood up, and suddenly realized how the Gut had gotten its name. Pausing for the instant it took the slimewater to make the route from my lips to my intestines, I begged the Master's pardon, requested his permission to withdraw, then ran for the trees with all my might.

I found a location adequately distant from our encampment to avoid annoying Mr. Overlock, and proceeded to obey nature's call. I disposed of my initial package in the manner of the fierce and squatting tiger, then scooched over a sheath of peaweed, stood up and proceeded with phase two. I felt a warm peace descend upon me as I did so, like a camel which has chosen to dump the contents of its spare hump. The operation was proceeding quite nicely, if lengthily, when I realized that there was an audience to my performance. A huge snake was sitting in the grass, lustfully eyeing my goods as it would a mouse éclair, and licking its lips. Then it lifted its head, opened its jaws to their fullest extent, and began hissing maniacally.

I was commending my soul to God in anticipation of one of my lower-ranking ways to die (#90: Deadly Snake Bite To The Genitals) when a shot rang out, and the serpent's head went whizzing into oblivion. I turned, and there was Vandemere Bibbons, smirking and holding a rifle, and pointing somewhat unceremoniously at my filial regions.

"Better zip up, Gravy. We wouldn't want anything falling out, would we?"

I took his advice, then bowed respectfully. "Thank you for coming to my aid, sir," I said.

"Shut up," he replied. "You don't think I give a barrelhouse frig for your life, do you? You're my prisoner. Move it."

"But sir!"

"I said move it, Grave. Unless you want me to pick up where that snake left off."

The concept lacked fascination, so I acquiesced. His rifle poking into my back, he led me through the night until we closed in on his encampment, a fire-lit series of tents quite aswarm with native bearers, food and supplies which quite dwarfed mine and Mr. Overlock's. Threading through the glaring assemblage, we paused in the center of the clearing, where Mr. Bibbons stood before me, gun cocked.

"Now then, Grave," he said, "let's have that map."

I attempted to feign ignorance. "What map?"

He sighed. "The map Overlock just gave you. I heard every word."

I drew myself up. "That, sir, is eavesdropping."

"And this, sir, is murder," he said, aiming the rifle at my eyes.

I swallowed. A rifle shot to the eyes was still only #50 on my list. "Here, sir," I said, giving him the map.

"Good for you, Grave," he said, smiling. "You haven't failed to meet my expectations of you. Now I shan't fail to meet yours of me." He aimed his gun once more.

I stood helplessly, and was glad that due to my recent evacuation I would be buried in clean khaki shorts. His finger trembled on the trigger.

Then he slowly lowered the weapon.

"No," he said. "It's worse to let you live."

My reprieve received, I gamboled for open spaces, but he stilled me with a cry.

"Wait, Grave." He tossed me a bag, cold from ice. "Here are some ducks for Overlock's meals. I figured you'd fail to pack them. We wouldn't want to lose time finding out who the winner is, would we?"

Joined by the laughter of his contingent, he shot several rounds into the air and I was off like an antelope.

I was wandering about, trying to find my way back to Mr. Overlock and thinking with mixed feelings that I might never find him, when a match was struck in the murk, and there he was. He was sitting in his same chair, lighting his pipe.

"So you're back, Grave," he said. "Where have you been?"

"I…I've been getting your ducks, sir."

"I see. And how is Mr. Bibbons?"

I blanched. "Mr. Bibbons is doing about as well as can be expected, sir."

"Is he finding his way without difficulty?"

"Eh—with less difficulty now, sir, I should imagine."

"Then you gave him directions?"

I trembled. "I suppose one could describe it that way, sir."

"You have been quite accommodating."

"Well, he was kind enough to show me his campsite, sir."

The Master looked at me, and I could no more easily read what he was thinking than if he had been a stone statue. Then he got up, flicked a speck off his cuff and stared skyward.

"Prepare my tent, Grave. I see by these constellations that it is late, and we must rise early if we are not to detain our followers."

"Yes, sir," I gulped, as mystified as ever. I dutifully pitched his tent, laid out his finest sleeping raiment, got him a book, a snack and a lantern, and bade him good night.

Then I plopped down on the naked ground, and preoccupied by fearful forebodings, dropped off to sleep as nightmare-riddled as it was short.

The wearying trip continued in consistent vein, one I might be forgiven the pain of detailed recollection. I will simply say that after two more days (the highlights of which included swimming across the Gut while towing Mr. Overlock in the open trunk, falling on a nest of fire ants while fetching wood and losing my other boot to quicksand), we reached the cave of Ganymede, which if it had not been for Mr. Overlock I would have identified as a simple pile of rocks.

"Clear the stones, Grave."

I feebly began to clear the pile, and was spurred on by the Master's whip, which he had had me make from a vine somewhere along the way.

As progress was made, a hole beneath became evident, as well as a stone stairway leading down to into it.

"Look, sir!" I observed giddily. "The cave!"

"Quite," he said, as dryly as a dead stick. "Carry me in."

We descended, where the light of the sky outside revealed a well-excavated foyer, upon whose south wall the well-known riddle was vaguely inscribed, and to whose east an ominous-looking black tunnel gaped. But to me, the coolness of the stone floor upon my bare feet was an aspect that rendered all others superfluous. It was glorious.

"Stop masturbating, Grave, and put the two missing stones in their places," snapped the Master.

Extracting the chunks from their bag within the trunk, I carried them to the wall and inserted them in the two places where words were missing. They fit together like newlyweds.

"Put together, its words will show…" I began.

"The only harmless way to go," finished Vandemere Bibbons.

I swirled. There was our adversary, looking typically smug as he brandished his firearm, while the two aborigines flanking him made threatening motions with spears.

"Thank you, Mr. Overlock, for proving so able a guide," he said. "And thank you, Grave, for furnishing the map which will lead us the rest of the way. You don't mind if I help myself to some of the stuff in your trunk, do you?"

He opened the container, and proceeded to help himself to the bulk of our supplies, including the bullets to Mr. Overlock's flintlock.

"I'm sorry Milo, but I rather prefer your dying the slow death of deprivation than the quick death of the gun. This will make up for all those antiques you got before I could."

He stood up with a self-satisfied sigh. "As you can see, the rock was genuine. Not that the riddle and its answer haven't been known for ages. But the map! Just where did you obtain such a rare item?"

"It is from my salt-mining operation," said Mr. Overlock.

"You mean they dug this up while mining for salt?" gasped Bibbons. "Remarkable. Well, I'm sure you know it to be genuine, or you wouldn't have come all the way out here. Farewell, Mr. Overlock. Good riddance, Grave. I'm taking these associates of mine with me into the cave. The rest will stay upstairs. Do feel free to feed them."

With that, he and his henchmen entered the cave, and disappeared from view.

Mr. Overlock chuckled a dry, quiet laugh, the kind he does without smiling.

"Pardon me, sir?" I inquired, mystified.

"The exit of one of my less-interesting rivals. He will be dead, lost or entrapped within the half-hour."

"But sir, he possesses the map! I regret to say that I gave it to him, two nights ago."

"Of course you did, Grave. Why do you think I allowed you to carry it? That map merely describes a route through an abandoned tunnel network in my salt-mining operation. I simply ripped it up and glued it back together. It served the same purpose as having you steal the rock—to lure Vandemere Bibbons to his doom."

"But I thought the stone was necessary to piece together the riddle, sir."

"Nonsense, Grave. The riddle is well-known, be it presently whole or incomplete. By stealing it, however, we aroused in Mr. Bibbons the suspicion that it possessed a usefulness for us, especially when we combined it with a sudden trip to the Dark Lands. I allowed him to follow us, then to overhear our conversation about the map. He pieced together the rest, and will now suffer the fate of the countless victims of Atwater Ganymede's final whim."

"Then may I ask, sir, what has become of the real map?"

"There is no map, Grave. None but the one which exists within this room."

He went to the south wall. "Note that the words themselves are surrounded, even connected to, a series of weblike lines extending in all directions. Many have believed that this in itself might be a map, but with no way of determining which path through it is safe. For this they've insisted on the existence, somewhere, of a written document whose words, when put together, reveal the 'only harmless way to go.' Unfortunately, they fail to see that such words exist before their very eyes, in this very riddle."

"Sir?"

"Attend. As I have pointed out before, each word in this riddle is etched in capital letters, and all the letters meet. The only lower-case letter is the final 'o' in 'go,' which connects at its side to the bar of 'g.' There are other ways of putting words together than merely arranging them. These words, meeting together as they do, are tunnels within the labyrinth, tunnels shaped like letters, which culminate in a circular room leading out of the 'g.' And while they connect, in endless varieties, with the other, deadly, tunnels, they themselves are the only safe conduits through the catacombs."

"Amazing, sir."

"Quite. And now that Mr. Bibbons has freed up some of our trunk space, we can use it to transport out Mr. Ganymede's treasure."

"But sir, how will we return it to civilization?" I asked. "We have been deprived of our supplies."

"We will help ourselves to the remainder of Mr. Bibbons', as well as to his servants," said Mr. Overlock, loading his flintlock with ammunition from his pocket. "Proceed, Grave. This being the beginning, you should find us at the base of the letter 'P.'"

I didn't like the term "should," nor the fact that I was to go first, but I need not confirm that the Master was as usual correct, and that after some toil transporting the fortune of gold and jewels out of the airless labyrinth myself, the Master and his flintlock cajoled the services of the cannibals, and we were home within the week. I was serving the Master his tea in the collection-room, gaping at the bounty of Ganymede goodies while he read the newspaper in an armchair, when he placed the paper down and made a surprising observation.

"The eldest son of Agony Bibbons should be old enough for simple mechanical actions by now," he said. "I shall put him to work in my cannery."

"But sir, won't it be difficult to procure the services of the child, as it has proven so frequently with those of the past?" I asked.

"Not in this case, Grave. You see, the child is mine, as are all of the Bibbons offspring. I found it the most convenient way of assuring proper cannery staffing for the foreseeable future. The only tiresome aspects of the operation were the compensation of the female and the inconvenience of the oblivious husband. Having arranged our recent expedition to secure the one and eliminate the other, I am free of their distractions. Some buns, Grave."

"Er—yes, sir."

And so it was that Mr. Overlock had bagged his elephant after all—although the answer to whether he had been first or not is one to which, I am afraid, I am unable to furnish a solution.

7

Chapter Seven
Milo Overlock At The Club

MILO Overlock belonged to a club, the Officers of Onwall, where he went occasionally and unfortunately always took me. I didn't belong there (it was an upper-class institution comprised of commissioned war veterans) and I'm not sure how Mr. Overlock got in, having never fought in any war. But we went anyway, so that Mr. Overlock could get the same absolute silence he got at home, and so that I could prepare him a duck in the club kitchen, in the same manner that I always did. On the day in question, we had arrived for lunch; Mr. Overlock was sitting at an elegant table in the dining room and I was standing at his side, marveling at how strictly the rules of silence (which Mr. Overlock had succeeded in extending to the dining area) were being obeyed, and wondering how so many clubmen could chew so soundlessly.

A noise suddenly announced itself, and although it was as soft as a cat's purr, seemed to shatter the sanguinity of the assemblage like a clap of thunder in a blue sky. It was an old man in uniform, a colonel it appeared, who had fallen asleep at his table and was snoring.

Mr. Overlock immediately summoned a waiter.

"Yes, Mr. Overlock?" said the young man, frisking up to the table with rather repellent obsequiousness. "What may it be my honor to obtain for you?"

The Master glared at him. "Milked duck," he demanded. "Grave will show you how it's made. And silence that pathetic invalid or I'll have you both smothered in mustard."

"Yes, sir! Right away, sir!" yipped the servling anxiously, and saluting, stumbled over to the sleeping colonel, rousing the old man with a shake.

"Accompany the child, Grave. See that the duck is doused in cream, but not swimming in it."

I followed the young waiter into the kitchen, where I saw him nervously wipe his forehead with a linen towel. He was the only person there, and it was clear that he also doubled as cook for the establishment. I began to see something of myself in him, some sixty years younger, and my heart went out to the poor fellow.

I put my hand on his shoulder. "Don't worry, son," I said comfortingly. "Mr. Overlock isn't going to—"

"Take your spider-veined, blood-deprived, skeleton-boned gropers off me, you crumbling sarcophagus bait, and find another boyfriend," he snarled savagely. "Overlock told you to milk a duck. So freaking milk it, you mummy's dick."

A certain degree of righteous umbrage filled my chest at this, and I eyed the wastrel with some hauteur. We Graves can only be pushed so far before we remember that we too fought at Goynes.

"Yes, sir," I responded humbly, and proceeded with my duties.

"Sir, may I ask what you're doing here?" demanded the boy brute peevishly, and I turned to see the person he was addressing.

"Oh. Jolly repentant, and all that. Needed eggs, boy. Needed eggs."

The speaker of these words was an old, buttery-looking gadabout-type floating amidst the cookery. He had a monocle and fob, and a fez which matched his polka-dot smoking-jacket.

"Sir, I would be delighted to fix you some eggs," said the waiter wearily. "However, I must insist that you leave the kitchen."

"Born in one, my boy, born!" said the gentleman beamingly. "I can make flowers from flour. I can make cakes from soap. Potatoes have eyes, elephants have nuts, but I can cook better than a stove."

"I'm sure that's true, sir, but I must ask you to leave anyway. This area is strictly reserved for subservient wretches."

The elderly gentleman looked over at me, and then nodded. "I see what you mean, my boy. Just let me finish battering up this crepe, and I'll be on my way."

"Sir, I must insist—"

"Fuck off, my boy, or I shall give you bad dreams!" said the senility case with a flourish, brandishing a spoon at the stripling.

"Fine." The boy turned his back on the man in resigned disgust, took a swig of sherry and grabbed a handful of ground beef. He spat on it and prepared to make meatloaf.

I quietly finished preparing the Master's duck and took it over to the waiter for serving. Although I didn't particularly crave the young man's company, the above exchange had left me curious.

"Excuse me, sir, but who is that?" I whispered.

"What, the one who looks like he could be your grandson? Captain of the Queen's Navy, the Right Honorable Gaylord Fortiscue. Served under Colonel Nethers, the snorer. Lost half his brain in the war."

"How did that happen?" I asked.

"He went to bed with his gun. Must have thought it was another soldier, and squeezed too hard."

"How dreadful."

"Gimme that gruel."

He snatched the milked mallard from my hands and we returned to the dining-room, only to find that the Master was not there. Then I heard the snap of fingers, and located its source in the adjacent but out-of-sight sitting-room, where Mr. Overlock, by some precognizance, had summoned us.

"I have decided to eat in here," he said. "Where is my duck?"

"Here it is, sir," said the young waiter, again the spirit of servitude. "I followed Mr. Grave's instructions to the letter."

"It shows," said the Master, his lip curled in distaste. "The cream is much too yellow, the bird too young, and there is a feather in my bowl. Take it back. I will have pollywogs, instead."

"Yes, sir." The waiter frowned, and eyed me as he would an uncut cutlet.

"And rouse the Colonel over there once more. His doctor brought him in a short while ago, and immediately put him to sleep with dull conversation. Commence!"

The Master spoke this command at a volume that made the Colonel's snores sound like a lullaby amidst a bombing raid, but no one seemed to notice. Everyone, instead, focused on the Colonel, each outraged by the gentle whirr that was proving so shattersome to their war-weary nerves. The waiter clicked his heels in obedience and immediately approached the sofa, where he shook the old man awake, rebuked him, then woke the doctor who had also fallen asleep at the Colonel's side. He had a few words with this physician, the physician went back to sleep, and the waiter returned to Mr. Overlock.

"The doctor thinks that something with a little sugar in it might keep him awake, sir," he whispered. "I'll bake him some cookies, as he's partial to them."

"They had better be successful," snapped the Master, full voice. "I am tired of having my equanimity disrupted, a state too frequent here."

"Yes, sir."

The waiter withdrew and all was quiet for a while. The strain of constant standing was proving quite trying to my feet, but fearing that shifting my weight might make a noise, I began daydreaming instead. Comforting visions of what my headstone might read one day ("Grave's Grave," "Grave, b. 1810 – d. End of Time," "Grave – His First Resting Place") filled my mind, though I was quite sure I could never afford one and that Mr. Overlock would probably just toss my corpse in the duck pond anyway. Then the Master saw me rocking on my beleaguered toes, turned around and checked me into stone-stillness with a glare. The waiter returned, gave Mr. Overlock his pollywogs, took a plate of cookies over to the Colonel and, patting the old soldier on the back, retracted. I stood emanating indulgence.

"Feed me, Grave."

I gently spooned each of the boiled pollywogs into the Master's face, while he slurped them down loudly and expressionlessly. When he was finished, I gently dabbed the corners of his mouth with my sleeve, and returned to my detached state of before.

"Make me a list, Grave, of every clubman and every servant present at this time. It should take you no longer than it took me to eat—ten minutes."

"Er—yes, sir."

These impromptu and seemingly meaningless commands of his flustered me no end. I immediately began running around the club, requesting in whispers the names of each guest and employee. The guests seemed revolted by my presence and generally refused to answer me, while the employees seemed delighted with my travails and also refused, if only to get me in trouble with the Master. Luckily, I was able to bribe the doorman with money I didn't have, and after receiving the information, ran back inside without paying him anything. It had taken me exactly twenty minutes.

"You have taken too long by half, Grave, and therefore your day's wage will be reduced by half," said the Master.

"I am improved by your discipline, sir," I squeaked.

Mr. Overlock took the list and perused it with pursed lips. He studied it for a minute or two, then he placed it in his coat pocket. He turned to me.

"Politely inform the guests and staff that Mr. Overlock wishes them to remain on the premises until further notice. Inform them that I possess this list, and that any unexplained absence will draw suspicion. There has been a death at the club."

I gasped. "A death, sir?"

"Quite. The Colonel is no more."

I looked over at the old man, shocked, and saw him slumped in the same position as before, his mouth open.

"Why, he's merely asleep, sir," I said.

"Listen."

I listened. Not the vaguest sound could be heard throughout the entire sitting-room, save the undulations of my stomach.

"He breathes not," said the Master.

I must have begun blabbering incoherent gibberish at this point, for the Master poked me in the flank with a pin, resulting in an outcry that served to sufficiently rouse the catatonic assemblage. Even the doctor woke up; alas, the Colonel did not.

"Excuse me, sirs," I feebly croaked out, "but Mr. Milo Overlock begs to detain you this afternoon, the purpose being this rather inconvenient death…"

A current of shock seemed to quiver its way through the undead throng, and sound was reintroduced to the crypt.

"Yes, sirs, it would appear that age, in its timeless tread, has crept upon a member of this honored establishment, closing its dreaded hand—"

"Silence, Grave," snapped the Master. "Go and inform the rest, as I've instructed you, and have them gather here. And spare them your poetry, or I will spare you your tongue."

I went to each of the uninformed and brought them up to date with the distasteful information, and was greeted almost unanimously with the attitude that it should have been me. Everyone congregated in the sitting-room and all eyes gazed transfixed upon the corpse, which was sitting there as though trying to think of a joke to tell.

Mr. Overlock went over to the body, and, putting one hand on the back and one on the abdomen, squeezed. A greenish ooze exuded from the mouth, which quietly dissipated. The Master and the doctor exchanged a look.

"His internal body has turned entirely to ectoplasm," said Mr. Overlock.

The doctor gasped. "But the only known cause for that is an overdose of corodium anide, or Pratt's softener, which in small doses aids constipation."

"Was the Colonel being given such a medication?" asked the Master.

"Why, yes. He was my patient."

"And did he receive a dose of the agent today?"

"Not by me. Whether or not someone else gave it to him is impossible to tell—the poison is untraceable in the bloodstream once ectoplasmic activity sets in."

Mr. Overlock glanced at the plate of cookies on the tray which sat on the adjacent coffee-table. He picked up the platter and studied its contents.

"One bite has been taken from one confection," he said, sniffing. "And the entire batch smells strongly of vinegar. The very fragrance of corodium anide."

He placed the platter back, then looked at the doctor. "Could one bite be sufficient to render death?"

"Depending on the amount that was mixed into the flour," said the doctor. "If it's an amount sufficient to smell, it is likely to be excessive."

"And one must doubt the likelihood of vinegar being intentionally added," said Mr. Overlock, eyeing the waiter.

"Not unless he put it in there," snapped the waiter, pointing at Gaylord Fortiscue.

"Why, of course I did," smiled the Captain. "Right into the bag. Nothing better for colds, you know. Except, possibly, octopus-ink."

"Has anyone else had anything made with flour since the Captain entered the kitchen?" asked Mr. Overlock of the waiter.

"No, sir. The cookies are the only things I've baked since you ordered your pollywogs…everything else on the menu requiring flour takes longer to prepare than the time that's elapsed."

"Are there any other cooks on duty?"

"Not with our budget," said the waiter. "I cook, wait, and even clean out the water closet between meals. I figure I'll have enough saved for college if I work till I'm sixty."

"Were you aware that the Colonel was on this medication?"

"I had to be, so as to hold the water closet for him. The doctor would always tell me when."

"Did he tell you to today?"

"No, sir."

The Master seemed to ponder. "I shall investigate the Captain's statement by examining the flour-bag. You shall all remain here, that the evidence may remain free of contamination. Grave, entertain them."

He departed, and I found myself alone in a coliseum of restless Romans requiring one good reason why they shouldn't release their lions. Lacking the option of reciting poetry, I couldn't think of one myself.

"I say, who's for a jolly game of whist?" I said brightly.

The members glared at me, like Romans who would just as soon keep the lions caged and eat me themselves. "I've got a better one," said the waiter-cook-cum-everything. "How about pin-the-tail-on-the-horse's-ass?"

The gathering smiled as one, and from the fact that several began extracting the toothpicks from their cocktail-glasses, I took this suggestion to have been the more favorably received.

I was plucking the last of some twenty or so olives from my crupper when Mr. Overlock returned, bearing the flour-bag.

"Captain Fortiscue," he said, "what was Colonel Nethers in relationship to you?"

"Superior officer, sir, superior," said the Captain. "And by superior I mean inferior. The old wart liked whipped cream on his pancakes! Positively berated me once for serving them sans."

"But was it congenial?" probed the Master.

The Captain rubbed his chin thoughtfully. "Congenial *and* pleasant, sir," he said. "I've never known a sweet tooth with less bite."

"Good. The evidence would appear to support you. This flour contains no additive other than vinegar."

The crowd gasped. "Then how could he have died?" asked one.

"He could've done it," blurted the waiter, pointing at the doctor. "The stuff was his. He could have poured it on the Colonel's cookies."

"Doctor, how long does it take a man to die from an oral overdose of this agent?" asked Mr. Overlock.

"About twenty-five minutes," said the doctor, glowering sourly at the waiter.

"Is there any other way for an overdose to be administered?"

"Why, yes," said the doctor. "It can be taken directly into the bloodstream by puncturing the skin. Administered this way, even the very smallest ammunt is deadly, and only takes fifteen minutes."

"Extract your vial," said Mr. Overlock.

The doctor did, and held it up for all to see. It appeared full.

"The container is far too full to have tainted the full contents of the platter," said the Master. "By coating the head of a pin, however, there would be virtually no discernable decrease in volume. The fact that I observed the cessation of the Colonel's life signs fifteen minutes after the arrival of these macaroons indicates that the fatal application was applied intravenously. The doctor at that juncture was asleep. The only individual in physical contact with the Colonel at the pivotal time was the waiter, who touched him on the back. Sufficient to prick him with a pin concealed in a hand."

The waiter's eyes turned white. "I did not!" he shouted. "All I did was tell him not to snore, like you told me to!"

"Doctor, remove the Colonel's shirt," said the Master briefly.

The doctor obeyed, and began examining the departed's dorsum. "There!" he said, pointing. The assemblees gathered, and gazed. Indeed, a tiny blood-dot encircled by the first bruise-marks of impending infection was visible just below the shoulder-blade, and a little ectoplasm was seeping out of it.

"But I didn't do it!" protested the popinjay in failing tones. "I had nothing against the fellow, and I don't possess a pin!"

"You feared that failure to control his incessant snoring would cost you your position," said the Master. "His death obviated that eventuality."

"And you're the one who suggested we 'pin' the tail on that horse's ass over there," added the doctor.

The waiter was over a barrel. He clearly reasoned that chances favored his youthful legs over further useless words, and he ran. He bolted out of the sitting-room and into the dining-room which adjoined the kitchen. I was glad to see him go.

"Apprehend, Grave."

My hands were down the seat of my trousers at the moment, massaging the line, and his abrupt command took me momentarily by surprise.

"Eh—me, sir?" I croaked out, my nimble fingers freezing in their slot.

"Quite."

"But sir, would not one of the younger gentlemen—"

He picked up the silver cookie tray, letting the biscuits fall to the floor, and slammed me on the backside with it. Not only was the region already traumatized with twenty toothpick-holes and a pin-prick, my fingernails had been pointed inward at the time of impact. I yelped, pulled out my beating knuckles and gamboled out in the direction of the hireling.

I spied the scamp galloping through the kitchen doors, and I think the sight of who his pursuer was encouraged him to ease his pace. Despite my begging his pardon and entreating his kindly abeyance, he continued to withdraw. I barged into the kitchen and slipped on a plop of fat on the floor, allowing me to dodge the cleaver he had heaved at me, which wedged into a wall. He then pulled a wastebasket into my path and sailed out a back door. I stumbled on the basket and toppled it over, strewing the floor with contents which included an open bag of very vinegary-smelling flour. I tottered out the portal and continued to chase the scoundrel, who was turning around the front corner of the building. My chest screaming and my heart alternating rhythms between bumblebee and mannequin, I clogged around the corner in time to see my quarry whizz past the doorman and around to the club's opposite alley.

"I say, my good fellow!" I heaved, lumbering up to the doorman. "May I impose upon your skills for a moment? That young man who just passed—"

He grabbed me by the neck with one paw. "Offer me money without paying, will you? I'm gonna beat the pumpkin-seeds out of you."

"But sir," I gurgled, "a murder—"

"Oh, it ain't gonna be murder," he said. "It's gonna be *worse*."

With that, he proceeded to thrash me within the proverbial inch of my life. I seemed to forget about the waiter after a moment or so, as numbness began to encoat my cerebral cortex, though not the fact that I had only bribed the doorman a buck. The doorman seemed to think my life its equivalent in value, and rampaged across the countryside of my carcass, leaving not a hill or valley untrammeled. In the midst of my comeuppance, when my insides were beginning to feel more or less like stewed cabbage, I spied the Master, directing the waiter doorward at flintlock-point, and bearing a smug expression of victory. I seemed to recall, from prior visits, another aperture on the side of the building to which I had last seen the waiter speeding, and now saw myself as the merest sheepdog, having herded the prey to Mr. Overlock's waiting gun. This object now pointing squarely at the stripling's spine, the Master paused a moment for the doorman to stop pummeling me and open the door—his only reason, I guess, for not merely taking his prisoner in the side door himself.

"Sir!" I blurted out, blood choking my words. "May I request the advance of one gold coin on my day's salary, so that I might pay this gentleman?"

"You failed to apprehend this criminal as instructed, Grave, so you shall receive no salary," said the Master. He turned to the doorman. "When you are through with him, he is wanted within."

"Yes, sir," said the doorman.

The Master withdrew, the doorman resumed, and after being finished with, I hobbled limply up the stairs and back inside. The lackey having spared me the use of my legs, I was able to return to Mr. Overlock's side, where I attempted, despite an occasional splutter and twitch, to stand as silently as before.

"The prisoner will approach the chair," said the Master.

The waiter, flanked by two of the more solid-looking members, approached and stood before Mr. Overlock.

"Do you admit to the crime?" asked Mr. Overlock.

The prisoner wavered.

"Keep in mind that if you accept guilt, your term of detention will be a finite one," said the Master. "Deny it and you will face death. Considering the evidence confronting you, you may accept as fact the impossibility of a successful defense."

The waiter waited.

"State your plea," said Mr. Overlock.

"I guess I'm guilty," whispered the young man hoarsely, a tear crawling out of one eye.

"Tie him up and contact the constabulary," commanded the Master coldly.

The waiter was taken away, to face the longest wait of his life.

All became quiet again, and I resumed my detached stance, with far more of myself being detached than there was before. I felt that home could not be long in coming, as there was no longer a cook in the kitchen. Then the Right Hon. Gaylord Fortiscue sauntered up, bearing a less-than-steaming plateful of crepe.

"Sorry to have forgotten, Mr. Overlock," he whispered. "The excitement and all. Oh! Here is your vinegar-bottle. Made wonderful flour. Nothing like a crepe made with vinegar."

"Thank you, Captain," said the Master. "Grave will see that you receive an invitation to dine with me next week."

"Yes, sir!" said the Captain, beaming. "I shall teach this underling of yours how to cook!"

The Captain departed, leaving me in a state of some mystification. This was not abated when the Master set the crepe aside uneaten, and rose from his seat.

"Home, Grave."

We exited the premises, to my great relief. The doorman gave me one last kick, and I aided the Master into the carriage. I drove home quietly, lost in thought. I must have conveyed some sense of this, for the Master had to repeatedly rap to keep me at attention. We pulled into the carriageway, and I opened the Master's door, wondering whether in my state of physical near-collapse I was missing something or merely imagining an element which did not exist. We went in, and I escorted Mr. Overlock to his room, where I helped him into bed for his afternoon nap and placed his tray at his side. I was feeling no more enlightened than before.

"Sir…" I ventured.

"You're a fool, Grave," he interrupted. "Surely you possess the faculties to answer the questions you are so clearly struggling with?"

"Sir, the old man—"

"His incapacities are his virtues. I asked him to make me a specially seasoned crepe, knowing that he would season the entire batch of flour before using it. I also provided the seasoning, knowing that he would never question what I told him it was."

"But sir, the list you had me procure…"

"Ask yourself why I would request such a list as soon as I finished eating, which was *ten* minutes after the waiter made his deliveries—when, even by injection, it takes corodium anide *fifteen* minutes to take effect?"

It finally dawned on me. All of it. The list he knew to request because he knew the colonel would perish twenty-five minutes after eating the cookies. The cookies which were tainted by flour which in turn had been tainted by his "seasoning." The pin he had used to prick me in the flank which he'd later used when holding the victim's back and stomach to create the telltale wound. The original, tainted flour which had fallen from the wastebasket, as opposed to the bag he'd brought out.

As I stood there visualizing all this, he extracted the vial the Captain had returned to him from a pocket on the coat hanging by his bed. The vial read "corodium anide."

"He who fails to uphold the rules of the club is almost as guilty as he who breaks them," he said.

He placed the container on the table, and turned out the lights.

8

Chapter Eight
Milo Overlock On The Train

"LOOK at the lovely choo-choo, sir," I said, as we stood on the loading platform.

"A steam locomotive is a transport, Grave. It is not lovely, nor does it chew. Assist the porter in loading my luggage. And by 'assist' I mean load it yourself."

"But sir, he won't let me," I protested.

The Master's eyes flashed with lightning. "I do not trust any of my belongings in the hands of strangers. *Make* him let you, or I shall have you shoveling coals from here to the Chasm of Death."

"Yes, sir."

I shambled wearily over to the luggage car, where the angry porter confronted me.

"What the hell are you doing over here?" he demanded.

I swallowed. "My Master—Mr. Overlock—requested me to load his baggage personally."

"It's already loaded. Get lost, dead man."

I drifted about, trying to verify the status of Mr. Overlock's luggage by peering through the windows, till a small contingent of nearby railmen began approaching, wielding pipes.

Having decided that I'd helped enough, I biffed back to the side of the Master.

"Everything's loaded, sir," I said. "The trunks were too heavy for the baggage boy, but I carried them in for him."

"Good," said Mr. Overlock. "Since you are so adept at lifting, you may carry me to my sleeping car."

"Yes, sir," I frowned.

Feeling as though the entire train was on my shoulders, I toted the small boulder that was Milo Overlock into the shiny steel snake. We were on our way to a dire little town known only as "Please Help Us," where the Master owned a leper colony that manufactured makeup. Production was down, and Mr. Overlock was on his way to improve matters, perhaps by threatening the inhabitants that he would cancel the weekly dance contest. I weaved my way down the aisles which were twice my width and half his, till we reached the culmination at drawing room 1-M.

Sweating, I opened the door and let Mr. Overlock slide over my head and to the floor. It was only then that I observed that the room was occupied. A young man decked in formal wear and a girl in a bridal gown were sitting on the chaise-longue, wasting no time in commencing the nuptial session.

"I say, chaps!" blurted the bridegroom, sighting us. "Play fair…this is our room, you know."

The Master gazed at them with curled lip. "Remove them, Grave."

The bridegroom rose. "Now see here…"

Mr. Overlock laid a paw upon the bride's shoulder, staring into her new husband's hot eyes. "I said remove them, Grave, before I decide to lay claim to all of the possessions I find in my sleeping quarters."

The bridegroom's mouth became pursed, and he appeared to grope for a retort. The Master's stone-cold gaze did not seem to aid him in his goal.

"Then where are we to sleep?" he demanded.

"In the water closet," replied the Master blackly. "Get out."

The bridegroom picked up his bundle of wife and inched past me to the door.

"We'll see who gets this room," he growled. "Come, Vulva."

"If you return, I will kill you both," said Mr. Overlock, extracting his flintlock and aiming it at the female. "Out."

The twosome, their honeymoon plans having been thus altered by the Master, withdrew in haste.

"And now," said Mr. Overlock, opening the platinum-lined box he had brought aboard with him, "I shall show my mice their bed for the trip."

I stared, aghast. The room had come with one bed and a chaise-longue, and I had naturally assumed that I would be sleeping on the latter. I endeavored to convey the point.

"Sir," I said, "surely you don't intend the mice to sleep in the bed?"

"Of course not, imbecile," he replied. "I shall use the bed. They will use the chaise."

"But sir, I thought I was going to sleep there."

"Don't be impertinent, Grave," he snapped. "These mice are your masters as well. They will occupy the chaise. You shall sleep standing up, over there in the corner."

"Yes, sir," I murmured dejectedly.

"Now, then," he said, opening the box. "Abigail. Abercromby. Templeton. Fiscus. Caroline. Piedmont. Winthrop. Adelaide. Honus. Marcel. Line up on your new bed."

Like little snow-white soldiers, they lined up dutifully on the chaise-longue, abreast. The revolting little milk-moustaches.

"Now," said the Master, surveying his troops like a sergeant-at-arms, "bite Grave."

Before I had an instant to prepare for the command, the walking cottonballs scurried down the chaise-leg, across the floor and up onto my trouser-cuffs. They whisked over these, past my waistcoat and onto my face, which they proceeded to bite hungrily. I screamed vociferously, but was too well-trained myself to raise a hand in defense. I just stood there and took it, until a few moments later when Mr. Overlock, judging me welted enough, snapped his fingers, and the mice retracted. They ran back up the chaise-longue and formed the same straight line as before.

"That will teach you not to be disrespectful to your superiors, Grave," said the Master. "Next, we will repair to the dining-car, after you have finished cleaning out this box…with your tongue."

The only good part about this experience was the fact that it left me entirely without an appetite for a meal which I would not have received anyway. I escorted (carried) Mr. Overlock and mice out of the room and toward the dining-car, threading through what appeared to be an ever-growing throng of angry travelers. We reached the dining-car as the train began to pull out. Only the bar was open, so I plopped the Master onto a barstool, placed his vile little sugartits on the stool beside him, and tried to force a bulging disk back into place by slamming my back on a dirty table.

"Silence, Grave," snapped the Master, and turned his attention to the barkeep. "Port," he ordered.

"Yes, sir," said the bartender, extracting and pouring the liquid.

"There seems undue commotion aboard this vessel," said Mr. Overlock. "Explain."

The bartender shrugged. "No one's come in here, so I don't know."

"Grave, ascertain the cause of the disharmony and report."

"Promptly, sir."

I exited the dining-car and found the commotion going on as tumultuously as before. Although he seemed to be at the center of all the ruckus and receiving the brunt of the negativity, a conductor-type suggested himself as the right person to ask. So I barged my way through, hushed the crowd with a gesture I meant to imply I possessed information, then tapped the conductor on the shoulder.

He almost jumped out of his uniform as he turned to confront me. "What!" he demanded.

"I beg your pardon, sir," I said, "but my Master has asked me to ascertain the cause of this disturbance."

He stared at me, his skin taking on a plumlike hue. "Oh, he has, has he? Get out of my face, you petrified pile of dinosaur crap. I've got a trainload of people with conflicting tickets, and you think I've got time to stand here talking to some extinct species' feces? Die, you casketful of bone silt. Your mother was a necrophiliac."

I bowed. "Thank you, sir."

I returned to the bar-car, where I saw Mr. Overlock's glass of port sitting on the barstool at his side, with each of his mice sitting on its lip and gulping furiously. The bartender was looking on with an incredulous expression.

"Now then," said the Master to the bartender, "you will mix me a Bloody Good—using duck's blood."

"I'm sorry, sir, but I can't do that," said the bartender. "All the duck on board is reserved for dinner."

"Then I shall have one made with your blood," said Mr. Overlock, aiming his flintlock at the man. "Unless you too are reserved for dinner."

"Like I said, sir, every duck on board is at your disposal," said the bartender. "One moment, please."

"What have you discovered, Grave?"

"The train is full of passengers with conflicting tickets, sir," I said. "Like the newlyweds of before."

"An oddity."

"Perhaps a printing error, sir."

"Count the passengers."

"Yes, sir."

I did, and reported. By this time, the excess passengers were beginning to fill in the open areas, and were filtering into both the dining and observation cars.

"Hm," said the Master, considering the figure I had given him. "Exactly twice the normal capacity of this train."

At this time, the conductor entered and made an announcement.

"I'm sorry, but due to the error, the sleeping-cars will have to go to the ticket-holders who come first alphabetically," he said. "We will try to make the rest comfortable where we can."

"Exactly what 'error' do you refer to?" asked Mr. Overlock, putting a peanut into Piedmont.

"Why, an excess of tickets sold, of course."

Mr. Overlock turned to the present passengers. "Who here intended to go by an earlier or later train, but found none available?"

The bridegroom, who by now had manifested here with his bride, was one of several who raised their hands.

"Vulva and I planned to take the evening train," he said. "But we found that there was a four-hour interval between this and the next one. We couldn't wait."

The Master looked at the conductor. "There is supposed to be only a two-hour wait between eastbound trains. Explain."

The conductor shrugged. "The next train was running late, due to mechanical issues."

"Why were the passengers not informed?"

"We decided just to cancel that particular departure."

"Why were the passengers not informed?" repeated the Master.

"We felt that the remaining trains would be enough to accommodate them."

"Why did you continue to sell tickets for this train after capacity was reached?"

"An unfortunate error at the ticket-booth."

"Are you saying that you accidentally sold exactly one train's capacity in extra tickets?"

"What do you mean, one train's capacity?"

"There are precisely two trainloads' worth of passengers on this train."

The conductor looked surprised, and began to resemble one of his own steam-engines. "Why, it's just a coincidence…"

"How many tickets do you sell per day, at the last terminal?" asked Mr. Overlock.

"It varies. Some days a handful, some thousands."

"And yet your ticket-seller was not aware that he had sold twice the tickets that this train could hold."

"Like I said, it's a coincidence."

"Coincidence, too, that this idiot behind the bar denied the fact that anyone had preceded me to the dining-car, when the very table that Grave struck his back against was already unclean. The bartender's motive in lying can only be that he resists admitting who has been in here or what they said. I can see from here that there are two mug-rings on the table. Having no reason to fear the passengers, it follows that the persons he served were of elevated station among the train's own personnel, and that their discussion was confidential. Am I correct, barkeep?"

The bartender looked away nervously, wringing weak quacks from the stomach of the dead duck in his fists.

"But what was his motive?" said the Master. "Here we have a free train, two sets of passengers, two sets of luggage…"

"I would rather you didn't continue, Mr. Overlock," said the conductor uneasily, extracting a tiny pistol from his watch-pocket. "I am far too busy to spend the afternoon discussing this affair at length with you or anyone else. I am under certain orders, you see, and too much analysis may trigger an unpleasantly premature action on my part. As soon as my associate with the keys arrives, we will leave you locked in here to ponder it. Bartender Cog, go to the next car and see if he's there yet."

The bartender nodded, took a swig of engine oil, and came out from behind the bar. He headed toward the door that separated our car from the one in front of us, passing between the conductor and Mr. Overlock as he did so. At that point, the Master quietly snapped his fingers, and in an instant his mouse army sped up and over the barman, down and onto the gun-wielding hand of the conductor, which the rodents proceeded to turn into Swiss cheese. The conductor screamed and dropped his gun. The mice, strips of skin in their mouths, continued to grip the besieged appendage, like piranhas. The bartender made a grab at one of the mice, and Mr. Overlock extracted his flintlock. Then the Master shot both bartender and conductor—the conductor in the mouth (which effectively silenced his screaming), and the bartender in the liver (depriving the engine oil of its destination). Mr. Overlock then put his flintlock quietly away, and stood stroking his chin musingly. Half of the passengers present had fainted.

We then heard a click proceeding from the direction of the door which led to the next car forward, and we turned to see a shadowy countenance peek through the little window in it, observe the bodies of the conductor and Cog, and quickly disappear.

"Rouse these passengers and assist them in informing any others to our rear, Grave," said the Master grimly. "Let them know that they have been the victims of a conspiracy and that I am now in charge. Quickly."

"Yes, sir."

Rousing those who had passed out by waving a bit of the Master's tobacco under their noses, I assembled an army of informants and we proceeded to spread the word to the rear of the train's occupants, for the passage forward, indeed, had been locked, apparently by the person we had glimpsed. The news was received with various degrees of disdain, the one constant being that everyone seemed to consider the whole thing my fault. Dancing past a variety of vigorously thrown objects (including a lady's shoe which effectively slammed me in the small of the ear), I returned to Mr. Overlock and found him sitting at a table, gazing out the window and ignoring the many questions which the other passengers were flinging at him.

I sighed, massaging my ear. "I'm very tired, sir," I said. "May I sit down?"

He eyed me as a knife would eye a slab of butter. "Not if you ever hope to stand up again, you pathogenic spore. Note the landscape. We are proceeding due north from our origins."

I scratched my head. "Oranges, sir?"

"Not oranges, you vacant husk, origins. Our eastbound train has changed course to the north."

I looked out. Indeed, the mountains which had been moving right to left were now coming toward us.

"Most disconcerting, sir."

The Master turned to the passengers. "What we have is an intentional rerouting of this train, indicating that the persons running it are aware of and in legion with those who have detained us thus far. We must assume that all personnel aboard are involved in the affair, for it would be impossible to conceal a change of course such as this, and just as difficult to suppress or do away with witnesses in the line's employ."

"Then what is their intention?" asked a passenger. "To kidnap us?"

"Unlikely," said Mr. Overlock. "They took pains to compress two trainloads' passengers into one train. Why the extra trouble and indiscretion—for added hostages? One load was enough; indeed, I alone am enough. I believe it is the second train which is of value to them."

"But if they're after the train, what's to happen to us?" inquired another passenger.

"Oh, we are to be dispensed with, undoubtedly," answered the Master.

A new selection of individuals fainted this time. The ones who'd been revived by Mr. Overlock's tobacco apparently decided that another go-around wasn't worth it.

"The question," said the Master, "is what they want with the second train. Grave?"

I started and bit my tongue, shocked that he would ask my opinion. "Sir?"

"Why do they want the second train?"

"Why—I don't know, sir."

"I think you do. How many other pieces of luggage did you see when you carried mine into the baggage car?"

I gulped. "Er—scores and scores, sir."

"Beware, Grave. If I catch you in a lie, I will have Adelaide chew your tongue off at the root and let her keep it for a bath mat."

I was less perturbed by the thought of losing my bleeding tongue than by the thought of tasting Adelaide. I hung my head.

"I'm sorry, sir. I…I never got inside the baggage car."

"Did you see my trunks go in?"

"They told me your luggage had already been loaded, sir. They chased me away with pipes!"

"Being bludgeoned to death with a pipe will sound like a dream-holiday after I'm through with you, if those trunks are not recovered."

I stared at the floor with abject humility, though knowing that his three trunks contained only two changes of clothes between them, changes he probably would not have made anyway.

"If we inspect the baggage car, we will find it empty," said Mr. Overlock to the crowd. "They have used the second train to transport our belongings to a destination of their choice."

"But what about us?" asked a woman. "What do they plan to do to us?"

"I assume that you are referring to the means by which they plan to rid themselves of us," said the Master. "They would not be likely to use firearms, for such would leave telltale signs upon their victims, and our provocateurs, I would hazard, desire both subtlety and simplicity. Perhaps our course indicates a possibility. We are presently proceeding into mountainous terrain. Certainly there is no way the train can be returned without provoking questions as to its inhabitants' whereabouts; an accident must be devised which may conveniently account for their demise. The Chasm of Death is a treacherous ravine quite negotiable as an uphill climb, but downhill at unmanaged speeds it could prove deadly. It may well be that we are destined to approach it from above, rather than below."

"Then how will the engineer and his cohorts escape?" inquired another of the uneasy audience.

"I am sure they will have no difficulty making their exit well before the train becomes a runaway, if they are wise and remain gathered together near the front of the train. As long as they do this, and keep the passenger cars locked, they need have no fear of the passengers attacking or escaping. They will have to concoct some plausible story, such as a hijacking, and claim to have been left to die in the cold mountains overnight. The other train will rendezvous with them, the valuables unloaded at some discreet location, and all will return heroes. The first will be praised for surviving a hijacking, the second for rescuing them in a faulty train whose departure was canceled, but which was the only one available to investigate when its predecessor failed to arrive at its allotted checkpoints."

"And we'll end up a mangled, haphazard heap scattered about some rocky valley," muttered the bridegroom of before.

"Quite."

"We must act," said one elderly occupant decisively. "We can still get to the rear. If we could stop the train, we could get off at the caboose and make a run for it. What do you think of pulling the emergency brake cord, Mr. Overlock?"

Mr. Overlock took the old man's cane, causing the man to tumble, and pulled on the overhead brake cable with it. Nothing occurred.

"It has been disengaged, probably from the start," he said.

"You mean, we have no brakes?" cried a lady.

"Only the ones to which the locomotive's remaining personnel have access," said the Master.

A certain uncertainty seemed to envelope the crowd. It was at this time that a little voice began to whisper "Get the hell out of there, Grave," and I began to inch toward the door which led to the onboard water closet. I had a dreamlike vision that if I flushed myself, I might end up in China.

"Grave."

I chastised my little voice for alerting me too late to my peril, but all it did was chuckle in response. Dismally, I wormed my way to the Master, wondering what agonizing denouement he had planned to this affair, and how it involved me.

"We must apprehend the villains in this case, Grave, which means that the engine must be taken. The only way to do this is for someone to climb onto the roof of the train and leap from car to car until reaching it. My mice can then take the situation in hand. As punishment for your lies, you will take them."

It's not as though I didn't see it coming, but my heart sank and my lip trembled anyway. To climb atop a cinder-spewing, coal-chewing railway train in my best tuxedo and "leap" from car to car with Mr. Overlock's malicious mouselings in tow seemed a trifle unsettling. The last time I had "leapt" from anything had been from my mother's womb, and I had never had the inclination to do so again.

"Mayn't one of the younger gentlemen go in my stead, sir?" I asked. "You may desire a drink, or your trousers pressed."

"None of your artificial panderings to service, you sniveling craven. Out the window and up. My mice shall cling to your vestments."

Just like that, the puffs lay grip to my faultless attire and the Master, using the old man's cane, busted a window.

"Out, Grave."

The window was still possessed of several clinging glass shards, but Mr. Overlock apparently had no patience for their removal. Gesturing restively and his mice biting me in turn, he ushered me through the aperture with no regard for scrapes and scratches, while I just hoped (fruitlessly) that the mice would get theirs, too. When only my posterior remained unfreed, and I was squeezing a shard to keep from whizzing into oblivion, the Master gave me a stinging whack with the cane and I burst through. I found myself clinging to the exterior of a tiny window on a two-hundred-ton metal monstrosity that was barreling through twenty-degree mountainous terrain at what felt like three hundred leagues a second. Although red-hot cinders were besieging my eyes like an insect swarm on a dead fish, and buttons were actually being blown, one by one, off my coat and vest, the mice held on as if it were all just a gentle breeze at a lakeshore picnic. Drat the perfect little things, I thought. Even *they* were Milo.

I saw the engine, several miles ahead, towing its endless string of subdivisions out behind it, with mine third to last. I gasped, but the rodents again began to nip, so I creakingly hoisted one leg up onto the lip of the projection which framed the window, and yanked the rest of myself up after it.

There is no overestimating the power of artificial stimulus. Perched on the tiny overhang of a railroad car's window, blinded by cinders and listening to my heart dance, the best I could do was drape my arms overhead and hug the sharp curvature of the vessel's upper body. But every time the wind threatened to take me (an event I'd have welcomed, not that I thought I'd actually die), a mouse would bite and my spontaneous reaction would create enough thrust to keep me affixed. It took one simultaneous empiercement by all the mice, centered on one particularly sensitive region of my central buttressing, to incite enough forward motion to propel me off the overhang and up onto the roof of the dining-car. Once there, I clung to it as if it were my mother's breast, while the exhaust of the distant smoke stile slammed my face in blast-furnace fashion and dried my sooty tears like the black streaks around a panda bear's eyes. Unable to see and barely able to breathe, I resolved not to move another inch. Then the horrid hellmice all ran down and up my pant legs, rendering a ghastly tickling so severe and hideous that I jumped up at once, shook them out and promised them that I'd continue. They resumed their stations on my beleaguered livery, and I totteringly wobbled to the next phase of my nightmare—the chasm between the cars.

The gap was eight feet. My height was six. To fail the jump meant death. I guess I figured I couldn't lose. I flailed back to the rear of the car like a scarecrow in a wind-tunnel, turned around and got my bearings. Then, imagining myself a track star with dozens of collegiate lovelies cheering me on, I set my eye on the next car and launched toward it. I could hear a host of bones waking up as I stumbled forward, and with every stride my arches slipped another quarter-inch, but the will of a Grave is not to be underestimated. I could see an invisible hurdle in my mind's eye, and a lanky but lithe lad prancing toward it with all the confidence of a roe eyeing a rivulet. I was going to make the leap. In my heart of hearts, I just knew it.

Then, two strides from the gap, one of the mice jumped off of my clothes and, running twice as fast as me, went and paused on the edge of the separation. I barreled forth, tripped on the little milkweed pod, and fell. My arms outstretched, I fit the gap like a cork, with finger and toe tips just extending past the lip of both cars. All the mice but one ran over me and onto the roof of the next car. There they stood and squeaked, motioning for me to join them. The other mouse, the one I'd tripped on, climbed onto my foot and bit my ankle. I yelped, while my feet became dislodged and fell into the gap. I found myself dangling from the car in front of me by my fingers. Then the mouse bit me again, deep enough to hit bone, and I involuntarily yanked myself up to where the horde awaited me, on the roof of the next section of train. One down, I thought, ten to go.

The unpleasantness of falling into as many gaps as this, tripping over as many mice and suffering an equal amount of marrow-sucking bites cannot be adequately described. But that is how each of the following cars went, one by one, with the only variation being an extra bite or two just to keep me running. Finally, the engine and its tender became my sole remaining objectives, and here the monotony was broken somewhat. I guess I was just too tired for the bites to have effect any longer, for as I dangled from the back end of the big, enclosed coal-car, I did not leap up to its roof as I had before. Instead, one of my hands slipped, and it appeared for a moment that my death was imminent, to be registered as manglement beneath the wheels of a Please Help Us special. Then the mice formed a line and, each taking the tail of the one before it, reached down and grabbed me by the coat collar. My other hand slipped, and I found myself hanging from the mouth of one mouse supported by nine others. They pulled and heaved, and little by little lifted me up onto the roof of the car with them. Then they panted and glared at me for a few moments before scurrying to the head of the tender and pointing over the side. I crawled wearily after them, looked over the edge, and saw what they meant. The engine's cab was large and open at the rear, and coupled in such close proximity to the tender that I could step onto its roof if I was careful. From there, I had merely to lower myself through one of its side windows, and I could sit back and watch the mice take over. Inspired, I made certain no one was in view, waited for the rodents to fasten themselves again, and moved into position. As soon as I was over the cab, I lowered myself toward the aperture. I then discovered that tossing myself inside was another matter entirely. For while the window was merely an open ventilation square, the wind here whipped ferociously, and I felt like a marionette dangling from a drink-happy puppeteer's knotted strings. I slammed against the side of the engine-car again and again, and one of my teeth flew out. Deliverance, however, was at hand. A giant, hirsute paw about the size of a watermelon suddenly thrust out and grabbed me by the neck. With an "Ack!" I felt myself being pulled inside, and in an instant I was on the floor, facing one of the most ideal studies in primitive man science could ever hope to find.

Before me, clenching and unclenching his wire-bristle fists, stood Homo erectus, accompanied by another, less advanced primate of equal bulk and similarly vague human characteristics. Their cage was a good-sized space at the rear of the engineer's compartment, which was also occupied by two others—the engineer and his assistant, I supposed—who came over and joined them in forming a semi-circle around me. The floor was damp with what I guessed to be a mixture of urine, oil and liquor; several bottles were scattered about, as though some celebrating had been going on. There were a variety of controls at the front end, and an iron grating, which I soon discovered gave access to the furnace, for one of my new acquaintances, after a grunt from his troop leader, went and opened it, and they each grinned at me as though I was to become the next round of kindling. I really did not know how Mr. Overlock's little mice could intimidate such a group, for these were apes not elephants, but after experiencing the rodents in action thus far I was not about to underestimate their capabilities. With a bold cry of "Get them!" I pointed at the cavemen and watched the mice jump down off my coat and go scurrying…out past our enemies and into the foremost part of the cab.

I sat on the floor, momentarily bewildered, utterly betrayed, shocked that the Master's mice had chosen such a time to go and play engineer. I sat facing my behemoth playmates with a simper on my as-yet unbloodied face. Then I extracted a little brush from my pocket and crawled up to one of the neanderthals, and proceeded to dust his feet. I say feet because he wasn't wearing any shoes.

He grabbed me by the pate and lifted me to a sort of limp standing position. He was huffing and puffing, and his breath smelled like the excrement of a sick goat.

"Some tea, sir?" I asked meekly.

I guess he didn't want any, because he and his bedfellows now proceeded to pummel me mercilessly. They began with my face, and worked their way down. I lost an eyelid right at the start, and was therefore able to witness each piece of the destruction as it wended its way southward. I marveled at how few people got to see their own collarbone, let alone taste their nose. I was surprised and gratified to know that there was enough blood in my body to actually spurt. My silk waistcoat, it appeared, really did resist stains, for my gruel slid right off of it; my trousers truly were as light as advertised, for I could feel the blows as if I didn't have them on. I was about to find out what it felt like to eat hot coals, for one of the more creative lads had taken a shovel's worth out of the furnace and was approaching me with it, when suddenly a great lurch yanked the train, my teachers and I went flying forward, and the hot coals went scattering over the well-primed floor, setting the compartment alight. I tumbled wildly into the front of the cabin, and felt myself grabbed and lifted off the floor. With my lidless eye I then perceived the mice, hanging in a long string by their tails as before. The top one was gripping the emergency brake chain on the ceiling, this being one which had apparently been kept operational. The bottommost one held me in its teeth. The engine-driver and his assistant, having no such fascination as bite-bait, had slammed full-force into the wall of mechanisms and controls, and were lying motionless on the floor, feeding the new flames. The ruffian who had fed me my nose had fallen on one of the bottles and was being charred on a shard, while the other fireman had gotten his head jammed in the furnace opening and was crackling at both ends. As soon as the train had slowed enough, I asked the mouse who held me to let me go; it spat me out, and I stomped out the fire as quickly as I could. I then tottered to a corner and collapsed, while the mice, who hung onto the brake chain till we came to a full stop, disengaged themselves and began shaking hands with each other. I wanted to lose consciousness, but one of my eyes wouldn't close.

A few moments later, Mr. Overlock walked up from outside. "Excellent work," he said, stepping over me and picking up his pets. "It is a shame that servants cannot be trained as well as mice."

The mice snickered, and the Master put them in their box, which he was carrying.

"Stop lying around, Grave," he said, giving me a kick. "We have a second train to apprehend."

"Yes, sir," I spluttered.

The second train arrived about an hour later, by which time the Master and some of the burlier passengers (using keys and weapons found on the persons of our adversaries in the cab) had made a thorough inspection of each car and captured the last of our remaining enemies. It came crawling up behind us and came to a stop, whereafter several of its malfeasants oozed out and approached our vessel. They came oiling up to our engine, whence the Master descended from the iron steps and stood confronting them with his flintlock.

"You have two choices," he said to them. "Death by pistol, or death by exposure."

Those whose next actions seemed to indicate a preference for the former got shot, and the rest, along with our captives, were tied up, to be left there in the snow. Then I was dispatched to bring all of the stolen baggage from Train #2 into Train #1, and after some of the more qualified passengers were elicited to help get the locomotive in motion again, we took off once more, at a much more leisurely pace than before. Mr. Overlock was hailed as a hero by every traveler aboard, while I generally received beratement for bleeding on people's bags.

As night softly and gradually fell upon our slow-moving ship, and the bulk of the passengers were raiding the contents of the train's galley, Mr.

Overlock began to wend his way back toward his sleeping quarters. I humbly followed.

"Your services will not be required tonight, Grave," he said. "The two newlyweds have chosen to express their gratitude by inviting me to spend the rest of their honeymoon with them. I have therefore decided to return to them the use of my cabin. I will be there for the rest of the journey."

"But sir…" I began.

"Another of the grateful passengers has donated his cabin as well, the one next to mine. You will sleep there."

I was enchanted to hear that someone had apparently valued my contribution enough to give me his room to sleep in. Bidding the Master a happy honeymoon, I proceeded there immediately, with the anticipation of my first good night's sleep in years.

As soon as I entered, my balloon burst like a bubble in my blood. Mr. Overlock's mice were lying everywhere…on the laid-out bed, on the chaise-longue; everywhere. The only spot where one was not strategically reclining was one location in the corner, where a person could sleep— standing up. With a heavy sigh, I took my station there dutifully, bade the beasts goodnight and proceeded to attempt to sleep. As the night wore on, squeaks and grunts assailed my ears through the thin wall which separated mine from the cabin of Mr. Overlock and the honeymooners. All throughout, my unclosable eye stared at the mice about me, who were always staring back and grinning.

9

Chapter Nine
Milo Overlock and the Anti-Milo

IT began with a message, and a messenger. The messenger himself had sent a messenger, who informed us that an important letter awaited Mr. Overlock at a wooded cottage not far from the main gates of our Queen's beautiful castle. It puzzled me why a messenger would send another messenger to convey the message that he had a message, and I expressed my bewilderment to the Master. To my surprise, even he did not seem certain.

"The question is why he did not deliver the information himself, or at the very least have his own courier deliver it," said Mr. Overlock, washing down a piece of cold duck from his plate with some cold duck from his glass. "The answer can only center on location. My presence at the location outlined is the desired element. Whether or not a message is truly involved is speculative. It may amount to a simple case of abduction."

He paused to wash down more duck with duck, as I effected concern and general disdain for the insensitivity of the modern criminal.

"Therefore, you will go."

A leg gave out beneath me, and I bit a well-inflamed canker sore. "M-me, sir?" I stammered out.

"Quite. We must ascertain the party's identity and intention."

"But sir, if their plans are indeed nefarious, what will they do when they find me in your place?"

"Kill you, I suspect."

He said this as if it possessed no more significance to the scheme of things than the cut of meat he would attack next, but to me his words bore potent effect. As often as I have wished for death, I've never enjoyed the thought of being murdered, even on nights of dinner-parties. I cringed, and attempted a meager defense.

"What if they refuse to give me the letter, sir?" I asked.

"Inform them that if they refuse to give it to you, it will go undelivered. They have gone to great lengths already…if such a letter exists, they will make certain I receive it."

"And if the letter does not exist, sir?"

"Then I will feed your body to my mice," he said. "At present, I am training them to be carnivorous."

Knowing full well that further argument would avail me at best a fork slung at my cheek, I sighed resignedly and awaited the conclusion of the Master's dinner before proceeding with my sudden "evening out." Having gathered the bones he had inevitably scattered about the table and blotted up the wine puddles, I sucked what encouragement I could from the napkin, sheathed myself in a moth-eaten (actually, mouse-eaten) overcoat, and went out to ready the horses. The decrepit plugs seemed shocked to wake up alive, but finding me to be the only passenger making the trip, allowed me to harness them with minimal kicks. I set forth, my objective being the little forested village which lay beyond the northern façade of my former post, Castle Overlock of Onwall, whose luminescent parapets stood towering against the night sky in the distance. My spirits rose as I rode toward it, much time having passed since I'd buttled amongst its buttresses. I had often encouraged the Master to visit there, but despite my persuasions and the fact that it bore his name (public demand), he rarely did, assuming perhaps that a seat of power could just as easily be at a dinner table as a throne room. I, however, had a fondness for the place stemming from my long-ago employment there, and as I approached the village resting peacefully under its gaze, felt comforted by the big, familiar presence nearby.

The cottage to which the messenger's instructions had guided me was a well-concealed little bungalow, deeply enshrouded in the wooden fringe of the town. I would have missed it altogether were it not for a formidable-looking man standing cross-armed by the roadside in front of it, waving me down with a sweeping gesture. He had a black beard, and was spitting sunflower seeds out of a toothless gap in the upper bridge of his gums. He was not young, but had the oak-like development of an older man whose life has been spent taking no nonsense from younger ones. I halted the horses and proceeded to approach the gentleman, cracking my knuckles in a way I hoped would convey menace and self-confidence.

He chuckled in a far-off thunderstorm kind of way. "Greetings, wraith," he said.

"That's 'Grave,'" I corrected him.

"Where's Overlock?"

"My Master has sent me in his stead," I replied, effecting a bold demeanor. "He does not enjoy subterfuge and neither do I. So kindly dispense with the preliminary folderol and give me your earth-quaking message, young man, or I shall see that measures are taken."

He put his hands on his hips and laughed robustly, looking like a Viking about to rape the village maiden. Then he extracted a wicked-looking onyx dagger from his pocket and pointed it at the conclave of my throat. "The only measures that are going to be taken are the ones for your coffin, wraith," he rumbled.

I would have gulped, but the resulting bulge in my larynx would have scratched against the tip of the knife. Instead, I sort of squeaked apologetically and dribbled out my mouth. He slowly retracted the dagger.

"Step this way," he said.

"But sir—" I gasped.

"Step this way, wraith, or I shall break the rules and kill you where you stand."

I suddenly felt quite obedient, and followed humbly as he led the way into the cottage. The place was rather plain inside, and seemed to possess only the most rudimentary elements of living. He led me to a large table made of rock, upon which many maps and similar paraphernalia were strewn. I was about to sit down, but he told me to remain standing, and, using a key that hung around his neck, unlocked a little black coffer resting on a mantle. He extracted a scroll, which he then handed to me.

"Give this to your owner, wraith," he said.

I was baffled. "Why didn't you simply deliver it to the house?" I asked.

A smirk creased his sedimentary features. "If I had, your master would not have sent you out here."

"But why do you want me?" I asked. "You're not...you're not planning to—"

"Kill you?" he growled. "Nothing on earth, in heaven or in hell would delight me more. But I cannot. Not yet, and not face to face. But I will, or someone like me will. And when it happens, you're going to get it painfully—at an angle."

His red, hate-consumed eyes bore into my perplexed ones with a heat that held me momentarily hypnotized, like a mouse confronted by a snake. In a desperate effort to disattach my gaze from the predator, I unrolled the missive in my hand and held it up in front of my face. As my vision cleared, I was able to read the following, which was inked in Tivoli script and looked like a royal proclamation:

I reign in the raiment of evil,

You govern in garments of good.

With nobles and chattel we meet to do battle,

Divided by weapons of wood.

But life is a series of colors,

And evil and goodness must mate.

With blood on the field, new scenes are revealed

Which only our conflicts create.

"I fail to see what this means, and why it couldn't have been delivered to our door," I said, somewhat brusquely.

"It is addressed to your master, and he will understand," said the ogre. "His first move was utterly predictable, putting you in motion. I fear that this will not become the challenge my master envisions."

"May I leave now?" I asked austerely.

"Physically, you may leave," he said, "but metaphysically you must remain where you are, until my destiny changes."

I was beginning to find this experience as exasperating as it was distasteful, so I rolled up the parchment and turned to the door. Still uncertain as to my host's real intentions, I picked up my step a little as I reemerged, and anxiously loped my way to the carriage.

"You can run but you cannot move, my counterpart!" he called after me, his bellow echoing off the trees. "You will not progress until I kill or die!"

I jumped up into the driver's seat and whipped the steeds, as the madman cackled maniacally behind me, abetted by a timely thunderclap.

"RECOUNT, GRAVE," said Mr. Overlock, as he unrolled the paper I had handed to him while dripping on the carpet from the sudden cloudburst I had encountered on the way home.

"He was a sizable gentleman, sir, with a black beard. He had an onyx dagger which he threatened me with."

"Why did he not make good on his threats?"

"He kept saying that it would break the rules, sir. He said that he could only assault me at an angle, not face to face, and that I could not move until he killed or died. Quite insane he was, sir."

"But you say he anticipated your arrival?"

"He called the action predictable, sir."

"Hm."

He perused the message carefully, while I stood in cold wetness, my damp clothes absorbing his pipe-smoke like a sponge in a tar-pit. I looked for an expression of interest or surprise on his part, but saw none.

"This riddle is so elementary, it was intended to be swiftly solved. The raiment of evil—black—and the garment of good—white—amass an army of royals and slaves and do battle with wooden weapons. The object, to mate. Very well, we've established that chess is our mysterious messenger's motif. But his identity? His object? He represents the black pieces, and clearly sees himself as 'ruler' or king. The lackey you encountered, black of beard and weapon, is a pawn, for a pawn may only attack at an angle, not face to face. My first, 'predictable' move, was to send you to meet this pawn, and as one who 'governs' we must assume that in this game I am the White King and you are the White King's pawn. You say he informed you of your inability to move—quite right. A pawn cannot move backward, so you stand as far as the cottage, unable to play a further role in the affair until the pawn before you kills or is killed, clearing a path for you to advance."

I was very dazed by all of this, but I did make a connection on the final sentence with the line "unable to play a further role in the affair." Could it truly be that I was to be spared additional involvement with something that was beginning to sound increasingly like another big misery? I hoped the "pawn" I had met would sit still for a nice long time. But then, another contingency concerned me.

"Sir, is it your intention to play this game, and by the rules?"

"Of course, Grave. It is the only reliable way to determine our adversary's motives."

I smiled, having received the answer I'd sought. He wouldn't move me, not until the Black King saw fit to change the other pawn's position. It meant that I could sit back and just watch the proceedings happen. I was so enthused that I went and procured the chess set that Mr. Overlock often used (playing both sides and somehow never losing with either) and gave it a prominent place on the parlor table.

"Where shall I position the pieces, sir?" I asked.

"You did not have to travel far from this vicinity. Place the White King's pawn at K3."

I did so.

"We can but assume that in the interest of setting the game in motion, our adversary's pawn traveled across the board to BK5, facing you. Our rounds can only be viewed as "passes" or elapsed-time forfeitures during this series, as we were unaware of the game's commencement. The only pawn that can have moved freely to BK5 is the Black King's, your 'counterpart.' Place it there."

I did, with a certain level of anticipation. The Master was a superb chess player, and it was folly for anyone to attempt such a confrontation with him. Hence, perhaps, the rather detached attitude he seemed to bear the strange proceedings. I was anxious to see which piece he would play next.

He stretched. "Mix me a wineapple cocktail, Grave, with pickled pigs' eggs, and bring them to my room. I shall retire."

"But sir, is it not your intention to take an action?"

"Of course not, you mental cyst," he said, ascending the stairs with candle in hand. "It is our opponent's turn."

The next day was one of some uneasiness for me, for the Master had risen with an appetite for hot cat, and was so single-minded in his desire that the chess problem seemed forgotten.

"You mean a hot dog, don't you, sir?" I said.

"I mean hot cat. One that has been feeding on wild duck. Obtain."

I had no choice but to set my worries aside and attend to this abrupt desire of his, although the sudden shift in mental gears left me somewhat shaken. Foreseeably, the task took me quite a portion of the day to arrange. First there was the time spent in local alleys fighting off the little lions, then the bright idea of luring one into following me by the use of fish. Then came the obligatory dip in the duck pond in order to feed the feline appropriately before its slaughter, only to find that by the time I was done being slapped red by the little hen I had chosen, the cat had loped off to oblivion with the biggest prize of the pond.

I went inside and was greeted by a cat-corpse tossed in my face by the impatient Master, who had shot our elderly neighbor's pet with a crossbow.

"Stuff it, Grave."

I went to the kitchen and dejectedly stuffed cold duck down the beast's throat, then deprived it (with rising nausea) of its coat. I cooked the thing, and returned it to the table with a pomegranate shoved in its mouth. The Master inspected the tabby, then snapped his fingers, whereafter a horde of his white mice swarmed in from nowhere, scurried up to the tabletop and devoured the meat ravenously. Wiping their mouths with a hearty and unanimous "Mm," they retreated once more to their haunts while Mr. Overlock graded their performance.

"Excellent," he said. "Tomorrow they will begin hunting their own felines."

I marveled how only Milo Overlock could train mice to track down cats, catch them and eat them, while instilling in them a proper taste for duck as well. Other matters, however, continued to perturb me.

"Sir, are you not concerned as to the action which your opponent has taken?"

"What?"

"The chess game, sir. He has had an opportunity to move."

"Do you know what that move is?"

"No, sir."

"Are you suggesting that I counter a move that we do not know of?"

I sighed. "No, sir."

"One of our bishops has gone out on a charitable tour of the area, KB-QB4, if that pleases you," he said. "I've sent a message asking him to linger near Allwon and report any unusual activity he encounters. When our opponent's move becomes evident, we will reply, no sooner."

"But what if he makes another move before we've discovered the first one, sir?" I asked.

"Give me your sleeve, Grave. There are crumbs on this plate."

And there the matter stood. The Master spent the rest of the day teaching his mice how to avoid leaving crumbs (a lesson he hadn't learned himself), how to appreciate a fine wine and to enjoy an after-dinner smoke. It was not until the next morning that a new development took place. I became aware of it right at the outset.

I had gotten up to use the water closet at about five a.m., an hour before my working-day tended to begin. I noticed a light emanating from the parlor. Repairing thither, I saw the Master pacing around, puffing on his pipe like a drainage bag attached to a catheter. I hastened to offer service.

"Ah, Grave," was all he said.

I felt hesitant. "May I...may I be of some assistance, sir?"

"I am agitated, Grave."

I looked, and perceived two new pieces in action on the chessboard.

"You don't mean, sir—?"

"Yes I do mean. Hang me for a fool the likes to rival you, but I failed to see it coming. The onyx dagger, the rock table. The pawn you encountered was a man named Stone, and he is the infamous manservant of my arch-rival, a being so shrouded in nefarity and stealth that to this day he is known only as the Anti-Milo."

"The Anti-Milo!" I gasped.

"Quite. One of the Queen's messengers arrived with the news last night. You being the dead sloth you are, I received him myself. He relayed the fact that an Allwon emissary, in the guise of a bishop, had arrived in town yesterday evening with the implication that he was preparing a seminar. He fit the description of a spy with whom we have dealt before. Allwon, our immediate neighbor to the north, is where the Anti-Milo implanted his dangerous influence many years ago, and where it has grown to parallel mine here. In his ascent to power, he replaced most of the original members of its royal staff with questionable individuals of his own choosing, which he uses as spies."

"But who is the Anti-Milo?" I asked.

"A rival of mine who formerly lived in Onwall. He calls himself Milo Overlock and has long claimed exclusive right to the name. I have never been able to vanquish him entirely, and as long as both of us live, the fight for supremacy must rage on."

"There are other pieces out of order on the board," I observed.

"Of course. The 'bishop' arrived bearing papers which contained his Queen's permission to come here. That makes him the Queen's bishop. For him to move, the Queen's pawn had first to be freed. I sent a messenger on horseback to our contact in Allwon, and the reply arrived just before you arose. An Allwon guard, on-duty, had been found drunk in an Allwon pub just outside the gates of his castle shortly before the spy's departure. He was the Queen's guard, her 'pawn.' She has left herself exposed in order to place her bishop in motion, an information-gathering tactic similar to my own. I was unaware of how deeply imbedded the Anti-Milo had become within his country's royal order. Chess is a game played with powerful pieces, Grave. Our entire monarchy is at risk."

I shuddered, though partially because my nightgown had a hole in the seat.

"I have already allowed our opponent two moves while we remained virtually dormant," he continued. "No longer. I have instructed the Queen to send a royal acolyte to investigate the so-called bishop's story, and to verify our suspicions about his true identity. The only one free to do so, in chess terms, is the pawn of the King's bishop. Approaching, as he does, at an angle, he will be free to apprehend our opponent's man, should the Anti-Milo make any move other than to address our pawn. If he does, his intentions will be proven, and his bishop will be in jeopardy from the knight. Thus the current order on the board. Tea, Grave."

I shook myself out of my stupor and went to mix his tea. When I returned, he was sitting in his armchair, his mouse Caroline resting on his forefinger.

"Pack my bags, Grave, and have the mice assemble in their box. We must move closer to the contest at hand. We will take occupation of the royal quarters at Castle Overlock. It is time, once and for all, for me to take the throne."

"Excuse me, sir, but may I use the water closet first?" I asked.

"No, but do get dressed in something less revealing. Your appearance suggests the Chasm of Death between two snow-covered mountains."

"Yes, sir."

Aching in the bladder, I piled together a suitable quantity of items and we went swiftly off to Castle Overlock in the early light of day. I was excited that I would be serving there again, among whose hallowed hallways I had so long buttled for our then-powerful Queen. Things had changed, though,

I saw as we entered. The walls I had once polished were now infinitely shinier, the furnishings were more aesthetically arranged, the tapestries hung straighter. Even the servlings' uniforms, which I had never been responsible for, were better pressed. All in all, everything seemed to have improved in my absence. It made me feel like a Christmas fruitcake.

"Show me to the throne room," commanded Mr. Overlock of the presiding butler.

"Immediately, sir," said the butler in dulcet tones.

I was glad he hadn't asked me to show him, for I could barely recognize the place and was cross-eyed with uro-retentive pain. Our dignified emissary led us down a long hall which culminated at two oversized arching doors; then, opening them, we were escorted into the ornate throne room where the morning sun gleamed down through stained-glass windows upon a golden chair, where sat our beautiful elderly Queen.

"The eminent Mr. Milo Overlock," intoned the butler with a respectful bow.

Mr. Overlock walked slowly up to her. She trembled in her seat.

"Off," he said.

She descended.

The Master stepped up to the throne and sat down. He gestured to our monarch.

"My crown," he said.

She took hers off, went up and placed it on his head. Then she descended again.

"How does it look?" asked the Master.

"Quite wonderful, Mr. Overlock," she replied.

"Hold up your scepter that I may see my reflection."

She held it up, and as she did so, I whispered "Hello, Your Majesty," to her.

"Silence, Grave," blared Mr. Overlock, while the Queen, the gentle sovereign whom I had so long served, glared at me disgustedly as though she had never seen me before.

"You have entrusted me to protect your kingdom?" said the Master. The room was so huge that it sounded like the voices of a hundred Milos.

"Y—yes, Mr. Overlock," answered the Queen. Her voice didn't echo at all.

"Then you shall address me as King Milo."

"Yes, King Milo."

The Master leaned back. "What is the fate of the acolyte?" he asked.

"He has not returned," said the Queen, great concern in her voice.

"He must have surprised the spy, who, fearful of reporting a total failure, rendered him a casualty of the game. Have my best knight advance immediately upon our opponent's bishop and eliminate him."

"But…but, Mr. Overlock—"

The Master glared at her ferociously, and she suspended her sentence with a slump of her shoulders. "Yes, King Milo."

"Grave, bring me a chessboard and my box of mice."

"Yes, sir."

"And no side trips, Grave. Man has ascended the throne once more, and we must waste no time in saving the country for this female."

"Yes, sir."

I galloped out, feeling grateful for my tiny bit of freedom. Ignoring the Master's order, I immediately began hunting around for a proper repository of my needs. Somehow, though, all the water closets I remembered were missing, with only row upon row of tapestries where I remembered them once being. Damn all tapestries, I thought. You can't pee behind them.

I spied what looked like a little broom closet, and in desperation I bolted in. It was dark, dusty and full of spiders, but it did have a bucket. Enclosing myself, I answered the tom-tom call of my beating loins until a warm mist seemed to fill the cozy confines of my secret privy. Then the door burst open.

"Hey, asshole."

It was the dignified butler of before, suddenly transformed into ignoble vulgus of the swinish multitude.

"I wash the floors with that bucket, fuck it."

"And a fine job you do, too," I said ingratiatingly.

The boot-licker wasn't having it. He looked both ways down the hall, then quietly rolled up his sleeves. He picked up the bucket.

"Open your mouth," he said.

I gathered that his was the simple gesture of one who knew I hadn't had any refreshment yet, but I much preferred coffee in the morning. I demonstrated this by knocking the container, curdling over with a sickly foam, upon his clothes, which sopped it all up like bread. I ran with all my flimsy might down the hall and into other regions of the citadel. After sustaining some hard looks from several other underlings of variable station, I slowed down my pace and looked behind me. The butler was evidently preoccupied with his morning toilet, and was not pursuing. I eased up, looked around, and found that I was completely lost. After some effort, I finally found a chambermaid I had once known, and with a certain reluctance she eventually helped me to find the place the Master's belongings had been stored. I hurried there (a gloriously ornate tower room) and found the mice, lying about like little royal children and being fed grapes by the castle handmaidens.

I begged the rodents to come with me, they sighed, and slowly assembled in their box. The handmaidens glared at me as one by one they reclothed themselves, then stepped on my toes as they left. I fumbled about in the trunks until finding the chessboard, then took it and the mice down, down, down, until we were back in the throne room.

I found the Master slouched on his throne, conversing with the Queen about sending spies into Allwon to monitor the moves of the Anti-Milo.

At the Queen's side stood the butler, who had reattired himself with the swiftness and decorum which no doubt had won him his post. I stuck my tongue out at him.

"Place the chessboard before me, Grave," said His Majesty Milo Overlock.

I did, and quickly organized the pieces in their current order. Mr. Overlock let the mice scurry about on the board, observing things.

"Our opponent is making his move now," said the Master. "We will not know for some time what it is." He looked at the Queen. "It may be necessary to send you in motion," he said frigidly.

She shriveled under his emotionless gaze, but nodded anyway. "Whatever you say, King Milo."

"If a missive from our spy arrives, report to me," said the Master. "Meanwhile, I will spend the day in contemplation. Grave, bring me a duck sandwich. You will be spending the night in the quarters of this lackey."

I gaped in horror, and saw a dim, reserved smile cross the butler's face. The mice snickered, as though cognizant of my earlier troubles.

"Dismissed."

I spent the day piling duck sandwiches into the Master's mouth. I prefer not to relate my experiences in the butler's bedroom that evening—except to say that he made me queen for the night. By early the next day, our adversary's next move was known and Mr. Overlock was preparing to counter it. I stood in the throne room, the Queen cowering before the iron-hard look of the Master, as he fiddled with her chess piece.

"The Anti-Milo is sending a knight-led contingent in from the northwest," he said. "We must prepare for an assault upon the castle. Therefore, it behooves us to conceal you. In the basement of this castle there is a grating which gives access to the sewers. You will go there, Queen-K2."

"But Mr. Overlock, the sewers!" she cried.

"Quite. And unless you address me properly, I will send you there by way of the kitchen drain."

She groaned. "Yes, King Milo."

"Lackey, take her down and drop her in the sewage," commanded the Master. "Do it quietly and inform no one."

The butler looked at the Queen. She nodded resignedly. "Er—yes, sir," he said, and escorted her out.

"Our informant has stated that the knight and his men have shown no sign of slowing up, save a stop at an inn called the Golden Turret for a night's rest," said the Master. "Let's interpret that as a rook's square. They are coming from the northwest. The 'west' or left side of the board, to us, indicates that they belong to the queen. Indications are that they will continue to advance today. Excellent. We have QN-QR3, followed by our move with the Queen, succeeded, most likely, by QN-QN5. We can now prepare our next action."

"Which is, sir?" I yawned.

"Setting you free."

I gulped my yawn down with a sharp intake of air, and stood staring at him tremblingly. "Me, sir?"

"Quite. You, and then I. This is reality, Grave. In a very short time an opposing army will be assembled outside our very gates, threatening all of Onwall. We must confront this menace at the source. We must infiltrate our enemy's fortress, capture his queen and place him in checkmate."

I nodded solemnly. "Indeed, sir."

"In order to set this plan in motion, your counterpart Stone must be forced into action. He must be tempted into attacking."

"But sir, could we not attack him?" I asked.

"We have nothing to attack with that would not be at an initiative disadvantage, and it would take too many moves to set one up."

I looked at the chessboard. "I don't think he will attack, sir. Look. He could have captured your knight already, but hasn't."

"Return to tic-tac-toe if this tasks you, Grave," he snapped. "An action against our knight would place him in jeopardy with both the Queen and the knight's pawn. No, we must move the Queen's pawn into attack position with Stone, and sacrifice him."

This little bit of information titillated me no end, for the Queen's pawn was her butler. I hesitated to celebrate, however, before thoroughly examining the scenario.

"Sir," I said, after studying the layout till my mind bled, "Stone could not take the butler at Q3 without placing himself in jeopardy with the Queen's bishop's pawn."

"He is protected by the knight, you pathetic wretch," he growled. "Now stop attempting to analyze a game that is as far above you as heaven is to hell, or I will give your services back to the Queen and you may act as her sacrificial pawn."

"I'm sorry, sir."

"Very."

We waited until the butler had returned from his duty with our country's matriarch, then Mr. Overlock gave him his orders. He looked at the board, appeared momentarily startled beneath his unflappable façade, then gazed at both of us keenly.

"You want me to attack the king's pawn," he said slowly.

"Do you question my instructions, servling?" said Mr. Overlock severely.

"No, sir. I merely wished to ascertain your intentions. I believe I understand them."

"Carry them out. Your objective will be a cottage in the neighboring village where Grave recently encountered the pawn in question. If you fail to report back by sundown, we will assume the worst and remove you from the board."

He lingered, an ironic smirk on his face. "I shall require Mr. Grave to accompany me, sir, to show me the way."

"Grave will write the directions down for you."

"I see. Very well, sir."

He proceeded slowly to the door, while I quickly jotted the directions on my handkerchief with an ink-feather. Pausing to receive this, the butler looked at me glaringly. "Should I fail in my mission, Grave, I hope you'll think of me when at last you fail yours," he said.

Not quite knowing what he meant by this, I merely said, "You're protected by the bishop's pawn."

"Mm. May you be as well protected when your turn comes."

He snatched the linen, and with as much contempt as he dared display while at his post, nudged me aside and pushed on out the door.

"As soon as that butler is dead, we move," said the Master. "Suitable traveling attire, Grave."

"Promptly, sir." I began to follow in the butler's stead, then stopped. "Eh—sir," I said, "what if the butler should defeat Stone?"

"Stone is the Anti-Milo's manservant, and your opposite in every way," said the Master. "I therefore know that I can rely on him *not* to ruin my plans. Proceed."

I didn't care for his reasoning, however true it was. Needless to say, the butler did not return at sundown and, having prepared accordingly, I rather gleefully flicked his piece from the board.

"Sir, I fear that the Queen is in some jeopardy, according to this arrangement," I said, helping the Master on with his coat.

"We must hope that our opponent is unaware of our moving her, and considers the turn a pass," he answered. "For now, let's concentrate on our advance into Allwon. I will move into the cathedral tonight, King to King's Bishop Two. It has a secret door leading out beyond the castle walls, designed to liberate the royal family in case of invasion. I will steal out before daybreak and take refuge in the now-empty cottage of the king's pawn. You will travel there on horseback tonight and sleep there. In the morning we will reconnoiter, then travel into Allwon territory using the maps in the cottage."

The only part of the last sentence I'd heard was "on horseback." I didn't know how to ride.

"Piedmont will accompany you, so as to manage the horse," he said, reading my mind and giving me the worst possible response. "The rest of the mice will come with me."

He opened the mouse-box and extracted Piedmont, whom he placed in my hand. The little cheese vacuum stared into my face with a menacing expression.

"He—he wants to bite me, sir," I said uneasily.

"Silence, whelp. These mice find you as offensive as I do, but will only punish if you give them poor service. On with your mission."

Palm outstretched, I dubiously escorted the rodent out and paddockward, my mind occupied with what a mouse might consider "poor service." Reflecting that I had once sneezed in the Master's soup and had ended up drinking it, I doubted that even my best intentions would fare any better with his miniscule counterparts. Steadying my hand, I walked carefully, and concentrated on handling my small companion with the greatest care. Then I was bitten for going too slow.

The stables attained, I held Piedmont up before each horse, to which he shook his head one by one. At last he saw one that he liked and nodded, so I had the stable boy prepare the steed for travel. "What's his name?" I asked.

"Gravedigger," the boy replied.

I was glad I had the youngster to help me mount the beast, for it would otherwise have required the propulsion of another mouse-bite to get me aboard. As soon as I sat on its back, it began to buck and rear, but Piedmont immediately dashed up, bit it on the ear and held on. Rather than causing the animal to jump through the roof as I'd foreseen, however, this stilled it into frozen submission. Slowly the rodent let go. Checking to see that I had hold of the reins (which I was clutching for dear life), it ran across to the horse's backside, which it sank its pointy little teeth into. With a violent paroxysm, the horse lurched into action, ignoring the stable door and plowing through a wall instead. It galloped haphazardly toward the stone bulwark of the palace's surrounding battlement, as though it could just as easily plow through this as it did the stable. As a scream began to make its way from my stomach to my lips, Piedmont once again scurried up to the horse's head and bit it repeatedly on the left ear. The horse began veering in the direction of the bite until we were in line with the castle gates. Fortunately, the guard saw us coming, and acting perhaps in the interest of his own survival, he quickly opened the portal. We flew out and into the countryside. For some reason, though we were now free, the mouse continued to keep the horse going full throttle with continued bites to the buttocks. He dashed onto my sleeve at every crossroad and looked at me with a quizzical expression, whence I immediately indicated "left" or "right." He then attacked the appropriate equestrian ear until we went rampaging our way around the corner and onto our new heading.

We closed in on our destination almost before I was ready for us to. We were screaming along at a pace that could have broken Onwall Derby records, when I saw the cottage for which we were destined go whizzing past us in a blur. "That's it!" I bellowed, and impulsively yanked the reins, forgetting that it was the mouse's responsibility to manage the horse. The horse slid to a sudden stop, I lurched forward and lunged into a sliding, face-first mound in the mud of the road. If I hadn't lived, it would have made a perfect grave.

I slowly extracted myself from the goop, and heard the horse whinnying with derisive laughter. The mouse was sitting on the bridge of the horse's nose, shaking its head. I had mud in my ears, but I could have sworn I heard the mouse say "You stupid idiot, Grave." I rose, dollops of light brown slop plopping off of my livery like the sludge of a stock-pond, and slithering from moustache to mouth. I tied the horse to a tree and sploshed suction-like to the door of the cottage, hoping to find a container or two of fresh water within, or at least a half-full chamber pot. It had none. There was no well out back, either. There was a closet, but no water in it.

I thought of stripping, but realized that what I could not do in front of the Master I could not do in front of one of his mice. The rodent having placed itself on the rock table in the center of the room and fixed its stare at me, I abandoned any hope of a jolly evening of freedom from Mr. Overlock and simply curled up in a squishy puddle on the floor, where I fell into a soggy sleep with wet dreams.

"Get up, Grave."

With a sudden lurch and an outcry of "Ugh!" I burst out of my coma and saw Mr. Overlock standing over me. It was still dark outside, but a vague blueness gave me to understand that morning was upon me, and that the Master had already crept out of the castle and through the woods to make our rendezvous.

"You are a pustule, Grave. A rancid, suppurating boil."

"I—I regret my shortcomings, sir."

"Your foolish attempt to take control of the horse could have killed Piedmont. As it is, it has merely rendered you a more greatly soiled stain on Life's napkin than usual. Bow."

I bowed, and he slapped me fiercely on the ear with his pipe. I couldn't help but wonder, amidst the stars that surrounded me, how he had known about my reining the horse. I could only assume that Piedmont, the hideous little ratling, had told him.

"I am not in the mood for foolishness today, Grave," snapped the Master. "I am therefore liable to be less tolerant than usual with you. A distressing event has taken place. Our Queen has been captured."

I gasped. "Not Her Temperance, the Royal Protectress?"

"Polygon of the seven virtues, yes," he said.

"But how, sir?"

"Stolen away in the night, through the sewers. The butler's replacement, informed of her secret hiding place, discovered that she was missing about four hours ago. The Bishop passed this on to me before I left. They will try to keep the matter concealed, but it will not be long before the entire castle knows of the disappearance, and is demoralized. That is why the Anti-Milo is building his forces up around the perimeter of the citadel, rather than attacking piecemeal. He plans a war, and seeks every psychological advantage. Indeed, I myself espied a knightly contingent to the east as I made my way here last night, which would have to be the king's, as the queen's is encamped to the west. They were quite close—had I been as attention-seeking as you seem to be, this game may have been a short one. He knows we're coming. He knows that our only hope lies in a showdown, and will accumulate his forces until we arrive. Should you and I fail, he will invade our castle and take it with a single blow."

"But sir," I said, "what has become of our Queen? Is she dead?"

"Unknown. All that can be determined, by the rules of chess, is that the king's pawn alone was in a position to attack her."

"Stone," I murmured.

"But how did Stone know?" he posed.

"A spy, sir?" I asked.

"Only one individual was entrusted with the knowledge of her whereabouts, and that is the individual we sent to engage Stone: the Queen's pawn, her butler."

My eyes widened. "So he told Stone how to find her!"

"Or he took Stone's place. The absence of a body here suggests that the butler arrived, brought Stone up to date, then assumed Stone's position as king's pawn. Stone returned to Allwon in order to report what he knew, and to be near his master's side when the inevitable showdown occurs. The butler returned to the castle, was admitted as always, and took the Queen away through the sewers. He can make no further moves at present—our knight guards against his promotion, and our Queen's bishop, if we choose to send him home, can remove his piece from the board."

"Sir—will we see the Queen again?" I asked.

"If she is alive, and if we win," he answered gravely.

"And if we fail?"

"Then our Queen, whom I believe they are holding as insurance against a possible attack upon their own, will meet the same demise which we will have already."

I brushed some of the dry crust off my panoply with a purposeful flourish. "Then we must Act, sir," I said.

"It would please me if you would merely act intelligent," he said. He then turned to the table, scooped up the maps scattered thereon, and shoved them into his overcoat. "Ready the horse, Grave."

"Yes, sir." I made my way to the door, where a nervous thought struck me. "Sir, why did Mr. Stone leave his maps behind?"

He smiled slightly. "One might call it an invitation."

I went outside, where with some effort I woke up the slumbering Gravedigger. It jumped up like a dragon about to lunch on an irritating little peasant, but I pointed at Mr. Overlock in the window and it immediately assumed the attitude of the most docile barnyard nag. I saddled it, and stood waiting for the appearance of the Master. Shortly, mouse-box in hand, he emerged, and I assisted him into position on the steed. The back of the animal bowed under his heavy body, which took up the entire saddle. It was now my unpleasant task to mount the beast behind the saddle, where I would have to ride on the base of the horse's spine in an uncomfortably crotch-to-rear position with the Master.

"Advance," said Mr. Overlock. "King to King's Bishop Four." The horse immediately complied, and we were off in the gloom.

Using the maps that Stone had so thoughtfully left behind for us, we were able to enter Allwon undetected before the full light of sunrise was upon us. The penetration required the use of some unpleasantly untrammeled little paths through the mountains, but I was not terribly concerned. I knew that ditches and pits which the horse might gladly have bucked me into were just road-dressing with the Master present. My only discontent was my situation so near the tail, which was lifted often and splashily as the horse walked along. By midday we were descending valleyward, and I thirsted for wine, but the Master was not to approach any populated districts under a lighted sky. Instead, we took the rockiest routes along creeks, where I was once permitted to free my broken back from its moorings and gulp from the yellow stream, looking up afterward to see the horse using it for other purposes next to me and the Master pouring exotic elixirs into his mice. Shortly thereafter we were back to our mission, and I was wondering with some dread what moves our opponent was making during the time it was taking us to complete our journey.

By the time night fell, we were in view of the castle. It was a pitch-black edifice looming spikily against the dark-grey sky, rimmed with the red of sundown. For the first time, we descended from the wooded fringes and entered the streets of a dingy little village called Headhorn. It seemed quiet. We clopped quietly down the street, and were only encountered once, by a peddler hawking his wares at us ("Shoe oil! Shoe oil!") at the top of his lungs. The Master aimed his gun at him and he went away. We slid down a side alley, between rows of sedimentary buildings, until reaching a little, slightly-lit stone hut at the end. A wooden sign hanging above the door, entwined in ivy, said "Pawn Shop." I knew we had reached our first destination.

We got off the horse and I tethered it to a post. Mr. Overlock went up to the door and proceeded to knock, scratch and kick it mysteriously. A man opened.

"The Bishop's Pawn, I presume," said Mr. Overlock.

The man ushered us in urgently, then hastily locked the door. He had a bald head with an undersized red wig perched atop it, was stout and wore the garments of a typical shopkeeper. He led us through the store and into a small living quarters in the rear.

"Good evening, Mr. Overlock," he said, sounding nervous. "Take a table. I'll get some drinks."

"No drinks," said the Master to my dismay. "Grave, this is our man in Allwon, the King's bishop's servant. Not a true king's, and not a true bishop's, but one of the Anti-Milo's spies that we've managed to win over to our side. He has been keeping me informed of our adversary's maneuverings."

"Pleased to meet you, sir," I said.

He gaped at me with upturned lip for a second, then reverted his attention to the Master.

"Mr. Overlock, I can only make so many more 'mercy missions' outside the castle before I am caught. My outward vocation helps me in relaying information, but I mustn't be absent when my master chooses to move me. It is quite possible that he will put me into action soon."

"How do you know?" asked the Master.

"He is systematically assembling his forces around your castle. Military contingents have been advanced to back up his knights to both the east and the west, which will begin to strike your castle's outer defenses soon." He blotted his brow.

"Our adversary is leaving his castle somewhat unprotected in places," said the Master, laying the chessboard out on a table.

"He knows you haven't advanced your forces," said the pawn. "He believes himself superior, and doesn't fear your coming alone."

"I do not come alone."

The pawn looked at me distastefully, then saw that the Master meant his mice, whose box he placed on the table.

"The overconfident always fail," said the Master. "It is a known fact."

"Is it overconfident to face one man with all of the resources of an armed stronghold?" asked the pawn incredulously.

"Anyone who ever hopes to defeat me under any circumstances is overconfident," said Mr. Overlock.

The pawn sighed. "Well, anyway, the diminished defenses will make it easier to get you in. Here are your papers. I will go in an hour before you, leaving word at the gate that two of my fellow acolytes will be arriving shortly to see me. Show your papers at the gate and the guards should let you in. Should," he stressed.

The Master yawned, and consulted his pocket-watch. "It is late. Have you any duck?"

"A little. We found one making a nest in the chicken coop, and cooked it for a spy."

"Grave, make us dinner," said the Master, not amused. "We will proceed with the plan as outlined."

I'm bound to say I didn't relish acting as servant to another servant, but figuring that I could at least lick my fingers while cooking, acquiesced readily. I foraged in and around the place, and while there wasn't much actual meat to be found, I managed to concoct a couple of duck egg sandwiches, topping them with duck poop (which the Master liked as a sauce) and serving them with two glasses of duck drippings. I was delighted to see that the pawn didn't touch his.

"Tonight you will go and inform our allies to act as I've written in this letter," said the Master to the pawn, handing him an envelope. "You must not be captured, and you must return to your proper position by morning. Upon this much depends."

"Yes, sir," said the pawn stalwartly. "I will set forth immediately."

"Grave and I will spend the night here, then continue with our plans in the morning. Proceed."

"Yes, sir."

The bishop's pawn departed on his mission, and I was left to arrange our sleeping quarters for the night. The Master, after finishing his dinner, took the upstairs bedroom, while I, after testing the remaining hard surfaces and comparing them, slept in the larder on a bag of onions. By morning, I was smelling so potently of mud and onions that I felt no one would want to come close enough to kill me.

Mine was the first move of the day, moving into an even position with the Master at his fifth square. Together, then, we proceeded to creep up the craggy escarpment which led to the imposing Castle Allwon. I felt like bullet bait as we neared the edifice, so cruel and sharp-looking it was even by day, and was particularly uneasy in that I was moving into direct jeopardy with the queen's pawn. The fact that Mr. Overlock was undoubtedly aware of this was little comfort, for I knew that he would gladly sacrifice me if it so suited his objectives. A general quietude seemed to pervade the parapets above, but I knew, somehow, that several vicious eyes were upon me.

As we approached the gatehouse, I tried to look benign and humble, to keep with our roles as priestly wards. The Master, I was dismayed to note, was looking as pompous and haughty as ever.

"What is your business here, peasant?" asked the guard at the gate brusquely.

"Eh—apprentices of the Bishop's cleric, sir," I said. "We are here to see him."

"Give him the papers, Grave," said Mr. Overlock with loud impatience, tossing me the parchments. "I grow weary of delays."

I gave the guard the papers, which he examined with squinted suspicion. "It appears to be in keeping with instructions as I've received them," he said. "However, you don't seem much like priests to me."

"If you don't open the gate, you will quickly discover how we perform funerals," snapped the Master. "Raise it."

The guard retreated to the wheelhouse, and slowly, the keep's iron portcullis began to rise. I was shocked by the thought that we were about to gain access to the enemy's stronghold, and nervous at the possibilities this portended. In moments, the pointed tips of the huge grille were above us, and we were walking with purpose toward the dual doors of the bastion's central structure.

It was, indeed, subdued. The outer guard had either advanced or taken up stations inside. The royal knights were nowhere to be seen, nor were there any faces peering out of the two turrets at the sides. At the Master's grim nod, I took one of the huge obsidian rings which fronted the building and knocked upon the door. The clang echoed over the entire grounds of the castle, so heavy was the knocker and so hollow, apparently, what lay beyond. No one, however, seemed to notice, until about two minutes later when the great obstruction began to creak open.

Quaking in my sandals, the first thing I saw was a dagger. An onyx dagger, in a hand. Then the door opened wider and I perceived that the owner of the hand was the infamous Stone, smiling darkly and casting his towering shadow over me like an eclipse. The Master's deduction had been correct.

"Greetings, wraith," he rumbled. "I hope you don't mind my opening the door. You see, I am now the Queen's pawn, and such buttling is part of my duties. Unlike you, who once served your queen but now work for your king, I who once worked for my king now serve my queen. An exact reversal, proving once again that I am everything you are not."

The Master interposed. "As butler, then, is it not your duty to admit visiting royalty?" he asked.

"Oh, by all means, sire," smiled Stone, gesturing broadly toward the interior. "Accompany me, if you will."

As we entered, it became clear to me why the knock had been so reverberative. For the entire interior of this huge stone body was hollow— a large hollow chamber like a cathedral, with a marble floor made up of white and black squares like a chessboard. There were doors leading out of it at the rear corners, which I supposed led to the two side towers we had seen flanking the building. There were windows above, fashioned from many colored segments, but the room appeared otherwise inaccessible. It was obvious to me that our opponent had had the entire castle outfitted to suit the purposes of the game, and that we were soon to take our places for the denouement of the contest. Confirming this, Stone pushed me onto a certain square, and motioned respectfully for Mr. Overlock to stand on the one to my right. Smiling, he proceeded to occupy the square one row forward, and one to my left, at a perfect angle from me. I then took full notice of the other occupants in the room. There were the two bishops' pawns; ours (looking nervous) and a Bishopless one backing up Stone. The two knights' pawns were still at their posts, and at the rear of the room stood our pawn's bishop standing kingside of two thrones. On one of the thrones sat a crow-haired old woman, and on the other, covered by some ten hissing black cats, our opponent: the Anti-Milo.

He was like Mr. Overlock, and yet he wasn't. He had a similar expression, one which conveyed a sense of superiority to all around him, similar sideburns (though they were straight instead of curly), similarly unpleasant tobacco (he smoked a long cigarette instead of a pipe) and a resemblant mode of dress, though his garments were darker and shinier. He was more narrow than Mr. Overlock, and taller, and his complexion was decidedly huskier. On close inspection I could see a wire-thin moustache curling out above his lip like two long individual hairs parted down the middle, and he held a lorgnette.

"Ah, excellent," he intoned, his voice as velvety-dark as burnt butter. "You have arrived at last, having given my knights all this time to penetrate your castle. I am grateful, sir."

"You have taken many liberties since leaving Onwall, opponent," said Mr. Overlock. "White must move first in a conflict such as this, not black."

"And so you did, years ago, when you drove me out of Onwall," said the Anti-Milo readily. "You made the first move then, and now that I have become King with my own country, I claim the right to continue the game where you left off."

"Your pawn took two moves in order to bring Grave your message. I claim that as forfeiture."

"And I claim that ignorance of a move is a pass. You wouldn't have accepted an invitation to receive my message here, would you? Enough, then, of technicalities—the true Overlock has won, brain against brain, and now it is time for you to denounce all claims to that title and throw yourself upon my mercy."

"I think not, imposter," said Mr. Overlock.

"Imposter, am I?" laughed the Anti-Milo. "Because I live in Allwon and wear the color black? Many would say that your actions in recent years have justified your playing my position, while I bear the color of heroic protector. We become more alike with time, leaving the red blood of our battles the only color of any remaining significance. Unless you wish yours and that of your manservant spilled as well, I suggest you surrender your campaign immediately."

"Your suggestion is declined."

"But why? Certainly you see that your position is a hopeless one, with only the two of you present. By now my forces have breached your walls, and will shortly diminish your defenses enough for my pawn to gain promotion, setting a new ruler on your throne. As I've always said, overconfidence was to be your downfall. Play it out if you wish, but the outcome is inevitable. You cannot win alone."

"Who said I was alone?" said Mr. Overlock. He gave a short whistle, and in an instant one of the stained glass windows above shattered, leaving in its place the crouched figure of an Onwall knight, aiming his arrow directly at the pawn of the king's bishop, who gaped.

The Anti-Milo, startled, grabbed at the chessboard which sat on a little table in front of him and adjusted the pieces accordingly. "Oh, excellent, excellent," he said with a certain lack of conviction. "He has advanced to his own fifth rank, meaning that he was moving while I was attacking your front guard with my two knights' contingents."

"While *one* of them attacked," corrected Mr. Overlock. "The advancement of the other allowed me to transfer the Queen's bishop—a former officer in the Onwall army—to my own bishop's fourth rank. The noise you are about to hear outside is the armed garrison he commands catapulting rocks at your outer wall."

In a moment, the tumultuous sound of thunderous pummeling sent shockwaves through the court. A rather foreboding aura seemed to encompass the Anti-Milo, as he slowly adjusted the pieces and surveyed the situation he had been unprepared for. His eyes flicked from the board, to the knight above, to the Queen staring nervously at him from his right. Then, coldly eyeing the Master, he made a curt flip with his left hand, and the tense-looking pawn—our ally—stepped one square forward.

The Master, seeing this, nodded quietly to the knight who was perched birdlike in the window-frame. The knight nodded meaningfully back, and jumped down. The leap, which would have broken my legs, seemed not to affect him (though I envisioned him yelling "Ow!" about a dozen times over in his brain), and he immediately sprang forward two more squares, sidestepped to a third and stood smiling at the bishop he now faced. He was within capturing distance of the rook, the Queen's pawn, and the Queen.

A pivotal move was at hand. Would the Queen step into action to protect her increasingly-jeopardized King, or step back and protect herself? I could see in the Master's eyes that he placed great importance on the action matching his prediction. The game itself may have hung in the balance, for if the Queen made an aggressive move and the Master countered it, a flurry of unpredictability would ensue which could potentially clear the court of its members and place either King in checkmate.

The Anti-Milo looked at his Queen. She stared back timorously, with a slight shake of her head. "Queen to Queen's Knight One," said the Anti-Milo.

A dim, dim smile wafted over the Master's face. It was a retreating move, a self-protective move. The Queen inched meekly over toward the door which led to the west tower, or rook. The chaos was momentarily avoided.

The Master then stepped onto the square in front of me and stared the Anti-Milo in the eyes. "Concede," he said. "Your queen is in retreat. You cannot move. In two moves, I will have Grave positioned in such a way as to checkmate you."

The Anti-Milo glanced tensely at Stone, who looked at me in astonishment, laughed and looked back. "Do not believe him, Master! This wraith must first pass through me, and then my brother behind me. He has neither the courage nor strength to do so! Do not concede when victory lies so close at hand for the one, true Milo Overlock!"

The Anti-Milo examined the chessboard for his options, while Stone pointed his dagger at me, quivering with bloodlust.

"You subhuman dog," he growled in a whisper. "What my Master said is true. There is no more good or evil, there is only birthright. You worked for your Queen before your master, but I've served my master since birth. Only I know who the true possessor of the name Milo Overlock is."

"On the contrary, I know perfectly well," I said.

He seemed shocked. "Who?" he asked.

"My Master was born of a common family and a common name," I said. "At a young age, he discovered that he was mentally exceptional and seemed offended by the lack of recognition his talents deserved. Obsessed, as he grew older, with receiving his due, he discovered that the real power in Onwall belonged to a secretive individual who controlled vital industries crucial to the country's prosperity. Determined to take this individual's place, he made himself available as business consultant to several foundering companies that he'd invested in at low cost. Under his guidance, these businesses flourished, and his investments made him rich enough to eventually take them over. Aggressively, some might say ruthlessly, he built them even further. He began to acquire so much power that he was able to drive out his principal competitor and control Onwall himself, appropriating his adversary's name and characteristics as a sign of victory. Now possessing the power and recognition he felt his due, he

225

pressed his own parents, servants of the Queen, into his personal service. His mother died shortly thereafter."

"And do you know who his 'principal competitor' was?" demanded Stone.

"I do now. It was your Master."

"Then how can you defend *your* Master, the man who calls himself Milo Overlock?"

"Quite simple. Because I am his father."

He gaped at this, but there was no time to respond further, because the Anti-Milo now made his move. With a nod to the Queen and a gesture to a square, he sent his matriarch into a position which he repeated on the chessboard. She now stood at Queen's Rook Two, and suddenly I felt that invisible-noose-around-my-neck sensation again. I was comforted, however, by the sudden stop of the pummeling noises outside, and the sudden appearance of the Bishop in the doorway, his company having cleared a path at last.

"I am ready if you need me, sir," he said to Mr. Overlock.

Mr. Overlock looked victorious as he eyed the Anti-Milo. The Anti-Milo, for the first time, began to exhibit a truly worrisome look, and he stroked one of his cats so hard that it screeched. He eyed the board, and he eyed Mr. Overlock.

"It is your turn, sir," he said. "However, do not be premature in your expectation of victory. My queen remains safe, and, coward though she is, is at my command. Any move by yourself other than retreat will place you in check, and an aggressive move by one of your pieces will only lead to the inevitable bloodbath of multiple sacrifices. Consider your action carefully."

Mr. Overlock paused, and looked each of his opponent's "pieces" in the eye. The grim Queen and the quavering Pawns, the counterfeit Bishop and the impotent Knight. All looked nervous except for Stone, who merely wanted to kill me. The Master, then, extracted his flintlock and quietly loaded it. To my horrible surprise, he turned and tossed it to me.

"Grave," he said, "kill Stone."

Everyone froze, including me. "No!" cried the Anti-Milo.

"Kill Stone, Grave," commanded Mr. Overlock again.

"But, sir—"

"Kill him!"

The Anti-Milo jumped up. "If he takes my manservant, everyone in this room shall die," he shouted. "Retract your decision!"

"I shall not," said Mr. Overlock firmly. "How many of this royal court, having proclaimed you their leader, will die for you? Stone, who changed places with the butler rather than put himself in jeopardy by kidnapping my Queen? Your queen, who instead of stepping forward when my knight first appeared, protected herself? This court agreed to cooperate with you because you convinced them that you could protect them through your own ingenuity. But they do not truly trust you, and therein lies our crucial difference. You see this as a conflict of opposites? Very well. By killing Stone and taking his square, Grave condemns himself to death. But for all of his faults, I know that Grave is willing to die for me, as are all of my people. Can you say the same for yours?"

The Anti-Milo stood in stunned silence for a moment, and I guess Stone felt that this was the proper juncture at which to break the rules. With a loud yell, he thrust his onyx dagger forward and charged at me. Perhaps it was reflex, perhaps it was a sense of self-preservation, or perhaps I was indeed emboldened by the Master's words. Whatever it was, I closed my eyes, steeled my hand, pulled back on the trigger of Mr. Overlock's flintlock and shot. A terrible roar filled the air, a bellow of agony followed upon it, and as I opened my eyes I saw the smoke issuing from the gun's deadly tip and the bulky form of Stone, incredulous of expression, crumpling over and falling before me. I had killed him. I goggled in frozen astonishment and disbelief, though my reaction did not stem from guilt. I was simply stunned to see that I had actually managed to effectively fulfill one of the Master's commands as intended, for the first time in my life.

"Well done, Grave," said the Master. "Take your square."

I became aware that the first command I had fulfilled to his satisfaction was also going to be my last. I was now in direct mortal jeopardy with two pieces—the Queen's Bishop's pawn, and the King's Bishop. The Anti-Milo was trapped. His only option was to set a chain reaction in order which would kill off just about every piece but the two opposing Kings. I would be the first.

The Anti-Milo had slumped back into his seat, and now his hand hovered, quivering, over his pieces. The Queen gasped as she saw him put his finger on the Bishop. She looked at Mr. Overlock desperately.

"It is time for you to decide who truly rules this country," the Master said to her. "A peasant, an outsider, who managed to penetrate your house with the intent of using you for his personal vendetta, or you. When this is finished, the ranking members of Allwon will all be gone and the only person left standing will be him. And for what—the improvement of your country? No. For a game. A game that could be played on a board, but which he decided to play with real lives. All to prove his claim to a name."

"A name that I possessed first!" demanded the Anti-Milo from his throne.

"But which you are not worthy of," said Mr. Overlock. "If you had been, you would never have lost it."

The Anti-Milo, looking furious, picked up his Bishop's piece. He looked at me. "Farewell, Grave."

"Stop!" shouted the Queen.

The piece remained shaking in his fingers.

"If you move that piece, you not only condemn this fool to death, but untold members of the court as well," she said. "Perhaps even myself! Is that your intention?"

"I am King!" the Anti-Milo thundered. "Your lives are mine to use as I see fit!"

"You are a peasant," she retorted. "You are not even of this country. Your words and actions are treason. I place you under arrest."

"No!' he cried. "Not until the game is over!"

"The game is over now," said Mr. Overlock. "You cannot move, and your pieces will not sacrifice themselves—a foolish act of desperation at any rate. Accept a draw now, or I shall view your turn as elapsed and move Grave one step forward and checkmate you."

The Anti-Milo rose. His cats, all ten of them, continued to cling growlingly to his limbs. "I'm sorry, Your Majesty," he said, addressing his Queen, "but as sole ruler I can only be dethroned by some sort of revolt— an act which the sickly, cowardly, inexpressibly incompetent cravens of Its Pathetic Dependency, The Embarrassment of Allwon, are hardly capable of."

"Traitorous villain," snarled the Queen, "you are not sole ruler. Not while I live."

"Precisely," said the Anti-Milo. He pointed at the Queen. "Look, my pussies. Does she not resemble a tuna?"

His cats licked their chops.

"Eat her."

The cats, a wild gleam in their eyes, leapt off of the Anti-Milo's frame and began creeping lustfully toward the Queen. She screamed.

Mr. Overlock, still carrying the box which contained his mice, extracted a key from his pocket and opened it. The mice all peeked out to see what was happening, and their attention immediately fell upon the cats.

"There," the Master said to them, "is your lunch."

The mice swarmed out of the box instantly, and went scrambling for the cats. The cats seemed stunned for a moment that they were under attack by mice, but seeing them scamper forward with gnashing fangs and barking, must have assumed that they were extremely small chihuahuas or something. Arching their backs and making a frightful siren-like whine, the felines bolted. They ran all around the large chessboard chamber, the mice snapping at their jugulars, until our bishop opened the door and the entire party took its discussion outside.

"If my mice have remembered their training, not even a bone will remain of those cats within the hour," said Mr. Overlock.

"Seize this imposter of a king," commanded the Queen, and the entire court aimed its weapons at the Anti-Milo.

"Stand fast," interrupted Mr. Overlock. "First must come the checkmate which will confirm my superiority."

"Not yet, sir," said the Anti-Milo. "You see, it is still my turn, and I claim the right to make it. I will accept a draw from you, sir, but not a checkmate. And if we draw, I must live to play another day."

He inched over to the door which led to the western turret.

"Where are you going?" demanded the Queen.

"I castle," said the Anti-Milo. "Farewell."

With that, he threw open the door and ran in, pushing the guard from the other side in with us and closing the door behind him.

"Guards!" shouted the Queen. "Apprehend him!"

Her fellow pieces abandoned their positions and charged the door to the rook's square. It was locked.

"Break it in!" ordered the Queen.

The younger and stronger of the personnel engaged in this task, while the Queen went out through the front doors and summoned more to help. She had the turret surrounded from without and the castle gates doubly manned by whatever forces remained on the grounds. Within moments, the door was broken open and an army of Allwon soldiers, followed by the Onwall troop the bishop had brought, plowed in. At the Queen's command, they scoured the tower from basement to battlement, examining every cranny while the forces outside awaited any appearance to the exterior.

But the Anti-Milo was not to be found.

The Queen was baffled and furious, but one sight of the Master's unmoved features seemed to relay the truth to her.

"We won't find him, will we, Mr. Overlock?"

"You will not."

She sighed. "I am sorry for all the trouble and misery this episode has caused both our countries. I shall immediately issue a royal proclamation declaring peace, and send emissaries with you back to Onwall to see that your Queen is safely restored."

"Accepted. In turn, I shall see that her captor retains his life, that he may replace the fallen Stone in your service."

"But that will leave your Queen without a butler, won't it?" she asked.

"I have plans for that."

A sudden hope filled my chest as Mr. Overlock looked at me. "Grave," he said.

"Yes, sir?"

"See that our ally, the Bishop's pawn, returns with us to take his position as personal servant to our Queen."

"Yes, sir," I frowned.

"And collect my mice, as soon as they've finished eating."

THE OUTCOME WAS as intended. We returned to Onwall, where Mr. Overlock received, as expected, a king's welcome. A new flag was unfurled with his face on it, the public honored him, and a holiday was declared. Our Queen was returned from wherever she had been kept, smelling somewhat rank but otherwise in good health. The Master deferred his royal authority back upon her and quickly returned to private life. Peace resumed in both countries, with my Master now a hero in both. As for the remaining pieces, most of them were returned to their usual stations on the board, while some found themselves in new arrangements as a result of the contest just concluded. The queens of the two countries, having both been manipulated by men, discovered a common bond that strengthened the countries' relations. The butler, charged with cleaning the Allwon castle, faced years of whitewashing when it was discovered that the castle's "blackness" was all due to the Anti-Milo's tobacco-smoke. The Bishop's pawn, our ally, forewent his new post as our Queen's new butler (our Queen having decided she could take care of herself) and became an Onwall oddity—an honest pawnbroker. And the mice, now fine catters, kept the local feline population from threatening any more of the Master's ducks. I, alas, still had to catch them.

I was dusting one evening and saw the chessboard sitting upon the table in the parlor, the pieces positioned on the final squares each had occupied during the game. Mr. Overlock had apparently placed them there, where he could see them from his seat in the armchair.

"Forgive me, sir," I said, "but shall I remove this board?"

"No, Grave. It shall remain there in perpetuity, as a symbol of my final victory over the Anti-Milo."

"But sir, the game resulted in a draw. Is not the question of the superior player still open to debate?"

"Not at all, Grave. The Anti-Milo's final move was to castle with the rook."

"Yes, sir."

"However, castling with the rook took him through check with our knight, rendering it an illegal move. The Anti-Milo escaped, but by doing so he proved me the superior player. Soon he will realize this, and we will never hear from him again."

It seemed strange to me that the outcome of a chess game could cause anyone to disappear forever, but the Master clearly regarded this as the only logical upshot, the same thing he would have done if he had lost. I began to ponder what kind of man would view life according to these terms. A man of tremendous ego, for whom the greatest intellect outweighed the greatest deed. A man whose every action determined the course of his country, whether in mortal combat or merely a game. A man who so deplored the conditions of his birth that he'd set out to become the Master of those who'd borne him. A man of strength, power and determination. A man of mystery. A man of duck.

In short, Milo Overlock.

Appendix

Sequence of chess moves in Chapter Nine:

White "passes" until made aware of the game when Black King's Pawn occupies his King's fifth square (BKP – K5). Turns begin formally alternating at this point.

White	Black
<u>White</u>	<u>Black</u>
1. KP – K3 (Grave picks up riddle)	QP – Q3
2. KB – QB4 (Milo trains mice)	QB – KN5
3. KBP – KB3	QB x KBP
4. KN x QB	QN – QR3 (The Golden Turret)
5. Q – K2 (into sewer)	QN – QN5
6. QP – Q3 (Butler confronts Stone)	KP x QP (Butler's piece is removed from game and Black King's Pawn occupies his square. Butler then assumes Stone's role as Black King's Pawn while Stone goes back to Allwon and becomes Black Queen's Pawn)
7. K – KB2	KP x Q
8. KP – K4 (Grave spends night in cottage)	KN - KR3 (Anti-Milo moving his forces)
9. K – K3 (rendezvous with Grave)	KN – KN5 +
10. K – KB4 (Milo and Grave travel into Allwon)	QRP – QR4
11. K – KB5 (Pawn Shop)	KRP – KR4
12. KP – K5 (entering the enemy's stronghold)	QN x QBP
13. QB – KB4	KN x KRP
14. KN – KN5	KBP – KB3 (to avoid capture by knight)
15. KN – KB2	Q – QN1
16. K – K6	Q – QR2
17. KP x QP (Grave shoots Stone)	O – O – O (Anti-Milo castles illegally)

www.ingramcontent.com/pod-product-compliance
Lightning Source LLC
Chambersburg PA
CBHW070616130626
46556CB00001B/381